RETRO

RETRO

An Amos Walker Novel

Loren D. Estleman

A Tom Doherty Associates Book
New York

RETRO: AN AMOS WALKER NOVEL

Edited by James Frenkel

A Forge Book
Published by Tom Doherty Associates, LLC
175 Fifth Avenue
New York, NY 10010

www.tor.com

Forge® is a registered trademark of Tom Doherty Associates, LLC.

Library of Congress Cataloging-in-Publication Data

Estleman, Loren D.
    Retro : an Amos Walker novel / Loren D. Estleman.—1st ed.
       p.   cm.
    "A Tom Doherty Associates book."
    ISBN 0-765-30448-1 (acid-free paper)
    EAN 978-0765-30448-3
    1. Walker, Amos (Fictitious character)—Fiction.   2. Private
investigators—Michigan—Detroit—Fiction.   3. Boxers (Sports)—Crimes
against—Fiction.   4. Fathers and sons—Fiction.   5. Detroit (Mich.)—Fiction.
I. Title

PS3555.S84R48   2004
813'.54—dc22

           2003071103

First Edition: May 2004

Printed in the United States of America

0 9 8 7 6 5 4 3 2 1

For Peter Spivak, a good man to have in your corner

There is no present. There is only the immediate future and the recent past.

—George Carlin

RETRO

ONE

What do you do with an old madam when she's peddled her last pound of flesh?

They never had any ambivalence about it in the old days. If she'd saved her money, they propped her up in a gondola bed piled high with satin pillows, parked her opium pipe among the crystal atomizers and pots of face cream and scent, and when the time came they carried her downstairs in a white coffin and buried her in a Protestant cemetery, Presbyterians and Methodists being notorious for their democracy. If her circumstances were straitened, the sisters of charity drifted to and fro past her bed in a ward smelling of quicklime and carbolic, put a damp cloth on her forehead when she moaned, and at the end gave the gravedigger's boy a coin to dump her in Potter's field.

That was in the old days. The new belonged to the self-employed, and whorehouse matrons had no more place than gondola beds or nuns in stiff linen. Why spring for a parlor and a bouncer when streetcorner space is free? Beryl Garnet was the last of her kind, and her reward for outliving all her contemporaries was the Grenloch Assisted Living Village in Farmington, an eighth of a tank of gas north of the house she'd run on John R in Detroit for nearly forty years.

The facility sprawled over six acres of greensward, with a retention pool—the Grenloch that had given the place its name—in front, where overfed ducks and geese paddled their feet and littered the surrounding walk with their waste. The building's façade had been made to resemble a Scottish hamlet, steep-roofed, half-timbered, and girded round with decorative ironwork for fat lairds to lean on and direct the monthly whipping of the serfs. The Dutch doors were plastered to solid brick. In order to get inside, I had to park in a half-empty visitors' lot and tug open a faux chapel door with a steel core.

The foyer was large, with shining black-and-white checkered ceramic tile and a white baby grand piano waiting for some old fish to sweep aside his tails and plunk himself down on the padded bench and trundle out Chopin's *Sonata No. 3 in B Minor.* Meanwhile the residents had to make do with the Dixie Chicks. The P.A. was cranked up to hearing-aid level.

I found Beryl's room number on a wall directory, black with white plastic lettering that snapped in and out, suitable for discreet editing when rooms turned over. It beat erasing names from a blackboard.

A maintenance worker installing a wall rail directed me to the nursing wing, where residents who needed a little more than just assistance were sequestered. This was separated from the rest of the facility by a fire door with a gridded window set into it. There the carpeting and potpourri ended and the linoleum and disinfectant began.

"Who you here for?"

I looked down at the man seated in a vinyl-upholstered armchair in the corridor. I'd have had to walk around him to ignore him. He was thin and bald, with long arms and legs in an electric-blue jogging suit zipped to his wattles. His withered-apple face was bright-eyed and he appeared to have most of his teeth, unless he'd had them made crooked on purpose. I told him who I was there for.

He shook his head. "Don't know her. I ran the Detroit Edison office downtown for twenty-seven years. Took a hundred thousand in a lump sum to retire. That was in nineteen seventy. If I knew I'd live this long I'd have taken the pension. You make your choices in this life and you stick with them. As if you could do anything else."

"I guess that's true."

"Don't just yes me because I said it. You don't know me. I might be a liar."

"You might be, at that."

"Well, I'm not. Back in seventy, a hundred thousand was so big you couldn't see around it. I've seen around it now, and there's nothing in back. What do you do?"

"I came to tune the piano."

"Horseshit. You look like a cop to me."

"It's the gum soles."

"Who'd you say you're here for?"

"Beryl Garnet."

He looked at the wall across the corridor. It was finished in corkboard, with childrens' pictures drawn in bright crayon thumbtacked all over it. He mouthed the name a couple of times. Then he shook his head again. "Don't know her. You make your choices in this life and you stick with them."

"As if you could do anything else."

He squinted up at me as if he'd just realized I was there. Then he pointed a finger at my chest. "You're pretty smart for your age. You take the pension when they offer it."

I said I would and left him. I turned a corner and stopped at a nurses' station. A plump, sweet-faced redhead in her twenties smiled when I told her who I was visiting. She wore a floral smock and had a blood-pressure indicator draped around her neck. Another nurse twice her age sat on a low turning stool speaking in murmurs on the telephone to someone she called Mortie. Lines 1 and 3 kept on flashing all the time I was standing there, and an oval glass fixture mounted above one of the doors in the hall glowed on and off with a querulous buzz. It didn't have anything to do with me.

"She'll be happy to see you," said the redhead. "She doesn't get many people."

"I think a gentleman around the corner may be in the same boat."

"You must mean Wendell. He stakes out that spot every day about this time. Did he tell you he used to run the Edison office in Detroit?"

"He advised me to take a pension."

"He tells everyone that."

"I don't get a pension," I said. "No one's ever offered me a hundred thousand, either."

"You should tell him. It might make him feel better."

I was tired of talking about Wendell. I'd expected the visit to depress me, but not before I'd made it. "How is Beryl?"

Her smile turned noncommittal. "Are you a friend or a relative?"

"Neither."

"She's in good spirits. She tells the most outrageous lies about her past."

"Any of them involve the old mayor?"

She looked down suddenly at a chart on the desk. I felt a little better then. It isn't every day you make a trained health-care professional blush.

TWO

The room was just a little larger than the handicap toilet that accompanied it, with the added advantage of a window looking out on a crew excavating a septic tank.

The walls were painted a cheery apricot, and a bulletin board had been bolted to the wall opposite the single bed for posting pictures of grandchildren and Get Well cards from friends and family. The only thing pinned to it was a black-and-white snapshot with pinked edges of a petite woman in her early twenties wearing chunky heels and a dress with padded shoulders, one hand resting on the radiator cap of a 1940 Packard. That was forty years before I knew Beryl Garnet, but I accepted it as evidence that she'd been young once and slim.

A woman with a puffball head of white hair with pink scalp showing through sat in a folding wheelchair, watching a couple in overalls spackling drywall on a sixteen-inch TV. The old woman had on trifocals, a pilled white sweater over a housedress mottled with explosions of orange and green, and a man's brown loafers with slits cut in the sides. I hadn't seen Beryl Garnet in twenty years, but I accepted this as evidence that she was still here and eighty.

I spoke her name. The old woman didn't turn her head or

blink. I raised my voice and tried again. For her I wasn't there, and neither was the couple on the TV. She was staring at them with the detached fixity of a cat watching fish swim in an aquarium.

"There you are, Lettie. We were about to call out the National Guard."

A woman younger than the redhead at the nurses' station, wearing a similar flowered smock and slacks, crept in, swung the chair toward the hall, and pushed it out. The old woman responded with a stammering squeal, like a bad pulley.

Beryl Garnet came in a minute later. I didn't know how I could have mistaken anyone else for her. She was still short and round and her hair was arranged in the soft, blue-rinse waves I remembered. Her complexion was paler, less like an enameled doll's, and she was using a walker, but apart from that, the last two decades seemed to have gone right around her like water around a snag.

"Turn that off, please. I wouldn't mind people wandering in and out if they wouldn't leave that thing yammering when they left."

I switched off the TV set. What sounded like the same program spilled out of several other open doors into the silence. Either home improvement was popular among the elderly or Grenloch got only one channel off cable.

She made her way over to the bed, sat down on the edge of the mattress, and spun the walker out of the way. I might have helped her if she'd asked. Maybe I should have anyway. You never know with old people. I did move over and push the door shut. That made the silence complete, if you ignored the crew jackhammering at the concrete outside.

She looked at me. She wore a dress of some pale green material like crepe, cinched at the waist with a wide belt of shiny red plastic or patent leather that matched her shoes, flat-heeled with tiny silver buckles on the sides. She was as tidy as a little girl in dancing school. When she was sixty, her back parlor had been the main payoff point for the old city vice squad.

"You're getting gray," she said. "But then so is the rest of your generation. How do you like it so far?"

"I like it fine. You look about the same."

She laughed. I'd forgotten that laugh; like Tinkerbell on crank.

"How would you know? We only saw each other that one time. How long has it been? On second thought, forget I asked. Who's keeping score?"

"You're hard to forget. You set your bouncer on me with a Great Dane chaser."

"Dear old Ulysses. I had to put him down finally. His hip went out."

I couldn't remember if Ulysses was the dog or the bouncer, so I didn't say anything.

She went on looking at me. I didn't know what she was seeing. Her eyes were still like bits of bright glass buttoned into her face. Her mouth was small and delicately curved, tinted Titian pink. She was Mrs. Claus, Martha Washington, and the Marquessa de Sade all rolled up into one lump of Silly Putty.

"I was surprised you were still listed," she said. "I thought you might be retired by now."

"I thought you were dead."

"Still the diplomat. Did you ever find that girl you were looking for?"

"She took a shot at me. It wasn't one of my more restful cases."

"I thought detectives thrived on danger."

"That's the gas company. Why the call, Mrs. Garnet? You can stroll down Memory Lane anytime with the clerks in Records and Information."

"They wouldn't remember me. I closed up shop when the police stopped arresting prostitutes and started arresting customers.

That was an open invitation to every streetwalker and call girl between here and New Orleans. With my overhead, I couldn't compete."

"You can confiscate a john's car if he uses it to cruise for hookers. More money for the city."

"I'm not complaining. I made a good living, and I spread it around."

"You and Magic Johnson."

She sighed. She was too good an actress not to have worked her way up from the bedsprings. If they all looked like Elvira there'd be no reason to leave home.

"Now you sound like a reformer. They were most of my overhead. Excuse me one minute."

There was an oxygen set-up next to the bed, with a pair of torpedo-shaped tanks and a pressure gauge. She turned the dial, placed the transparent plastic mask over her nose and mouth, and took two deep gulps. Then she put the mask back on top of the contraption and turned it off.

She looked embarrassed, and she hadn't the experience to put it over. "I have a touch of emphysema. My blood pressure would kill most people half my age, and three operations have failed to locate the source of my internal bleeding. I wear diapers, to put the comic point on it. It's all been very dreary so far and not at all the adventure I'd been led to believe."

I said nothing again. This conversation was outside my specialty.

She scratched the back of one plump pink hand. It had a Band-Aid on it. "I've made all the arrangements except one. I'd like my son to have my ashes."

"So call him."

"If it were that easy, I wouldn't have called you. We haven't had contact in thirty-four years."

I added backwards. Everything in my life seemed to add up to that year.

"What happened in nineteen sixty-eight?"

"Vietnam. You might have heard of it."

I said I had. I dreamed about it now and then, but not as often as I used to. "Draft dodger?"

"Such an ugly term. You can't say it without sneering."

"I didn't coin it. I didn't coin *amnesty,* either. He could have come back anytime in the last twenty-five years."

"There's a little more to it than that. The FBI has been looking for him all this time."

"How hard?"

She laughed again, scraping a nerve.

"It's funny. Del was a sickly boy. He missed a lot of school and only managed to graduate at the bottom of his class. No one would ever have predicted he'd place among anyone's top ten."

THREE

Delwayne Garnet had worked his way onto the FBI's Ten Most Wanted list by default. The two bottom slots opened up when a pipe bomb went off prematurely in a car headed toward the Federal Building on West Fort Street in November 1968. Forensics experts scraped together enough organic material to identify a pair of fugitives sought in the bombings of recruitment centers on the campuses of Wayne State University and the University of Detroit, struck off their names, and added Delwayne's. He had already been known to the Detroit field office as the one the local urban guerrillas sent out for coffee. Whatever else he knew about the internal organization besides who took sugar and cream and who drank it black was more important to Washington than Delwayne himself.

He'd been adopted by Beryl Garnet in infancy. She wouldn't say who his birth parents were, but accidental pregnancies were as common in her work as cavities, so I didn't press her for an answer. I'm not as curious as I once was about things I can't use. There are worse ways to be brought up than in a brothel; there is always someone to babysit, and you get to have your own room outside business hours. Sometimes several of them. Possibly his early life had contributed to his choice of associations later—

you can't watch your foster mother hand a fat envelope once a month to the officer on the beat without forming specific opinions about the nature of authority—but that was happening all over, with a lot less personal exposure to explain it. Whatever the circumstances were, at eighteen, Delwayne's senior picture moved from the Murray-Wright High School yearbook to the nation's post offices.

Beryl gave me a print of it from a drawer in her nightstand. It was a narrow, dusky, sullen face, possibly part black or east Indian. The expression looked furtive, but that's not unusual in school. I didn't think I'd like him, although not for any of those reasons, or even his background. To hell with what modern science says about the practice of physiognomy; certain faces belong in the dictionary next to *trouble*.

He'd moved out of the house on John R several weeks before the blast. Beryl didn't know where to, but he'd been around to borrow money on a semi-regular basis, showing up each time with longer hair, scruffier whiskers, and less pleasant manners than the time before. The visits stopped about the time his picture appeared in newspapers. The prevailing wisdom was he'd fled to Canada under an alias with falsified documents to match, but that was just speculation because Windsor was only three minutes away by bridge or tunnel. That was the story on Delwayne Garnet so far as I could obtain from his next-of-kin. I'd found people on less, but not after the largest intelligence-gathering organization in the world had failed.

"I can get right on this if you want to hear from him," I said, slapping shut my notepad. "No guarantees on whether I turn him or if he'll do anything about it if I do. He might think it's a trick to lure him into U.S. jurisdiction."

"That won't be necessary. Whatever we had to talk about would only depress me, and that isn't how I intend to spend my time." She took another hit of oxygen, bigger than before. Her age had begun to etch itself into her pallor.

"What do you want done with the ashes if I don't find him?"

"Suit yourself. I just don't want the State of Michigan dis-
posing of them. I've stayed out of their hands this long."

I looked at Delwayne's face again, not liking it any more
than I had the first time, then stuck it inside my notepad and put
the pad in my pocket. "I charge five hundred a day, not counting expenses. They promise to go high on this one."

"You can discuss all that with my lawyer. He has your number. He'll be in touch." She smiled primly; I remembered all
her girls had called her Aunt Beryl. "Don't worry about my estate going bankrupt. I didn't turn it all back into sex toys."

On my way out, I told the nurse at the desk that Mrs. Garnet
was ready to be put to bed.

"Did you have a pleasant visit?"

I got out Delwayne's picture and showed it to her. "Have you
ever seen this man?"

She looked at it. "I'm afraid I haven't."

"Then no."

Around the corner, Wendell of Detroit Edison had surrendered his seat to the maintenance man I'd seen earlier, who was
eating his lunch out of a greasy paper sack. He didn't have any
words of wisdom for me, about pensions or anything else.

That was in March. I was running surveillance for Workers
Compensation, collecting video on a bricklayer with a spinal
injury claim that made me tired and sore just watching him play
softball, paint his sailboat, and dip his wife on the dance floor
at the Roostertail. The Comp people settled anyway. I also had
a couple of dead-beat dad jobs outsourced from North Dakota
and Texas, an employee theft at a Best Buy in Troy, some insurance work, and a credit confirmation that was probably the
last one any private investigator ever got in the era of afford-
able software. I considered framing the check and hanging it
next to my stuffed dodo. Instead I cashed it.

All this time no one shot at me or hit me on the head, I didn't
find any dead bodies, I stayed out of jail, and my license wasn't

threatened even once. My luck couldn't hold. Meanwhile I filed my notes on Delwayne Garnet and his picture under my blotter with the rest of the unfinished business and forgot about him. Inasmuch as any lone eagle can ever forget about paying work.

By June, the spring had dried up. Prom Night had come and gone without a single date-rape complaint, all the bridegrooms had been background-checked on behalf of all the fathers of all the brides, the philandering spouses were planning their separate vacations or patching things up for the sake of the cruise booked last Christmas. I couldn't even score security work. It's like that sometimes; just when you think you can afford to hire someone to arrange the magazines in the waiting room, a good wind comes along and blows nobody ill. I'd spent last season's bounty on the cigarette tax and a new flush valve for the water closet. The superintendent who was paid to take care of that promised he'd reimburse me the next time he made contact with the out-of-town syndicate that owned the building. It was the only income on my horizon. When the telephone rang I went for it like the cord on the reserve parachute.

"A. Walker Investigations."

"Amos Walker, please."

"Who's calling?"

"Is this Mr. Walker?"

"I asked first." I like to throw three balls and then strike them out, the way John Hiller used to do for the Tigers. The difference in his case was they had to pay him even if he walked the side.

A throat got cleared. It sounded like someone riffling through Blackstone, always an encouraging sign in my work. "My name is Lawrence Meldrum, with Meldrum and Zinzser. We're attorneys, representing the estate of Beryl Garnet. I believe Mr. Walker knows what this is in reference to."

"In that case, I'm Mr. Walker."

"Pardon?"

"When did she die?"

Water gurgled on his end. I was pretty sure it was water. It didn't cut the phlegm the way alcohol did. "Last night, shortly after eight. She'd had a stroke and was paralyzed for two days. She'd prepared a living will, but she passed before the decision could be made to remove her from life support. She was a woman who knew exactly what she wanted. Refreshing, really."

"That's what they said in Detroit Vice. When's cremation?"

He said it had taken place, and we negotiated; he as if it were his money, I because it was mine. I stood firm at fifteen hundred to start up, and he waggled the white flag suddenly as if he'd been intending to do that all along. I had an idea I'd need a lawyer to sue the lawyers for the rest. Fortunately I knew a couple who sucked other lawyers' skulls for practice.

Meldrum told me to expect a messenger that afternoon with a cashier's check and the ashes. He called them "cremains." The conversation was over before I could come up with a response to that.

The UPS driver on that route was a former second-string guard with the Lions who looked like Baby Huey in short pants. He was used to bringing me flat parcels containing affidavits. He thumped the tall rectangular carton onto my desk. "Heavy. What's in it, a bust of Beethoven?" He thrust his electronic gizmo under my nose.

I signed it and handed back the stylus. "Just an old acquaintance."

When he left, I got out the switchblade I use for a letter opener, sawed through the tape, and lifted a bronze urn out of a mess of Styrofoam peanuts I'd still be sweeping up come the Fourth of July. It was shaped like a miniature milk can, with a brushed finish and a sealed lid, and had probably set Beryl Garnet back eight hundred dollars. The little shield-shaped plate designed for engraving a name, dates of birth and death, and a tasteful sentiment was blank. I shook the urn. It sounded like a can of baking powder.

I stood it up on the desk, fished the envelope containing the cashier's check out of the box, put it in the safe, and took out my little blue book. A third of the names in it belonged to dead people, but I was too sentimental about Nate "The Nose" D'Innocenza and Jimmy Three Fingers to strike any of them out. Of what's left, half would gladly strike out the other half for me, if they knew about the book. I found the name I wanted and dialed a number in Plymouth, Michigan. A bosun's pipe blew in my ear and a canned voice told me the area code had changed. I didn't think it had been that long since I'd called; but then Mammy Bell shuffled the codes around by the week. I drew a line through the old one, wrote in the one the recording gave me, broke the connection, and tried again.

"Yes?"

It's an education just how flat one syllable can sound coming from the right mouth.

"Red, this is Amos Walker. Most civilians say 'Hello.' How long since you retired?"

"Almost half as long as I was in. This a land line?"

I said it was. He never spoke on a cell or a cordless telephone and refused to speak with anyone who was using one. He said any ten-year-old kid with a scanner could intercept a radio signal.

"What do you need?"

"This one's got dust on it. It goes back thirty-four years."

His arithmetic was faster than mine. "Shit."

"I couldn't have said it better myself. What's it going to cost?"

"How much venison you got in the freezer?"

"I haven't been deer hunting in years, Red. It's too much like my work week. How about a case of Scotch?"

"I quit. Promised my daughter."

"Tigers tickets. You used to be a big fan."

"Used to."

I breathed. "That just leaves cash."

"Uncle gives me more than I need just to keep me from writing my memoirs."

We were at an impasse.

He said shit again. "Come on up. I had enough of my own company today."

I said I'd see him in thirty minutes.

"Take Ford Road and you'll see me in twenty."

Red Burlingame had been with the Detroit field office of the Federal Bureau of Investigation for more than thirty years, the last ten as Special Agent in Charge. He'd personally engineered the arrests of five fugitives on the Ten Most Wanted list, which was three more than his nearest competitor. Even more impressive, he'd managed to do it without calling attention to himself and away from J. Edgar Hoover, thus avoiding transfer to the field office in Anchorage. If he didn't know where I could start looking for Delwayne Garnet, I was going to have Aunt Beryl as an office mate for the rest of my life.

FOUR

Plymouth is a good-size town, too far from Detroit to be counted as a suburb, and trying hard to remain a village, with some success. Its business section is a playground of gift shops, antiques stores, and aromatic bakeries, which moved in about the time the last hardware store closed. Its annual show of ice sculptures draws visitors from all over the state. In June, there was not a six-foot peacock or Father Christmas to be found, just a pretty park and strollers in khaki shorts licking ice cream cones and dodging in-line skaters. I left them behind and drove through well-maintained streets lined with sleek brick split-levels and historic houses like wedding cakes and parked in an asphalt driveway behind a pickup truck the size of my house, with dual wheels and a hammered steel toolbox bolted across the bed. When Red Burlingame left the Bureau, it hadn't taken him more than a week to go rural. He'd turned all his three-piece suits into greaserags except one to be buried in, planted tomatoes in his backyard, and inundated all his friends and relatives with birdhouses handmade in his basement.

We'd hooked up back when he was still in harness. His daughter had fallen into an abusive relationship, and he'd needed an independent to dig up the boyfriend's background, to avoid anything being traced back to Burlingame's office and a charge of using government personnel for private purposes. I came lowly recommended by his colleagues, for the same reasons that made me right for the job. I'd spent three days finding the boyfriend's arrest record under his real name. The daughter obtained a restraining order against him, and when he showed up at her apartment anyway, I was following him. I wasn't there when the police came, but he wasn't going anywhere with a collapsed lung.

Burlingame answered the door wearing a short-sleeved Madras sport shirt with the tail out over an old pair of slacks bagging in the knees and no shoes on his stockinged feet. He was a big man, thick through the shoulders and thickening in the waist, with rusty streaks in his white hair and a granite jaw against which a thousand alibis had dashed themselves to pieces. He wrung all the circulation out of my hand—from habit, not a contest of strength—and let me into a widower's living room with scattered sections of newspaper and a half-eaten sandwich calcifying on a saucer balanced on the arm of the sofa. Forests of family photos stood on the mantle of a gas fireplace and on top of the TV set, where a roly-poly talk-show host was grilling a movie star in dungarees without sound. Burlingame snatched up a remote and flipped off the power.

"Twenty million dollars a picture, and he spends the whole interview talking about his colonic," Burlingame said. "I may be senile, but I don't remember Gable discussing enemas with Louella Parsons."

"Maybe she edited it out."

"Maybe I left public life just in time. What would you say to a beer?"

"I only start talking to them after three."

He tipped a hand toward the sofa, carried the saucer with the fossilized sandwich into the kitchen, and came out a minute later with a Tall Boy in each hand. He gave me one and slung himself into a recliner.

I asked him if he missed his job. The only sign in the room that he'd been in government work was a framed letter on the wall near the front door, signed by William Webster, the FBI director at the time of his retirement, congratulating Special Agent in Charge Randall Burlingame on his years of service.

"Just the field work. There got to be less and less of that near the end, and more pencil-pushing. The newbies had a hard-on against all the senior men who served under Hoover, so they buried us in paper, trying to make us quit. I hated the sawed-off son of a bitch, but when he didn't like someone he fired him, and that was that."

"Is it true you called him a fairy to his face?"

"Hell, no. He canned trainees just for looking down at that little platform he stood on when he handed out the diplomas." He sipped from his can. "For the record, I never thought he took it in the ass. He never dressed up like a woman, either. You'd think what he did to King and the Kennedys would be enough without making shit up."

"Ever hear from the Bureau?"

"Not if either of us can help it. Couple times a year a snot from the Feature page calls me up asking for an interview. I'm thinking of changing my number again."

"Think they'll send a hit squad?"

He wriggled his toes in their argyles. It was the only tell that he was agitated, and all the time he'd been in the field it would have been hidden in black Oxfords and parked under his desk.

"If you think that's funny, you haven't been reading papers or watching television. Just now the Bureau's living out Hoover's favorite wet-dream. They probably wouldn't waste a cartridge on a brontosaurus like me, but they'd truss me up with the IRS so tight my great-grandchildren wouldn't be able to breathe."

I didn't have anything for that. I took out the picture Beryl Garnet had given me and reached it over.

He took it, stood his beer can on the arm of his chair, and fished a pair of steel-rimmed glasses out of his shirt pocket, but didn't put them on. Instead he held them in front of the photograph like a magnifying glass.

"I'm getting something," he said. "Jewel name of some kind. Ruby?"

"Garnet. First name Delwayne. There's a place for you on the Psychic Hotline if you ever get restless."

"I always had a good memory. Back then it was an asset. Garnet, I remember that little fish. Swam right through the net we rigged up for the keepers. He never would've made the list except for what he knew and how easy he'd crack. Look at that face. Like a skinny Humpty-Dumpty."

"Maybe you're selling him short. He's stayed hidden all these years."

"That's because for most of them he hasn't been worth looking for. Anything he'd have to tell us we can get off a Golden Oldies album." He handed back the picture. "Anyway, I know where he is. Or was when I quit."

I put away the picture next to my notepad and left them both in my pocket. Burlingame's mouth healed over whenever anyone started recording his words.

He drank some more beer, delicately. He used to fist back Scotches like fizzwater, but now it was like watching someone kiss his ex-wife. "Inside secret. It might not be so secret anymore, but I make it a point not to keep up. We never put anyone on the Ten Most Wanted list until we knew where he was. That way, we could time things and pop him just before the evening news. I know that shoots my legend all to hell, but who cares. If I don't do it, some revisionist prick with a press card in his hatband will do it after I'm dead. Why give him the scoop?"

I'd known most of that, but I didn't say anything. I assumed he knew reporters no longer wore hats or used words like "scoop."

"So why didn't you pop Garnet?"

"We found out the two geniuses who blew themselves up on the way to blow up the Federal Building were the whole organization. Washington wanted to go ahead anyway, for cosmetic purposes, but I convinced them we'd wind up looking like idiots when the case went to court. We rotated Garnet off the list and plugged in an armored-car bandit holed up over a TV repair shop in Cleveland. We'd been saving him for just such a rainy day."

"But you continued to keep up with Delwayne."

"He was my hobby. Well, not just him. After the Chief died I thought it might be a good idea to update my files on some of the investigations that didn't go into the showcase at headquarters. A lot of the agents involved were busy reinventing themselves, which is hard to do as long as there's a pin on the wall map who Knew Them When. You think twice about pulling out a pin and throwing it away when it has points on both ends." He looked at a thumbnail that needed manicuring. It had probably needed it since he'd stopped wearing suits. "What makes Delwayne hot after all this time? His timing's off if he wants back in this country. Even a bomber by default makes Customs nervous."

I told him the job. There wasn't any reason not to. The client was dead and I was in charge of an ashcan.

"Huh. I thought Aunt Beryl died years ago."

"You knew her?"

"Better than she knew me. I put her place under surveillance after Delwayne rabbited. That was S.O.P. with a long successful history going back to Dillinger, but it hit the wall in the sixties. Those revolutionary types had discipline; cut off all ties to friends and relatives when they went underground. In most cases the ties were half cut already, but even so." His eyes got a distant look. It didn't last more than a second, and afterward I wasn't sure it had been there at all. "You learn a lot of shit when you plant a bug in a whorehouse."

"Yeah?"

"Yeah." He drank.

I gave up waiting. There was more there than a couple of off-color stories, but I wasn't going to get them then or ever.

I took a swallow, teetered the can on my knee. "So did any of these files come home with you?"

The den was small and pine-paneled, with a dartboard on the door, a half-grown rolltop desk, and more family pictures on the walls, most of them much older than those outside. A boy wearing a first draft of Burlingame's square features posed in a cap and knickers in a monochrome snapshot with a pretty girl about fourteen, who might have been an older sister. I'd never heard him mention family apart from the one he'd started from scratch.

He'd gone in five minutes ahead, then unlocked the door. A portable file box stood on the desk with its lid open. It had probably come from a floor safe, possibly under the desk where he'd have to pull out a bottom drawer to open it. Other security features would apply. He knew the black-bag boys back to front.

The tabs were labeled AUTO, CHECKING, DENTAL, HOUSE-HOLD; domestic dodges like that. They might have stood for ABSCAM, CASTRO, DALLAS, and HOFFA. Then again the files might have contained automobile receipts, checking statements, dentist's bills, and his homeowner's insurance policy. The file might have been a decoy to distract me from a secret sliding panel or a hidden midget with a photographic memory.

"No computer?"

He shook his head. "You can burn or shred paper, but no one can totally erase a hard drive. I gave notice the day I came back from lunch and found the office troll hooking one up in my office. I didn't train to be a typist." He handed me a gray cardboard folder with dog-eared corners.

I looked at the tab. " 'Office supplies'?"

"Don't waste time trying to figure out my code. It's been

tried. You're holding the sum total of the Bureau's knowledge on the subject of Delwayne Garnet."

I hefted it. It was an inch and a half thick, with a gusseted bottom to prevent bursting. "You collected this much on a punk fuse? Hoover must have sent the chairman of the senate appropriations committee a fruitcake that year."

"This is nothing. You should see *your* file."

With his deadpan, you could never tell when he was serious. "How long can I keep it?"

"You can't."

I stroked the plastic tab with the ball of my thumb. "We never did establish compensation."

"I told you I was bored. Did you think I was jacking you up? The file doesn't leave this room. All I need is you getting broadsided by an Escalade on the way home and some cop finding it and tracing it back here. On second thought, give it back." He stuck out a square hand.

"Hang on, Red. A beer doesn't make us brothers. I get jacked up so much they call me Jack. I was suspicious the minute you said you had all the money you need. Nobody does. And the last thing anybody ever gave me for nothing was a swat on the butt in the delivery room."

He withdrew the hand. "Well, you're right about that. I want something back."

"How much?" I hadn't stopped to cash Lawrence Meldrum's check on the way from the office. It meant an extra round trip.

"Not how much. What. Just let me know how it comes out."

"It?"

"Delwayne." He slapped the carry case on the desk. "I've got a box full of files with no last page. When I was contributing to society, I never once saw a case through from start to finish. At some point I stopped solving crimes and started cataloguing them. When you find Garnet, tell me, and tell me if he told you anything. At least then I can close one file out of fifty."

"That's all you want?"

"It'll give me something to look forward to between now and when my daughter visits next Christmas."

I blinked. He was every retired car salesman who couldn't keep from hanging around the lot. I hoped he wasn't contagious.

"It doesn't promise to make much of a story," I said.

"I'd rather it was Deep Throat." He rolled a shoulder. "But hell."

"Deal."

He closed and latched the lid on the file box and carried it out, shutting me in the den. The cloak-and-dagger may all have been for show. The rest of the stuff he'd spirited away from the field office might still have been sealed somewhere in the room, where even a fellow who is handy with a pick couldn't get to it. For some people, a corkscrew is the shortest distance between two points.

There was a comfortably shabby armchair in a corner, with an ashtray on a little table. I lit a cigarette, crossed my legs, opened the folder, and looked into the faraway eyes of a corpse.

FIVE

E *ye,* actually; the right was occluded by a dark sludge, un-
mistakable even in black and white printed on grainy non-
reflective police stock. The left was staring at something
halfway between it and infinity.

It was a head shot, and until I knew what I was looking at I
turned it sideways trying for vertical. The head lay on glistening asphalt, presenting a three-quarter view of a fine-featured,
African-cast face with a thin Little Richard moustache that
clung to the full upper lip like liner. A pale collar with long tabs
encircled a muscular neck with custom-made fidelity, spread
just enough to display a glossy knot and under it the top half of
a medium-wide necktie with an Art Deco pattern. I saw one
lapel of a houndstooth overcoat, broad and notched. The man
wearing it looked surprised and knowing at the same time. I'd
seen the expression before, always with a combination of envy
and relief.

I glanced at the back. A faded stamp read PROPERTY OCSD
12/31/49 DO NOT REMOVE FROM PREMISES. I didn't know what
an Oakland County Sheriff's Department crime photo was doing in a folder with Delwayne Garnet's name on it.

The next item of interest was an original birth certificate

issued by Wayne County, recording the appearance in Detroit General Hospital of Delwayne Lance West, boy, on June 11, 1950. The mother's name was Fausta West. It rang a leaden bell somewhere in the part of my brain I kept shuttered with sheets over the furniture. The space for the father's name was vacant.

A smeary carbon bearing the heading of the Wayne County Probate Court, signed by a judge whose name I couldn't make out, assigned guardianship of Delwayne Lance West, a minor infant, to Beryl Garnet, widow, aged 35. The document was dated June 14, 1950. She would have been waiting at the hospital exit when Fausta was released.

Just for fun I paged through some other official-looking sheets, hunting for a record of formal adoption. There wasn't any. Assuming the file was complete, it stood to reason. In 1950 it was a great deal more difficult for a single woman to adopt a child than to obtain a guardianship, particularly if the single woman kept a brothel. Delwayne West had become Delwayne Garnet through repetition rather than by court order. The process was just as legal. All you had to do was stop using the original name and use the new one exclusively.

The file was a jumble, with no order and a lot of things that made no sense in any context, much like a person's life. Transcripts from Murray-Wright High School reflected an academic career strong on English, history, and fine arts, and on its way out the back door as to science, math, and geography. I could rule out looking for him behind the counter in a pharmacy or at a bank window. Not knowing where to find New Zealand on a map is no handicap except to explorers.

There were two newspaper clippings, coarse-grained and brittle brown, both stamped CONFIDENTIAL. You had to wonder how the Bureau pulled that one off short of buying up every copy on the stands and mugging the delivery boy. Both were obituaries of sorts. One took up two half-columns to announce the suicide of Fausta West, a former MGM contract player who had appeared in the chorus of a number of Esther Williams musicals before her option ran out. She'd been employed for the past two years as a cocktail waitress in Long Beach, California, where the stunt gaffer she'd subleased her apartment from found her on the floor of her kitchen with all the gas jets open on the stove. A faded pencil notation on the bottom edge dated the clipping: "Sept. 9, 1952." There was nothing to tell me what paper had carried it.

I looked at the postage-stamp size picture that accompanied the article. It showed an unremarkable-looking blonde with a pretty face and an Ipana smile, the kind booking agents kept around in stacks of eight-by-ten glossies and used to plug mouseholes in their offices. How she'd landed even bits in *A* features was an argument in favor of the casting couch. Fade to black at twenty-seven.

The other clipping, folded twice, had taken up most of the front page of the old *Detroit Times* on New Year's Day 1950, with a banner:

LOCAL FIGHTER SHOT TO DEATH

Pictures included a pub shot for the sports desk of a smooth-muscled light-skinned black in satin trunks and lace-up boots, gloved fists raised in defensive position. He looked more focused without an eye full of blood. Another shot, horizontal, showed a sheet-draped gurney rolling through a crowd of beefy men in crumpled fedoras, baggy overcoats, and neckties that reached only to the second buttons of their shirts. One of them glared at the camera with his thumbs jammed inside his belt and a short cigar plugged into his face, eyes glassy in the Speed-Graphic flash. That closed out the composition. If police personnel hadn't provided him, the photographer would have had to inflate one from his kit.

I read the article, then turned it over and read a photocopy of an Oakland County Sheriff's Department case file: fourteen pages typewritten by someone who would never be a Kelly

Girl. It was filled with strikeovers, smeary erasures, and one whole line that had been produced from the wrong row of home keys. The clipping and the report told a complete story except for an ending. Curtis Smallwood, known to the sports page–reading public of 1948–9 as the Black Mamba, had been on his way to a lightweight championship with a 23 and 0 record (eight knockouts) when he dropped his guard and took an unjacketed .38 bullet through his right eye in the parking lot of the Lucky Tiger, a roadhouse seven miles north of Detroit in the wilderness that was then Oakland County, an hour short of midnight on the last day of the 1940s, making him the Motor City's final murder victim of that decade. Plenty of witnesses had heard the shot and the squealing of tires indicating the killer's escape, but none had seen the actual event, which had taken place after Smallwood parked his week-old Alfa-Romeo and before he got to the entrance. He was dead on arrival at the pavement.

The suspects were in large supply. Archie McGraw, his manager, had had words with him over his flamboyant lifestyle, which included a relationship with Fausta West, a Hollywood starlet who'd been photographed with him at a Detroit nightclub during a personal appearance to promote a film. A producer at MGM named Wellstone, who'd been pruning West for a career as a featured player, was rumored to have threatened Smallwood with a drubbing by studio goons if he didn't "lay off the white meat." There was a name on the list I hadn't thought of in years: Ben Morningstar, who had inherited the territory formerly belonging to the Purple Gang, including labor racketeering, drug peddling, and the local fight game. If you had a budding Joe Louis and you wanted to show him off against a legitimate contender, you had to go to Morningstar first. No animosity reported between him and Smallwood; being Ben Morningstar was suspicious enough when an acquaintance succumbed to lead poisoning in the open air.

The file didn't mention any arrests. A much smaller newspaper clipping without pictures told readers there were no new leads in the Curtis Smallwood killing. Nothing after that. There were too many other things going on in 1950 to allow room for a murder mystery without a solution.

I could guess the thinking in the sheriff's department. Archie McGraw hadn't cracked, and a Hollywood honcho like Wellstone was always and forever outside their jurisdiction, or for that matter any jurisdiction that involved lawyers on retainer to a major studio. Morningstar bought inspectors and better by the package, like Gilette blades. Fausta West's suicide two years later would have given them someone to point to later if they ever felt the need; dead people made handy horizontal surfaces to pile things on, without fear of complications. Even if they hadn't evidence to close out the case based on that, they would be satisfied there weren't any untagged murderers walking around. Contrary to fiction, even lazy cops prefer to tie things off, however loosely. I found a Long Beach Police Department photo of Fausta, pale with bruises beneath her eyes, stretched out on her back on the linoleum floor of her kitchen with her ankles crossed and her head resting on a sofa cushion with palm fronds embroidered on it. She looked peaceful.

An FBI blowup of Delwayne Garnet's senior picture followed. I thought he looked a little like Curtis Smallwood. Then I didn't. I didn't see any Fausta in him, except maybe a little around the eyes. You can't trust a photograph. At best it's a flat illusion of a three-dimensional reality.

There was some sixties stuff: a mimeographed handout on yellow-jaundice paper with "fascist" misspelled three ways, inviting freedom-lovers everywhere to join something called the Moroccan Army of Liberation; front-and-profile mugs with fingerprints of Delwayne's revolutionary colleagues from early arrests; color photos taken from different angles of a mangled van containing scattered body parts, what remained of the M.A.L. after the bomb went off prematurely and Delwayne fled. Pictures of whomp-jawed men in snapbrim hats standing behind a bed with pistols and revolvers and automatic rifles spread out on it, personal effects of the deceased. It all seemed more dated than the stuff from almost twenty years earlier, but then that whole decade smelled like bare feet.

The feds had traced Delwayne to Toronto, where in 1987 he'd been putting his fine-arts education to use, drawing storyboards for local television commercials and assembling newspaper and magazine advertisements from clip books. Up there he'd gone by the name Lance West. It was as if he'd known he was pathetically easy to trace, so hadn't bothered to wander too far afield when putting together a new identity. A contact sheet showed him at thirty-six, carrying a large portfolio along a bleak wintry street in long shot and telephoto close-up. He'd grown a chin beard and filled out a little, but his classmates would recognize him at a Murray-Wright reunion if he bothered to show up. I doubted he would, and not because he was technically a fugitive. Nothing about his background suggested the kind of young man who formed long-standing relationships.

Law enforcement files are always the same. You always open them with the feeling you've been invited to visit an exclusive club, and close them thinking you've seen it all before, in a better version.

I drummed the material together, slipped it back into the folder and the folder onto the desk, and returned to the living room. Red Burlingame had his recliner fully extended and was cable-flipping with the remote: half-second explosions of bilious congressmen, stick-figure cartoons, self-important authors, reheated romantic comedies, dumbed-down documentaries, marathon breast-cancer discussions, a clever but unpleasant sci-fi comedy, and country music videos with no country and music that had supported different lyrics in more talented throats. He gave up finally, long after I would have, and settled on a 1970s sitcom whose entire cast was long since dead or in jail. The laughtrack was borrowed from *I Love Lucy*.

"This how old G-men spend their time?" I asked.

"I thought about greeting at Wal-Mart. Too drafty. Who do you like for Curtis Smallwood?"

"Ben Morningstar."

"Yeah, me, too. I was ready to take him down on a couple of hundred years' worth of RICO violations when he up and died on me."

"Ungrateful son of a bitch."

"You ever meet him?"

"I worked for him once. That's how I met Beryl Garnet."

He squashed the POWER button with his thumb. The picture on the tube folded up and blipped out in the middle of an abortion gag. "What did you do for that crumb?"

"Blew up a bus full of kindergarteners. It was an insurance job."

"Okay, pardon the hell out of me. I assumed you had standards."

"Standards are for steady work. I'm saving up for a bail fund." I sat on the sofa. "A girl he had custody of went missing. I went looking in the usual places. That restore your faith?"

"Find her?"

"Kind of."

"Dead?"

I shook my head. "She may be out now. It's been twenty-two years, and all she did was commit a couple of murders. It didn't have anything to do with this. Was Curtis Smallwood Delwayne Garnet's father?"

"Could be. He was born six months after Smallwood was killed. Oakland County sent investigators out to Hollywood. They ran into a very polite brick wall. Miss West was shooting on location in Italy, some little mountain village without telephones, inaccessible by automobile. You read the report."

"It didn't say if they bought it."

"It might've been true. She was only back in Detroit for the birth later, and she was probably registered here under a phony name. By the time the certificate became public record, she'd have been back in L.A., minus one baby and getting back her figure for some part she'd never land."

"Why leave L.A. at all?"

"Press, probably. Hospital staff out there didn't live on their paychecks even then. Here, no one expects picture people to check into a public facility. All she had to do to become invisible was lay off the peroxide."

He put aside the remote. "Oakland County cops didn't have much choice but to buy what MGM was selling. The studios were sovereign nations in California. They lost their national clout when Antitrust made them sell their theater chains, but the sale money gave them plenty of juice to tend their own backyard. The old whiskers who invented the system were still in charge. They treated the local law like their own security, and why not? It was a factory town. It's damn near impossible for out-of-town talent to gain a foothold without cooperation from the natives. They watched Van Johnson mince around a closed set and flew home."

"They talk to this producer Wellstone?"

"If that was his name. I haven't looked at the file in years."

"It's incomplete. There's no catalogue of evidence, to begin with."

"The case was almost voting age when we inherited Delwayne," Burlingame said. "Files get moved. Things slip out and fall behind cabinets. Also there wasn't any love lost between the feds and the locals in those years. Anyway, we weren't out to solve any old murders that fell outside our jurisdiction. We just wanted a line on our fugitive."

"The paper said Wellstone threatened Smallwood with a beating if he didn't stay away from Fausta West. The studio had invested too much in her to see her throw it all away on an interracial affair."

"That was the *Times,* right? You're quoting the Hearst Press."

"You're right. Reporters are so much more reliable now."

He blew air out his nose. "It's not impossible. Harry Cohn at Columbia sent thugs after Sammy Davis Jr. when he took up with Kim Novak. They say that's how he lost his eye."

"He lost it in an automobile accident. But I heard the story too. Maybe whoever told it was thinking about Smallwood."

"Whoever shot out the fighter's eye was pretty good. He used a revolver, and there weren't any powder burns around the socket."

"The revolver ever turn up?"

He shook his head. "That's a vote for Morningstar's people. Those connected boys throw away guns like tinfoil."

"Everybody does. Guns are cheap." I got up. "I'm not being paid to solve any murders either. Thanks for the look, Red. I'll start with Toronto."

"Dress warm."

"I'll farm it out first. Delwayne could have moved fifty times in sixteen years. How's your daughter?"

His mouth remained a straight line across his square face, but the corners of his eyes creased humorously. "She's okay. She and my son-in-law are adopting a baby boy."

"Junior G-Man."

The creases flattened out. "If that's what he wants. I hope I'm dead by then."

SIX

On the ground floor of the Detroit Public Library on Woodward Avenue stands a world globe, nearly a story high and rendered obsolete by international events of fairly recent origin. No one consults it anymore, but it screens the afternoon sun from the derelicts who stretch out at its base. They're always sleeping, no matter what time you visit the building. Dumpster-diving must be exhausting work.

The library serves pretty much the same purpose, except to those of us who draw a distinction between information and raw data cut with spam. I went to the out-of-town telephone directories and spent quality time with the Toronto yellow pages before settling on the Loyal Dominion Enquiry Agency on Queen Street in Toronto. I figured any group of detectives still arrogant about siding with the loser in the American Revolution had the pluck necessary to track down a thirty-year fugitive from U.S. justice. Its display ad featured the Maple Leaf flag and a Mountie. I wrote down the number, along with a couple of others in case we fell out over free trade.

While I was there, I used a microfilm reader to study up on Curtis Smallwood. I didn't know why he fascinated me so, except the backdrop was a very different Detroit from the one

I knew. Three major department stores took out full-page ads every day in all three daily newspapers, nightlife boiled through clubs both legal and tucked behind steel-reinforced doors with screw-you panels, and the only thing Japanese to be found on Jefferson at rush hour was the occasional gardener commuting to and from Grosse Pointe. George Kell was batting .343 for the Tigers, Henry Ford II dropped broad hints about a whole new division to be built around a luxury car designed to boot the Cadillac out of its market. Walter Reuther, president of the United Auto Workers, was asking what was in it for labor.

Smallwood, the "Black Mamba," got plenty of press with a stunning series of knockouts, T.K.O.'s, and decisions, one of which took place before ten million viewers during the Friday night fights on NBC. He had a lethal hook, an explosive cross, and the legs of a Triple-Crown champion. America was in love with boxing in 1949: It fit neatly on a bulbous nine-inch screen, and you knew which one to root for by the shade of his trunks. Smallwood's were black, with a white satin stripe that contrasted nicely with his medium-dark skin. I wondered if the televised fight was available on tape.

I didn't learn anything about the shooting that hadn't been in Burlingame's file. Reporters kept the story on life-support for weeks, mainly through feature interviews with the dead man's acquaintances—not counting Fausta West, who was shooting outside the country and unavailable for comment. A picture of her and Smallwood taken near the entrance to the Oriole Ballroom showed her in a striped fur coat, chinchilla or Siberian tiger, him in what might have been the same houndstooth he'd worn the night he was killed, with a fringed white scarf draped around his neck and a borsalino hat tugged down rakishly over one eyebrow. Neither was smiling, and their heads were turned toward the camera as if the photographer had called out their names to get their attention just before he pushed the button. It was the shot said to have drawn the threat from Paul Wellstone, the producer at MGM, and possibly a bullet. White supremacists were mentioned as well. It had been only thirteen years since Detroit police broke up the Black Legion branch of the Ku Klux Klan in connection with another fatal shooting.

Wellstone was interviewed, in his leather-upholstered office in Hollywood. He came off charming and jovial, good-naturedly denying rumors of hard words between him and the deceased. The *Free Press* reporter assigned to the story might have been influenced by a VIP tour of the studio, including a visit to the set where Lana Turner was filming, extensively detailed, but I doubted it. That was a tough generation of news-hawk, who had covered the gang wars of the 1930s, the 1943 race riot, and a long string of Grand Jury investigations into city corruption, including the murder of a United States senator in 1945. In a photo exclusive to the paper, the producer smiled from behind a couple of hectares of desk, dressed in a terrycloth sportcoat with patch pockets and a silk foulard. He had a moon face, a silly little chevron-shaped moustache, and eyes as hard as asphalt.

The byline belonged to someone named Edie Van Eyck. I don't know why I noted it down, except that it was rare for a woman journalist in those days to land an assignment from the city desk. But then the story had passed to the feature section for lack of progress. She was probably as dead as most of the principals.

Closer to home, Archie McGraw, Smallwood's manager, ducked the center spot. He forted up behind a pair of former light heavyweights and gave no interviews. There were no pictures of him.

Ben Morningstar was equally elusive. He was in Havana, scouting a site for a casino to be built and operated by a coalition of Detroit businessmen. Joe Zerilli and Sam Lucy were among the partners. Respectively, they sat on the national governing council of La Cosa Nostra and ran the sports book in southeastern Michigan. A swarthy, more ferretlike version of the Morningstar I'd known scowled at a contraband camera in a morgue shot snapped on the back terrace of Al Capone's vacation home in Miami Beach. I'd seen it before. It was the only known likeness taken of him between a group shot struck at the time of a Detroit Police Department sweep in 1931 and ghosty Kinescope footage of his appearance before the Kefauver Senate Committee to Investigate Organized Crime in Interstate Commerce twenty years later. He hadn't given Congress any more than he'd given the cops or the press, citing his Fifth Amendment right to avoid self-incrimination seventeen times. He'd worn his trademark heavy black-framed glasses only in the Florida picture, removing them when he'd been arrested and before his televised testimony in 1951. His nickname in the bad old days was Specs, and he'd hated it.

Edie Van Eyck had written the McGraw and Morningstar non-stories. Those old-time sob sisters never let the grass grow under their chunky heels.

The stuff from City had even less substance. The Black Mamba had threatened the referee in the Rodriguez fight for delaying the count, or maybe it was a ringside judge for shaving points; no one could pin down the details or their source. An unidentified contact in the police department hinted that Smallwood had placed bets against himself in the forthcoming fight with Joe "Rock" Candy, a Philadelphia native who had to go through Smallwood to get to Jake LaMotta, which opened the nationwide gambling racket to smoky speculation and a dead end. Someone reported overhearing the deceased agreeing to meet what sounded like a female caller on the telephone just before he left for the Lucky Tiger and his death in the parking lot. Again, the information went unattributed.

You could almost hear the first thud of earth striking the lid of the coffin containing the Curtis Smallwood case. Whenever the mysterious-woman card came up, the investigation was as good as buried. Both the cops and the papers were busy kicking dirt into the hole. I scrolled forward to 1952, missed the local coverage of Fausta West's suicide, and had to go back. She got a paragraph on the obituary page, taken off the AP wire, with no photo and no mention of her connection to the Smallwood murder, which by then was strictly of historical interest. In the meantime, President Truman had survived an assassination attempt, King George VI had died, and the Tigers had traded Vic Wertz to the Cardinals. Edie Van Eyck was busy that week interviewing Clare Booth Luce.

After an hour and a half among the Studebaker advertisements I left the library and staggered blinking out into the twenty-first century. I drove back to the office, collected the mail from under the slot with no interference from the lack of clients in the reception room, and wastebasketed the circulars and second notices while waiting for someone to pick up at the Loyal Dominion Enquiry Agency.

The quasi-English-accented female voice that finally came on the line listened to me, then put me on Hold. I heard part of the score of *The Phantom of the Opera*. I reached out and patted Beryl Garnet's brushed-bronze cap. "Patience, old girl."

Just before the chandelier let go I spoke to someone named Llewellyn Hale, who sounded American, and of course he was, although they prefer to call *us* Americans and to hell with the shared continent. He didn't spill his tea when I told him I was working a thirty-four-year-old missing-person case. He asked a few questions. I heard computer keys chuckling. We discussed terms—in U.S. dollars, he was no provincial bumpkin—and he said he'd be in touch. Politeness is Canada's chief export, after Moosehead beer and stand-up comics.

I didn't pat the urn again or speak to it when I'd hung up. We hadn't been that friendly before the incineration.

Lawyer Meldrum's check was giving my wallet heartburn. I went out to sock it in the business account, holding back a few hundred for bribery and gasoline, deposited a sandwich and a cup of coffee in my personal account, and let myself back into my hobby room.

The telephone was ringing. It was Llewellyn Hale at Loyal Dominion. He'd found Delwayne Garnet in just under fifty minutes.

SEVEN

The customs agent on the foreign side of the Ambassador Bridge looked like trouble; but then that was the idea. He was six-two, with his cap squared off across his sandy brows and a jaw that ached for a chinstrap. The morning sun was at his back, limning his uniform in purple.

He glanced at my driver's license, handed it back, and asked what my purpose was for visiting Canada. When I said, "Business," his gray gaze went to the urn strapped into the passenger's seat. "What's in the container?"

"Cremains."

He waved me over for the full treatment. I climbed out of the car for the patdown and smoked three cigarettes while a pair of uniforms pawed through the upholstery and lifted the hood and felt the trunk lining and poked at the undercarriage, looking for terrorists and undeclared fruit.

I'd left the munitions behind, which was a wise choice, because they found the catch to the gun compartment I'd tricked out under the dash and sprang it open. They'd seen my investigator's license and carry permit, so they didn't ask any questions about it. One of them tugged the cover off the urn, slid out the aluminum canister, twisted loose the top, and stirred the gritty contents with his fingers. He was older and darker than the others and might have been American Indian.

"Who is it?" he asked.

"Client. I'm delivering her to her son."

"I always thought human ashes would be more fluffy."

"You wouldn't if you knew her."

He put everything back together and held it out. "Sorry for the inconvenience, sir. These days we have to be careful."

I cradled the urn in one arm like a loving cup. "It was 'cremains,' wasn't it? I should've said ashes."

"Enjoy your stay in Canada."

I shook loose of Windsor by way of Queen's Highway 401 and followed it for two hours through miles of forestry the lumber sharks of Fifth Avenue and Pall Mall hadn't managed to get their hands on, then took 2 along the shore of Lake Ontario, which on a cloudless day in June offered no horizon, rolling unbroken into blue infinity. Miles out, the occasional turnturtle profile of a laden ore carrier crept among the waves like dragons on an Old World map.

Toronto's a clean city, not much crime of the violent kind, and no place for a professional who pays his bills with the interest accrued from human misery. From that perspective, there isn't a thing wrong with it that twenty years of crooked politics and a casino or two couldn't cure. The motorists obey the law without much horn action and the swarms of Hollywood second units that shoot there on location have to send back to the states for bags of trash to make the place look like New York City. Even the little man on the pedestrian WALK signal has good posture.

Loyal Dominion appeared to be doing well, despite the inequity in abductions, blackmail, and street thuggery; but then I supposed even Canadians stepped out on their spouses and ran away from home. A discreet sign bearing just its name stuck out perpendicularly from a four-story brick building that sparkled from recent sand-blasting. Its neighbors included the local office of a large United States travel agency and one of those places that sell coffee in giant cups with whitecaps. I drove two blocks past the building and beat a BMW into a spot freshly vacated by a delivery van. The driver of the BMW tapped his horn and drove on without gestures. I hoped I wouldn't need an interpreter.

The air was crisp, on a day when Detroiters were testing their air conditioning and wondering if they could get by without bringing a jacket to work for the drive home. There was a virile breeze blowing off the lake, and in the dead of summer you can still draw a horizontal line from there to the Bering Sea on a map. I pulled my suitcoat out of the back seat and shrugged into it as I walked.

A hidden gong went off when I opened the door to the detective agency. The reception room was a done-over storefront, with pale green carpeting, antique excursion posters framed on the walls, and a pair of panoramic aerial shots hung side by side above a doughnut-shaped work station of Horseshoe Falls roaring into a ravine full of smoky spray. I thought for a moment I'd entered the travel agency by mistake.

A freckle-faced towhead sprawled across the work station interrupted his conversation with the receptionist to look my way. He had on a denim shirt over a gray T-shirt and jeans with the cuffs turned up, the way U.S. youngsters used to wear them in the fifties. The scuffed sneakers seemed to be overdoing things, but then I didn't keep up with fashions on either side of the border. Maybe I looked like someone who'd bled through a seam in the time-space continuum. He said something to the woman seated inside the doughnut, then undraped himself and strolled out through an open door in back.

The woman at the work station smiled up at me. A plastic hairband kept her pale brown bangs in place. She wore a white sweater with a gold chain holding it together in front and a blue silk blouse, and when she moved her hand, a charm bracelet on that wrist jangled and clanked like armored cavalry.

"Amos Walker. I have an appointment with Llewellyn Hale."

"Yes, the American detective. Mr. Hale says to go right in. His office is at the end of the hall."

This was the owner of the virtual English accent I'd talked to the day before. I said, "When did he say that?"

"Just now."

The hallway led past two rows of open doors, beyond which young, casually dressed people sat in lozenge-shaped offices, cricketing computer keyboards and speaking over headsets. In between the doors were framed letters of official appreciation, signed by ministers and home secretaries. The door at the end was open as well. I raised my fist to rap on the frame.

"Come in, please, Mr. Walker. We don't stand on ceremony here."

I recognized this voice, too. It belonged to the freckled towhead. He sat behind a small blue-enameled desk, immersed to his elbows in what looked like a tangle of black seaweed on the composition top. The walls were hung with floor plans of Byzantine temples and a small window behind him looked out on a street that was identical to the one that ran past the front of the building.

He extricated himself from the tangle long enough to shake hands and point at the plastic scoop chair that faced the desk. "I have to say you look like my idea of what an American private detective should look like."

"Broke?" I sat down.

"Resilient. We've an easier time of it here, I think. The law is quite specific about what we can and can't do. So long as we color inside the lines, it lets us alone."

"It's the same where I come from."

He smiled. "Only you don't always color inside the lines."

"It's a four-hour drive, Mr. Hale. Not a spaceship. The work's the same."

"You didn't fly?"

"You have to be at the airport two hours early. By then I was in St. Thomas."

"Next time you ought to take the train." He caught me looking at what he was doing, and grinned broadly. "An industrialist in London found our surveillance equipment in his ceiling. This is how he delivered it. Whenever I have time on my hands I untangle another ten or twenty feet. Do you do divorce work?"

"Every time I get the urge I slam a car door on my hand and it goes away. My tag's missing persons. Like Delwayne Garnet?"

He accepted the prod with a forgiving smile. "Mr. Garnet is no longer missing. He never was, actually. He's been observing the statutes and paying the taxes of Canada right here in town for more than thirty years. That's how we found him, by accessing the tax rolls in Ottawa." He twitched an elbow toward a computer console on a stand. "He uses the name Lance West, as you suggested."

"Where's he using it?"

He slid open the deep drawer of the desk with a toe, dumped the ball of wire inside, and kicked the drawer shut. Then he spun his chair and lifted a marbled gray cardboard folder off a neat stack on a credenza under the window. "His address is on the first page," he said, turning back and holding it out. "He works at home."

It was printed in boldface. "Where's Yonge Street?"

"Just round the corner. I wouldn't be surprised if I passed Mr. West every day on the street. Shall we bill you, or would you rather leave a check with the receptionist?"

I read the report in my car. Lance West, 52, was employed by Lost Galleon Entertainment, publisher and distributor of a line of graphic novels, which Llewellyn Hale had described as "Comic books with a glandular condition"; complex stories of conflicted superheroes, disgraced police officers, and other societal misfits pitted against even worse antagonists in stories told through panels, speech balloons, and spelled-out sound effects. Personal details were sketchy. There was no mention of marriages, children, or club memberships. But then all I'd authorized Loyal Dominion to do was find Garnet/West. A run through court records hadn't turned up so much as a ticket for jaywalking, much less making or detonating bombs. International flight to avoid prosecution seemed to be the universal cure for political principles.

The Yonge Street address belonged to the second story of a building containing a seafood-and-pasta restaurant. I found a spot across the street and got out with the urn under my arm to read the menu posted in the window. It was placed conveniently next to a door with a gridded glass, behind which a flight of narrow steps led to the next level. The specialty of the house was ravioli cooked in squid ink. I should have packed a lunch.

A narrow alley separated the building from a stationery shop next door. I took it around to the back, where three cars shared a hundred square feet of brick paving with a pair of locked Dumpsters, and looked up at the second-floor windows. There were four, including two half-size crankouts that would probably belong to bathrooms. The square butts of air conditioners stuck out of the others. No easy exits there. An accommodating town, Toronto. I liked it more the longer I stayed.

The door to the front stairs was unlocked. The well had been painted recently, a pleasing shade of teal, and I breathed through my mouth to avoid taking in fumes. The steps creaked. There was nothing I could do about that. I missed my .38. Most serious injuries take place on staircases, particularly when there are felons at the top.

I made it to the landing without taking on any fresh holes. The place appeared to be in the middle of a spruce-up; a wainscoted hallway stretching to my right glistened with fresh varnish, but the floral runner looked as if it had been pressed between the pages of a book for sixty years. The jury was still out on the vintage bowl fixtures hanging from the ceiling. They were either part of the retro remodeling craze or left over from when they were new.

There were two doors, paneled and painted, with numbers in scrolled brass fixed with brads to the center. The number on the second door was the one I was interested in. I used the section of wall between for a shield and knocked.

"Who is it?" The voice was muffled by the door. I never try to read anything into one in that situation.

"Delivery for Lance West."

He was silent just long enough for me to wonder if he took deliveries of any kind.

"Okay, just a second."

Bolts slid. Chains jingled. Latches turned. I got ready to put my foot in the door.

It opened wide, a surprise. A slightly older version of the Delwayne Garnet I'd seen in FBI telephoto shots stood in the doorway, wearing a gray hooded University of Toronto sweat-shirt over brown cords with the ribs rubbed shiny at the knees, carpet slippers on his feet. He'd put on weight and lost hair, but the chin whiskers looked the same. At close range I was sure he was part black. Turpentine fumes rolled out of the apartment behind him.

Time and lack of interest from the other side of the border had blunted his reflexes. He blinked at me from behind half-glasses, then at the urn I was holding. "What the hell's that?"

"Delwayne Garnet?"

He took in air and tried to put the door in my face. I got my weight against it and swiveled inside.

"I'm not a federal agent," I said. "I'm not even a cop. I really am here just to make a delivery."

He'd stepped back, expecting an assault. "My name is West."

"Your mother's name was West."

He turned and ran.

I said hell, set the urn on a coffee table covered with artistic clutter—paintbrushes sticking up out of glasses, stained rags, stubs of charcoal scattered like droppings—and followed him down a short hall. The door he'd slammed behind him was locked, but it was one of those bathroom locks with a straight slot, designed to slip with a butterknife in case someone fell in the tub and needed rescuing. I used my pocket knife on it and found Garnet with one foot on the toilet, wriggling to get his hips through the narrow crankout window.

I grabbed the waistband of his pants and pulled him back inside. His foot slipped off the toilet and he sat on the floor hard. Ten Most Wanted, my ass.

EIGHT

How do I know these are Beryl's ashes?"

Perched on a tall stool upholstered in black vinyl and silver duct tape, Delwayne Garnet had the top off the canister and was glowering inside. The stool was the only place to sit in the living room/office, apart from an unmade bed and a plaid armchair with a brick inserted in place of an amputated leg. I was sitting on one of its arms. The seat, sprung and sunken, looked like a miniature Bermuda Triangle.

"I can't swear to it myself," I said. "You hear stories about crematoriums. Does it matter?"

"I guess not." He put the top back on and slid the canister into the bronze urn, balanced on the rail of a tilted drawing board. "Who was it said if we really believed in an afterlife, there'd be no need to visit a cemetery?"

"Billy Graham. I've got a receipt from the lawyer for you to sign. You get a copy, if it helps." I found it in my pocket and held it out.

"Lawyers are fascists' tools." He took the receipt and read it. "What about the rest? The house on John R, all the money she squeezed out of her girls? A starving family in the Dominican

Republic could live for a year off what she paid the Detroit Police Department every Tuesday."

"City turned the house into an empty lot years ago. The rest never came up in conversation. I suppose she made other arrangements."

"She would. I was just a tax deduction to her." He took a fine-line pen off the drawing board rail, started to write "Lance West," then drew a line through it when I cleared my throat, and scrawled "Delwayne Garnet" instead. I took it, tore off the original, and gave him the carbon.

"She didn't pay taxes. Her business was cash and carry. She raised you as a favor to your mother, because having a baby in Hollywood and no wedding band didn't fly with the morals clause in a player's contract. She didn't have to. She went on supporting you after you ran away with the circus. She didn't have to do that either. Then you stiffed her for better than thirty years without even a postcard. In her place I wouldn't have given you my ashes. But that's just me."

He pouted. I was beginning to see why no marriages had appeared on his record. There was a patch of dried blood on his cheek where he'd scratched himself trying to poke a thirty-six-inch waist through a thirty-inch window. The effort had taken the starch out of him, and he'd moped in from the bathroom and climbed up on the stool and listened to my spiel without interruption. It helped that I didn't look like FBI. The Bureau wasn't disguising its undercover men in cheap suits and tired faces that season.

An oversize sheet of drawing paper was clipped to the tilted board, with two rows of panels roughed out on it in pencil. The action appeared to have something to do with two men wrestling on top of a tall building. The speech balloons were blank. Finished sheets of panels were thumbtacked to the walls. He was a good representative artist, with an eye for subtle expressions. The anatomy looked accurate, but then I can barely draw a conclusion.

"You've come a ways from the Moroccan Army of Liberation," I said.

"That was Stu's idea. He thought it sounded exotic, and that it would convince the pigs we had branches in both hemispheres. He was the idea man. Karl made the bombs. He had a chemistry scholarship at the U of M before he dropped out. He showed me how to make an explosive device out of used kitty litter."

Stuart Pearman and Karl Anthony Mason were the anarchists the Detroit forensics team had shoveled out of the wrecked van in 1968. I said, "I would've thought it was explosive enough without help. Ever blow anything up?"

"Only on paper." He swept an arm toward one of the tacked-up sheets, filled with flying debris and body parts and a *Ka-rumpph!* in fat letters. "I'm hot stuff with a pencil or a brush. Any other tool—"

"Ka-rumpph. How's the money?"

"Pays the rent. The General Service Tax is killing me. These streets don't clean themselves. Lost Galleon Entertainment is four guys and a PageMaker program. If I could hook up with one of the big imprints in the States I'd be set. They're making movies out of graphic novels now."

"Spiderman."

He screwed up his face. "No, that's a comic book: steroid freaks in long underwear. I mean dark, really complex pictures, where the camera crawls inside the heads of serial killers and psychotic gangsters. The originals are practically storyboards for the production team. All they have to do is cast the parts."

"I remember when they used to make movies out of real books."

"If you mean those gasbags on the *New York Times* list, they still are. I'm talking about the difference between a seven-course meal and a Twinkie. This is a respected art form."

"So what's stopping you from making it big in the States?"

"I'm a fugitive. I have to lie low."

"No one's looking for you, Delwayne. The feds have known where you are for years. Who do you think I asked?"

"If that's true, how come I'm not in custody?"

"They lost interest a week after you rabbited. They have bigger shrimp to poach these days, suicide bombers and video pirates. They use old hippies for target practice."

He frowned. He picked up a soft-lead pencil and added an ear to one of the men duking it out on the skyscraper. He threw the pencil down on the rail.

"This could all be a ruse to coax me across the border and arrest me. I bet you're a veteran."

"You might re-think *ruse* before you make the trip," I said.

"Yeah, I served. I don't owe the feds a thing."

"Neither do I. A pig's a pig. I watched them belly their way up to the trough for eighteen years. This one fat lieutenant asked me for a blow job once. Next time I saw him was on TV, accepting a commendation for valor from the mayor."

"Maybe he earned it." I got up. "I didn't come here for your backstory. I had that already. I don't care if you come back home or go on drawing pictures for mooses and Mounties. I got what I came for." I folded the receipt and put it in my pocket.

His eyes followed me up. He unhooked his reading glasses. Without them, his face resembled one I'd been looking at in pictures lately; fuzzy ones made up of tiny dots in fifty-year-old newspapers. "I guess if you thought about it you'd hate my guts."

"You'd be surprised how little time I spend thinking about your guts."

"I do. I think about it a lot. Not what *you* think. I didn't know you existed until a little while ago. I mean that whole idiotic episode, picket signs and combat footage and throwing buckets of blood in people's faces. I tried to do a story about it. The images wouldn't come. It's not the block; I don't believe in that except as an excuse not to work. After thirty years it all seems childish, even for a comic book."

"Graphic novel."

"You know what I mean. Or maybe you don't. A lot of people who lived through it can't get past it, no matter what side of it they were on."

"So don't write about it. Do what they did then: Tell it as a western, or a comedy in Korea. You draw good explosions. Your sound effects need work. They go boom, just like you always heard."

"I wouldn't know. I wasn't there when Stu and Karl were killed. I used to have nightmares about it, though, where I was. I saw myself lying in pieces and wondering how I was going to stick them all back together." He looked at the drawing sheet, picked up the pencil, put it back. "Sometimes I had them when I wasn't asleep."

"Flashbacks are cheap entertainment."

"I haven't had one in years. I guess if I was going to use the material it should have been then."

"What are you going to do with the ashes?"

He put his glasses back on, as if he couldn't see the urn without them. "I haven't thought about it. I'm not the kind of person who can live with something like that on the mantel, even if I had a mantel. Toss them in Humber Bay, I suppose. Think she'd mind?"

"I didn't know her well enough to know what she'd mind. All she told me was she didn't want the State of Michigan to have them."

He showed his teeth. It might have passed for a raffish smile in one of his panels. "Same old Aunt Beryl. That was one area where we agreed."

"Put on old clothes. You never know when the wind will change." I fisted the doorknob.

"The story I really want to tell is my father's."

Just pull on the knob and walk out. Like climbing in from a ledge. Nothing easier if you prefer solid earth under your feet to having it come at you from forty floors up. The job's done.

Forget about a hotel room or supper. Just pull on the knob and walk out and gas up and drive back across the border and don't look back.

Being smart is more than just knowing what to do. It's knowing what to do and then doing it. So what I did was turn around and step off the ledge.

NINE

He was looking at me, with his head tilted back so that I couldn't have been more than a smear seen through lenses designed for close work. It was probably as much as he wanted to see. A smear is a lot easier to talk to than a human being.

"You know so much about me, you must know who my father was."

"I don't. Unless Beryl told you, you don't either. I'd bet plenty she didn't."

"You said you didn't know her that well."

"She ran a whorehouse in downtown Detroit for forty years and bought two generations of cops. You wouldn't be just now taking delivery on her ashes if she were the type to spill secrets to adolescents."

"It wasn't that big a secret. People hear things and guess the rest. They gossip. You'd be surprised what a boy can learn through an open transom in an old house."

"Or hiding in closets. Under beds, too. I guess you picked up a real education there."

"Oh, sex. I found out all about that by the time I was eleven. I graduated with the help of a forty-eight-year-old whore named

Rose. It was my first time and also my last. I'm still disgusted."

"I was the same way with mushrooms. Now I like them fine. Maybe you just got hold of a bad mushroom."

"Maybe I'm just not the mushroom type." He took off his glasses and rubbed them on the front of his sweatshirt. "I admit it, I was a snoop. I lived in a house full of babysitters, and each one thought one of the others was keeping an eye on me. Five days a week after school and all day Saturday and Sunday I had the run of the place. I found out every method of birth control and all the remedies for crabs and worse, all by observation. And I found out my family history by eavesdropping. It was a glamorous life for the son of a movie star and a contender for the lightweight championship of the world."

"Movie stars don't take bits in musicals, and Smallwood had a lot of contenders standing between him and the title. Romanticizing them doesn't make your childhood less glamorous." I shot my watch out of my cuff. "I need to get back on the road. The trucks start piling up on the bridge at four."

"What do you charge for an investigation?"

"Depends on the investigation."

"You must know I'm talking about solving a murder."

"That's police work."

"Are you saying you never interfere in a police case?"

"I never take a job to interfere in a police case. There's a difference."

"I don't see it."

"The police do."

"Are you afraid of the police?"

"Terrified. They're armed and they drink a lot of coffee."

He held the glasses up to the light. They looked dirtier than before he'd tried to clean them. "If everyone felt that way, we'd still be fighting that crummy war."

"Give it up, Delwayne. Even the cops gave it up in the end. There was a bushel of suspects, too many motives, and not enough incentive after the press lost interest."

"Because the victim was black."

"Partly, probably. Also it wasn't the only murder in town. Automobile production was up, employment was up, births, too. Somebody had to make room for all those babies."

"So it's not a police case anymore. You're free to accept it."

"I always was."

He scratched his chin whiskers with the earpiece of his glasses. "Sounds like we're still on opposite sides."

"I can't afford to turn down work on that basis. Homicide's different. It can be contagious, for one thing."

"This one's more than fifty years old. What's the half life?"

"Same as the statute of limitations. It can still burn you after a hundred."

"I'm not convinced you're as cowardly as all that."

I grinned. "That won't work either."

"Let's quit chasing rabbits. How much to overcome your fear of death?"

"Authority, too. Don't forget authority. I only adjust my rates for inflation, not for risk." I gave him the usual numbers.

He goggled. "U.S.?"

"Cigarette machines in Detroit don't take Canadian."

"What kind of expenses?"

"Mileage. Long distance calls. Stitches. Bail, since cops are involved. Cold cases are like extinct volcanoes: no such thing. That's why I need three days up front. It saves running back to you every time I come out of cardiac arrest."

"What if the expenses run higher than your fee?"

"You pay them, same as when they don't."

"What kind of a payment plan do you offer?"

"The traditional one. If you stiff me, I call a collection agency. They nose around among your neighbors and business associates, ask embarrassing questions, stand in the middle of Yonge Street and call you a deadbeat through a bullhorn. If that doesn't work, they get a court order and seize your assets."

He tried to make a sneer. It looked better on paper. "I've got eighty-nine dollars in savings. Don't spend it all in one place."

"In that case, we're wasting time. You can't afford me."

"Can you recommend anyone?"

"Not for eighty-nine dollars."

"There's a check coming when I deliver this book in the fall. I can pay you then."

"Call me in the fall. What's three more months on top of fifty years?"

He scooped a gum eraser off the rail and rubbed out the ear he'd drawn earlier. It seemed to take all his concentration.

"I'm impetuous," he said. "I imagine you knew that before. If the mood I'm in passes, I'll never know the circumstances of my father's murder and my mother's suicide."

"A lot of people with that background pay plenty to therapists to help them forget the circumstances you want to pay an investigator to find out."

"At least they have that option." He redrew the ear. "Sometimes I think being the child of death unresolved must be like living life as an amnesiac. You can go for long periods behaving normally, without wondering about the blank. Then, suddenly, it's urgent you know. The feeling passes, it always does, but in the meantime you age at an accelerated rate. Who said swinging a bat and missing consumes more energy than swinging and connecting?"

"Al Capone. You might prefer the blank."

"Do you always spend this much energy talking yourself out of a job?"

"Truth in advertising. You can't exchange an unsatisfactory answer."

"Does anyone ever change his mind when you give that speech?"

"One did."

"Just one?"

"He came back later."

He leaned forward, blew away the eraser shavings and graphite dust, and sat back to examine the new ear over the top of his glasses. It didn't look any different to me, but then I once hung a Picasso print upside down.

"You're as curious as I am," he said. "You know too much about something that happened years and years before I left home. You didn't need it just to find me."

"Don't read too much into that. I'm a forties buff."

"What?"

"You know: Glenn Miller and *Casablanca* and the Bataan Death March. Nobody worried about cholesterol and you could smoke in a supermarket. We didn't have civil rights or penicillin, but you could get a T-bone steak for a buck at Berman's. I like hats and big cars and black-and-white movies. I can get lost in all that. Then the lights come up and I have to fill up the tank on the way home, at twenty-first-century prices. I've got twelve hundred and forty-two dollars in savings. Eleven hundred of it came from your Aunt Beryl. Call me in the fall, when you've got fifteen hundred to blow." I foraged, found a card, and stuck it between two of the brushes sticking up out of a glass on the coffee table.

"How do I know you're worth it?"

"You asked me. I didn't drive four hours to make a pitch."

"You're pretty independent for a man in a J.C. Penney suit."

"Sears. And I'm not independent. Just a lousy salesman."

"I wouldn't say that. I like the way you talk. When you're not making speeches, I mean. Those big word balloons get in the way of the action. How'd you like a part in a graphic novel?"

"Would I have to wear long underwear?"

"That's a comic book, damn it! Did you listen to a word I said?"

"Yeah. I was just clapping your erasers. No, I wouldn't like a part. I'm afraid of tall buildings."

"You're just a big scaredy-cat." He flipped over the sheet he'd been working on, picked up his pencil, swooped down on the blank sheet he'd exposed, tore it off, and turned it around to show me. He'd drawn a cartoon cat with a nervous expression and quaking lines all around. It wasn't a bad likeness, except for the pointed ears. He had a problem with ears.

TEN

stopped at a duty-free shop to buy a box of putative Havana cigars. The transaction took five minutes, just long enough to ensnare me in traffic at the border. I took the tunnel to avoid the trucks backed up at the bridge, which stuck me square in the biurnal stream of international commuters, all of whose horns were in order. When the big moment came and the U.S. Customs agent asked me if I had anything to declare, I showed him the cigars. He took one glance and waved me on through. That settled the argument about whether they were genuine. I wasn't planning to smoke them anyway.

Red Burlingame was backing his truck down his driveway when I pulled in behind him. As I got out and approached the cab, he powered down the window. He had on a felt hat with a braided band. I'd never seen him wearing one. I don't know where old men still find them.

"I'm meeting my daughter for dinner," he said. "I'm late."

I poked the box of cigars through the window. "Thanks for the lead. I found Garnet, just where you said. He goes by Lance West now."

"Sounds like a porno star." He sniffed at the seam. "Cubans?"

"I wouldn't trust it. The label's bordertown Spanish."

"They're overrated anyway. Like their music. What'd the little prick have to say for himself?" He laid the box on the passenger's seat.

"He tried to hire me to find out who killed his father."

"Smallwood? He never knew him. Take the case?"

"Not for what he was paying."

I delayed him another five minutes answering his questions. He still had more FBI in him than parent.

I drove to my building to pick up mail and call the service for messages, but I couldn't go up. It's a neo-gothic design, fierce faces on the rainspouts, and after business hours, when the cut-rate endocrinologists, Romanian hearing-aid technicians, and teenage website designers go home and the maintenance crew is trailing its cables and scraping gum off the wainscoting, it's as bleak as a decomissioned cathedral. Even the ghosts have decamped to deserted buildings in more stylish neighborhoods. I was wrung out from eight hours on the road, suffering the post-partum depression that sets in after a job. It was no mood to take into an office where the telephone hadn't rung and the mail was full of nothing but work-at-home opportunities for the terminally unemployed.

I smoked a cigarette on the sidewalk, stalling. You never knew when the Monopoly millionaire might come puffing up the street, one hand holding down his silk hat, looking for a detective to trace his stolen sports car. But by the time the stub burned my fingers it was clear he'd decided to hire the guy from Clue. I snapped the charred filter toward the storm drain and got back behind the wheel.

By bedtime I was feeling better. I had a bellyful of Tuna Helper and whiskey, an hour of Julie London on the stereo, and had identified the murderer fifteen minutes into a two-hour first-run TV movie. I could still figure out everybody else's mysteries. It was a bullet-point to consider for my next Yellow Pages ad. I went to bed.

The next morning, business picked up. I had a new client and an old murder.

ELEVEN

My old answering service had closed its doors. If it had doors. All the operators whom I liked to picture plugging and unplugging jacks, cracking gum and wise during breaks, and clicking out the door at quitting on five-inch heels with seams up the backs of their stockings, were out on the street. Since my business is too fragile and most of my prospects too timid to spill their problems to a machine, I'd had to cast my lariat over five states to find a replacement. The new outfit was a subsidiary of a telecommunications company with offices in sixty-seven cities and had changed its name three times in eighteen months. Some of the operators were men, and all of them spoke in the disconnected singsong cant of a Calcutta tour guide. They probably wore baggy jeans to work and wouldn't know a slingback pump from a Flying Wallenda.

The one I drew the morning after Toronto was named Michael. He stumbled over apostrophes. I stroked him gently, milked out six messages, hung up, and broke a pencil. Five of them were from Lance West, asking me to call him back. He didn't leave a number. When I remembered who Lance West was, I went down to the car, where I'd left Llewellyn Hale's report on Delwayne Garnet, and paged through it on my way back upstairs. I found his number on page fourteen and dialed it standing up at my desk.

"Hello?" He sounded out-of-breath.

"Delwayne, this is Walker."

"Sorry, friend. You've got the wrong number." He hung up.

I dialed again. I'd have used my gun butt on the buttons if I didn't have to unlock the safe to get it.

"Hello?"

"Lance West, then," I said. "Someone should have told you it sounds like the lead in a gay porn film."

"Walker?"

"Sorry, friend. I must have dialed the wrong number." I hung up.

When the bell rang I was sharpening a fresh pencil. I sighted down the barrel, tested the point with my thumb, blew off the cedar shavings, and slid it eraser-end down into the cup. Then I picked up. "A. Walker Investigations."

"Damn it, Walker, this isn't a game. Just answering to 'Delwayne' on an open line could be interpreted as an admission of my identity."

"No one's listening, Lance. You called me first, remember? Also second, third, fourth, and fifth. Sixth, if you count this one. I didn't think I made that big an impression."

"You didn't. But I don't know any other investigators in the U.S. I want you to take the job I offered you yesterday. You know the one."

"Hollywood call?"

"What? Oh, money. I borrowed against what I've got coming this fall. Turns out my friends at Lost Galleon had a few doubloons lying around I didn't know about. They like my work. Which translated means I come cheaper than Steranko."

"What's a Steranko?"

He sawed air in and out. "Do you always work this hard at not working?"

"It's still a police case, Lance."

"I'll pay you a bonus at the end." He breathed again. "Five thousand, if you deliver."

The mail slot in my door creaked and three envelopes dribbled to the floor. Real checks don't come in envelopes with windows. "Put fifteen hundred in the mail. The clock starts when I cash it."

"I won't be using the mails. I'm flying out in an hour."

"Flying out where?"

"Detroit. I'll be paying you in cash."

"What broke you loose? You're still lukewarm here. The Washington spooks might throw a net over you just to keep in practice."

"I'll take that chance. When I was growing up with my ear to the wall, I learned some personal information about my mother and father that might help with the investigation. I don't want to tell it over the phone and I don't want to wait four hours while you make the drive up here. Can you meet me in the dining room of the Airport Hilton at noon?"

"There hasn't been an Airport Hilton for years. It's the Marriott now."

"Thanks for that. I may reserve a room. Is the hotel still attached to the terminal?"

I said it was.

"Good. I don't plan to visit the old neighborhood or take in the sights. I'm keeping my return ticket in my pocket. One rotten whiff and I'm on my way to the gate. Will you meet me?"

I said I would, and the connection broke. I used my freshly sharpened pencil to enter the time and place of the appointment, no name, on the Word-a-Day calendar. The word was *mesoblast*. I didn't see me working it into a conversation any time soon.

I returned the only non-Delwayne-related call I'd had waiting, and used the pencil again to note down the names of elusive witnesses to a tanker crash on the Jeffries Freeway the Monday before. It was an insurance job, easy in, easy out, good for a new set of radials for the car. I did a little sleuthing over the telephone, snared some unlisted numbers, left messages, and made appointments. Just to be prepared I broke a stack of blank affidavits out of the file cabinet and put it in the belly drawer, along with a gold Cross pen for that professional touch. I slit open the mail, wrote out a check for the only third notice in the batch, sealed and stamped it, and stuck it under the hinged lid of the elk's-foot inkstand I use for an outgoing basket. Then I started some tobacco burning and got to work waiting for it to be time to leave for the airport. Some days are like that, end on end. Then business slows down.

The Marriott convention center hotel at Wayne County Metropolitan Airport may be unique in our country, although not for long. It's the only one I've ever entered where I had to pass through a security checkpoint in order to drink at the bar, dine in the restaurant, or take a room. This is because it's directly attached to the Smith Terminal and the gates where planes take on and disgorge passengers. The federal annexation of security has made for polite personnel who can speak in polysyllables without having to come up for air, but the beef medallions are as good as most places, and you don't have to empty your pockets and take off your shoes in order to get a table.

Despite these precautions, a stewardess was raped and strangled in one of the rooms a dozen years ago. The long-range result was the recent arrest of a suspect implicated in a similar murder in Lansing, based on DNA fingerprinting. The immediate result was the Hilton chain was forced to sell the hotel to Marriott when people stopped booking rooms. A new name outside a building works miracles of faith.

I parked in Short Term and hurdled the fresh barriers the airport had installed to discourage people from using the spaces within car-bomb range of the terminal. The traffic inched along the four-lane driveway in lock-step, all the driver's faces in profile behind the windshields, looking for an opening to jag into and unload passengers and luggage. A big county deputy with a stainless-steel whistle plugged into the middle of his face kept busy breaking up clinches at the curb. He had an angry man's tan, red as a scraped shin.

The dining room staff was holding its breath for the lunch crush. I took a corner booth. It was still early, so I ordered a glass of fizzwater with a twist and browsed the menu while the room filled up. The party of six seated around the center table got loud fast. They were dressed for first class and had started the drinking day on the ground in whatever city they'd started from; I guessed New York from the braying honk of the alpha male, a curly-haired skeleton in sharp lapels and egg-shaped gold-and-enamel cufflinks who kept offering his mussels to his fellow diners and when they declined, shoveled them onto their plates anyway.

One of the reluctant recipients was a trim redhead seated at his right in a smart pale-pink suit, with her hair cut short and very close to the nape of her neck, smoking a cork-tipped ciga-rette. She looked cool and tolerant and bored, in a well-bred way. Her quietness made the host seem even louder.

"Still waiting, sir? Would you like something from the bar?"

I pulled my gaze away from the redhead and looked at the waiter, who had crept up silently on rubber soles and oiled muscles. He was a fine-featured young black with a bump on his nose that saved him from being pretty. "Chloroform, if you have it," I said. "Bring it to the center table with my compli-ments."

His smile went no deeper than the dimple in his necktie. "I'll ask them to hold it down."

"Thanks. I can't hear the jets taking off." I ordered a Tom Collins.

He went off on cat's paws and came back five minutes later with the drink and a message. "Mr. Walker, Mr. West called and asked you to meet him in his room. He's in three-twenty-two. Non-smoking floor."

I was tapping a cigarette out of the pack. "How'd you know I was Walker?"

The dimple returned briefly. "He has a gift for description."

"He's an artist."

"That would explain it. Would you care to order?"

I asked him to bring the check. I paid it, finished my drink, and walked out past the center table. The entrees had arrived and Mussel Man was scooping some of his pasta onto the cool redhead's plate. At closer range he looked vaguely familiar, like a pale copy of an original that hadn't been any too clear to begin with. The monogram on his cufflinks read J.M. I wouldn't have noticed it except hardly anyone wears French cuffs these days.

TWELVE

The hallway on the third floor was quiet, with even the scream of accelerating jets muffled behind triple-paned windows and yards of insulation. It smelled of that sweetish disinfectant housekeepers use, made up of lilac, aniseed, and weapons-grade ammonia. A young Japanese in a gray uniform went up on tiptoe to beam at me over the top of the towels folded and stacked on her cart, then turned around and charged through an open door at her back armed with a toilet brush.

I knocked on three-twenty-two and stood back to give Garnet a full view of the stalwart form through the peepsight. After thirty seconds I knocked again. I waited, then put my ear to the door. Nothing was moving around on the other side. I couldn't hear a television or radio or a shower gushing. Something ran up the back of my neck on needle heels and vanished.

I checked the number again for fun and strolled back to the housekeeper's cart. The girl came out of the room, grasped a plastic squeeze bottle by the waist, and paused when she saw me. I smiled and opened my wallet, showing her the deputy's star pinned to the bottom half.

"Good afternoon, miss," I said, still smiling. "We have some routine questions to ask the guest in three-twenty-two, but he won't come to the door. Can you use your passkey?"

Her eyes brightened. "Terrorist?"

"Nothing so certain as that. Just a random check. His name came up in the lottery."

Her face fell. She shuffled through a collection of key cards on a ring, powered past me, and slipped one into the slot. She started to open the door, but I grasped the edge before she could push it more than three inches. I'd caught a bitter whiff from inside.

"Thank you, miss. We'll take it from here."

" 'We?' " She looked up and down the hallway.

"Your country is grateful."

"Green card come up renewal soon."

I selected a business card from my wallet and held it out. It belonged to a satellite dish salesman who'd tried to hook me up last year. The company logo was an eagle with spread wings overlaid with gold foil. "Williams is the name. If you experience any difficulty, just call that number."

She took the card, stared at it long enough to convince me she didn't read English, and stuck it away in her apron. "Okay." She went back to her cart.

I waited until she resumed cleaning, then stepped inside Garnet's room and clapped the door shut behind me. The place reeked of sulfur and saltpeter, an odor you never forget, and which in my case is a headlong plunge through parts of my past I'd pay to avoid. It was fresh; I could almost hear the echo of the shot ringing off the porcelain in the bathroom.

I didn't want to move from that spot. I wished I'd thought to grab something off the housekeeper's cart for protection. A squirt of bleach in a gunman's face plays hell with his aim.

From where I stood I could see into the bathroom on one side and half of the closet on the other. The shower curtain was open and the tub was empty. A man's worn leather jacket drooped from a hanger in the closet. A pair of mirrored sliding doors hid the other half.

I performed a swivel and a reverse, shoving the bathroom door until it banged against the tub and heaving the closet doors together along the track to the other side. I was prepared to throw myself either way if I flushed anything. Both spaces were unoccupied.

That took off some of the pressure. Bathrooms and closets are the hiding places of choice of nine out of ten hotel felons.

I walked into the room and hesitated near a lamp on the low bureau, but there was no one to throw it at. The place was standard size, with a pair of those beds that desk clerks think are queens, a nightstand between, and a maple hutch with the doors open to expose a nineteen-inch TV set. One of the beds was rumpled slightly, as if someone had been sitting or lying atop the spread, and the blinds were drawn over the window. Delwayne Garnet lay on his back on the carpet between the far bed and the TV. He was dressed pretty much as he had been the day before, in the gray college sweatshirt and distressed corduroys, but he'd traded the carpet slippers for sooty-looking Trainers. The sweatshirt had acquired two holes since I'd seen it last. He hadn't done much bleeding through them because they'd stopped his heart.

I leaned down far enough for a sniff. The shooter hadn't stood close enough for the powder to burn the material. Garnet's mouth was a little open. His eyes, open also, looked surprised and a little hurt, but wise with a knowledge we're not to have until there's nothing we can do with it. He never looked more like his father.

I straightened. I was breathing through my mouth, and I could already feel my throat growing itchy from the brimstone air. For all that, it had already begun to fade. His skin would still be warm.

He had a key card to the room in one pocket, nothing else on his person. The drawers in the bureau and nightstand showed only a Gideon Bible and two mammoth metropolitan directories. I looked under the bed and took another tour of the closet and bathroom. I wondered if the killer had taken his luggage.

I found an airline ticket folder and a fat wallet in the leather coat in the closet. I opened the folder, holding it by its edge like a phonograph record, and read the return date. He had an aisle seat on a nonstop to Toronto leaving at 6:19 P.M. That explained no luggage. He had a U.S. Social Security card and a Canadian driver's license in his wallet, both in Lance West's name. The Social Security card was a good copy, but it's a pathetically easy design to counterfeit, with the name typed on an ordinary typewriter. Fake credentials were a cottage industry during the sixties, when the demand among draft-dodgers and other fugitives was at an all-time high. If they were good enough you could use them to acquire all the legitimate papers you needed at your final port of call.

The money compartment held a little over sixteen hundred in U.S. bills, nothing smaller than a fifty. After paying me my advance he'd have had just enough to buy a magazine for the flight home, and maybe a drink aboard. I didn't find any credit cards. He'd probably paid cash for the room. I wiped off the wallet and put it back, money and all.

A careful man, Delwayne Garnet; but then he'd had thirty-four years to practice. No wonder he looked so surprised when two bullets went into his chest.

What a mesoblast.

The TV remote lay on the rumpled bed near the foot. I left it there and pushed the Power button on the set with a knuckle. Bette Davis shrieked at me. I jumped and muted the sound. Filmed in black-and-white, she was talking with what looked like a trim British official in a room furnished in rattan with a fan turning slowly from the ceiling, a tropical set. I knew the film: *The Letter*. It was an early scene. The movie opened with a fusillade from a revolver. That would explain none of the neighbors reporting the shots. I switched off the set.

I wiped off everything my fingertips had touched, conned the hallway, and went out. A vacuum cleaner whined in the room where the housekeeper was cleaning. I'd thought about hanging the DO NOT DISTURB sign on the door of Garnet's room, but decided against it. The police would probably consider that obstruction of justice.

My young waiter was busing the table that had belonged to the noisy party of six, stacking soiled plates and silver on a butler cart. The diners had spilled drinks and food on the cloth, filled the ashtrays, and from the tight look on the waiter's handsome dark face—quickly abandoned when he looked at me—hadn't left much of a tip.

"Just a guess," I said. "Ten percent."

He smiled his brief smile. "It's a privilege to work here on salary alone, sir. Would you like a table?"

"I'd like five minutes." I held up a ten-spot folded into quarters.

He resumed scraping crumbs. "I only serve food."

"I'm not a pervert, just ignorant. I seek enlightenment."

He looked around. The headwaiter was in conference with the woman at the reservation stand. Customers had begun to trickle out. We had the section to ourselves. He executed a graceful movement and the bill was gone. "Okay if I keep doing what I'm doing?"

"Sure. You look like a fellow who can work and think at the same time. Boxer?"

"I didn't know I stuttered."

"I boxed a little in college. You learn what to look for." I pointed at the bump on his nose. "Left jab?"

"Steering wheel. I was sparring when most people my age were taking drivers' ed. How much of the ten have I used up?"

"That was small talk. You told me Mr. West called down to ask me to meet him in his room. Did you take the call?"

"The hostess did." He cocked an eyebrow toward the woman talking to the headwaiter.

"She probably wouldn't know if it was him calling. I doubt he came down after he checked in."

"Didn't you ask him?"

"There didn't seem to be any point in it."

I was using my poker voice, but he had an ear for inflection. Hearing is almost as important in the ring as seeing. He stopped working and faced me.

"Two from a nine-millimeter," I said. "Maybe a thirty-eight. Anyway they were too big for a thirty-two, and forty-fives and magnums chew up more meat. He might have been the one who called down. It was pretty fresh."

He looked me up and down. "Police?"

"Private. Whoever did it cost me a client."

"Then you can't spare this. I don't keep what I didn't earn." He slipped the ten from his apron pocket and held it out between two fingers. There was a little scarring on the knuckles.

"You won't get far in sports with that attitude." I looked down at the table. A cork-tipped cigarette had smoked itself out in one of the ashtrays. The redhead wore pink lipstick to match her suit. "I'll let you work it off. What name did the skinny guy sign on the check?"

"Is he a suspect?" He put away the bill.

"Not unless he could be in two places at once. He just caught my eye. Also my ears."

"He didn't sign anything. He paid cash."

"Did he pay for anyone else?"

"Everyone else."

"Who pays cash for a party that size at these prices?"

"I wouldn't know, sir. I just wait tables." He dumped the ashtray into a lined bag attached to the cart.

"Guess."

"Movie stars and gangsters. They don't like to give away autographs."

I remembered the high-pitched bray of the man who insisted on sharing his meal with his guests. "Ever see this one in a movie?"

"I work out evenings. I don't see many movies."

"You wouldn't have seen him if you had a season pass. That voice would knock the earphones off a sound crew."

His forehead puckered. "Wait, I remember someone at the table called him by a name. Something German. Morgenstern? Mr. Morgenstern."

It didn't do anything for me, besides suggest he hadn't borrowed the J.M. cufflinks. "Do you know if he's staying in the hotel?"

He shook his head.

"Okay. Where do you work out?"

"Kronk."

"Good club."

"Great club. It turned out Tommy Hearns."

"You don't have his reach."

"Neither did Ray Leonard. That didn't keep him from wiping the canvas with Tommy."

"Twice."

"I don't count the second time. That was a bad decision."

"Ever hear of a fighter named Curtis Smallwood?"

He nodded. "The Black Mamba. He was way before my time."

"Mine too. So how come you heard of him and I didn't?"

"I'm a student of the art."

"What's your name?"

"Joseph Sills."

I grinned. "Jersey Joe?"

"I'm from Philadelphia."

"The Philly Kid."

"I prefer Joseph Sills."

"I'll look for it on the bill at Cobo."

"Look fast. I plan to make my stake and get out while I can still do simple arithmetic."

"What then?"

"Open a restaurant." He finished stacking his cart and peeled up the tablecloth.

On my way past the reservation stand, the hostess asked me if I'd had a pleasant meal. She had a big woman's sense of fashion: strong colors, minimal makeup, and a bright scarf coiled loosely around her neck.

"Tell you after the next course."

I went back up to Garnet's room and found the hallway not as quiet as it had been. A gang of bellmen, black-suited security, and Wayne County Sheriff's deputies in uniform were gathered in front of the room, whose door stood wide open. There were more inside, clustered around the Japanese house-keeper. She looked like an imported doll in a crowd of G.I. Joes. The tallest of them, a slick-haired forty in a suit blacker than all the rest, bent over her like a question mark to hear her broken English. She shook her head and spotted me.

She pointed. "Him."

Shadows fell over me from all sides, like lowering clouds. The tall man who'd been asking the questions straightened, looked at me, and crooked a finger.

THIRTEEN

The tall man's name was Hichens. He was a captain with the plainclothes division of the Wayne County Sheriff's Department, whose jurisdiction covered everything at the airport not claimed by Washington. His suit was black enough to swallow galaxies. It looked as if it went on all of a piece, shirt, tie, and all, and zipped up the back. He had an ordinary sort of face, memorable only for its bleak eyes and hairline that went straight across the white marble forehead without a peak or a part. His hair was as black as his suit and glistened like a roll of unexposed film. I didn't know you could even buy Brilliantine anymore.

He ran six foot seven in loafers, and one look told me no one had ever asked him if he'd played basketball in college.

"Ever play basketball in college?" I asked him.

He worked his lips and held up a business card. It had an eagle with spread wings on it, overlaid with gold foil. "Who's Aaron Williams?"

We were seated on either side of a gray steel desk in a gray office in the Smith Terminal, a holdover from when the sheriff's department ran all the security at the airport. The walls shone with fresh paint, without decoration except for a rectangle of paper the size of a bedsheet, spelling out the suspects' rights. It was where they stripped and searched suspicious passengers.

"Door-to-door hack," I said. "He tried to sell me a sports package. I gave up sports when the Tigers moved out of the old ballpark."

"The maid says you told her you were Williams."

"She jumped to a conclusion. I told her Williams was the name."

He flicked the card a couple of times with a finger. Then he put it down and picked up my wallet. "Where'd you get the star?"

"I used to serve summonses. Back then the department handed them out like plastic whistles."

"A long time ago. Now you can lose your license just for flashing it around. I think I'll just hang onto it."

"Not without a warrant, and not until you quit the county, join the state police, and work your way up to lieutenant. My ticket belongs to Lansing."

He tapped each corner of the wallet against the desktop, rolling a square wheel. "I guess you read a book. Come across anything about the fall for impersonating an officer of the law?"

"I memorized it. In order to find me guilty you have to show I told someone I was an officer of the law. All I did was show a badge and a card from a satellite company. I even told her whose name was on the card. I can't help it if she couldn't read the rest."

"You're missing the bigger picture. You're our Number One for West."

"Garnet."

"According to you."

"It'll check."

I'd spun him the tale twice: once in room three twenty-two and again there in the office. I'd started with Beryl Garnet's ashes and finished with Delwayne's corpse. There was no embarrassing either of them anymore. I'd even mentioned the cranked-up volume on the TV, which a deputy had confirmed by turning it on and taking it off Mute; the mood music behind Bette Davis and Herbert Marshall nearly blew all the buttons off his uniform.

Hichens counted the bills in my wallet, ticking off points as he separated each with a thumb. "You con the maid into unlocking the door to the room. Ten minutes later she finishes cleaning the room next door, lets herself into West's, and finds him, dead with two holes in his clock. She calls security, security calls us. You can still smell the powder stink, and the stiff is a long way from room temperature. We're just nicely getting started when you wander back onto the set. You were gone just long enough to ditch the weapon." He gathered the bills into a stack on the desk, smoothing the edges with the heel of his hand, tidy as a brick.

"Or to ask the waiter who gave me Garnet's message if he got it straight from Garnet." I'd left out J. Morgenstern, whoever he might be. I couldn't see a spot for him, and that would only aggravate a man like Hichens, who liked things in neat stacks.

"You said. He'll probably confirm it. I'd cover my ass the same way if I decided to go back up and brass it out. You still had time to toss the gun down a laundry chute."

"How'd I get it inside the hotel? My watch set off the metal detectors."

"You hear of people smuggling all kinds of hardware through airports. It happens at least twice a year, like the lunar eclipse."

"Damn lucky it happened the very day I came in to kill Garnet."

"Someone got it through."

"Why'd I do it? I can't keep my murders straight."

"You say he came in to give you information that might help

you find out who killed his father—if it was his father—back in nineteen forty-nine. That's a stretch, but say he really wanted a murder tied up that's run loose all this time. Why now? Maybe it was you who said you had information. That might be enough to make him cross the border. Old jungle fighter kills war protester. That'd play at the Fisher Theater."

"Pretty thin."

"Maybe. Motives aren't as important as they used to be. All you have to do is have issues with your mother. And who doesn't?"

"Someone should read me my rights before I respond to that."

"Someone will, when we arrest you for Murder One."

I took out the pack and showed it to him. He shook his head. I played with the cellophane. "I told Garnet that murder's a crime without a sell-by date. What if someone killed him to keep from getting tied up?"

"You mean one hand on the walker, the other on the gun? All the other suspects are dead or on oxygen."

"Even a senior citizen can tug a trigger. Ask Marvin Gaye."

"Say he taped *Matlock* and took the bus. Why didn't he kill you instead? You're the one with the shovel."

"Garnet would just hire another digger. Stop the client, stop the investigation."

"Who else knew there was one?"

"That's your job. I've already got one murder on my plate."

"So do I." He returned the bills to the wallet and shoved the wallet across the desk. "Only my murder cancels out yours. Your bankroll's on its way to the evidence room." His eyes got even bleaker. "What the hell are you doing?"

"Taking inventory." I riffled through the bills and put the wallet away. He hadn't palmed any. I never thought he had, but I was getting tired of the cold war. I wanted to see what it took to touch him off.

"You're a goddamn masochist," he said calmly. "I'm about to clank you in County as a material witness."

"I've been. Tonight's corned beef hash. All I've got in the refrigerator is a box of Arm and Hammer."

"I've got a tuna casserole and a wife who couldn't cook her way out of a telephone booth. I can wait all night for a story I can file downtown." He rested a hand on the desktop. There was nothing else on it. I was betting there was nothing in the drawers either. The room was just a space between walls. In another six months it would be a Cinnabun. "Touch anything in Garnet's room?"

"Just the door on the way in."

"Yeah. If you wiped anything off we'll know it."

"You just insulted the housekeeping staff."

"That Jap woman's a pip," he said. "She wouldn't open up until I agreed to put in a good word with Immigration."

"Not even then, if you called her a Jap to her face."

He pointed at the wallet. "You've got a permit to carry. What caliber?"

"Thirty-eight. I left it in the car."

"Ballistics will want it."

"I'll bring it around. Am I clanked or can I go?"

"I'll decide after you sign a statement. Are you seriously planning to go on chasing?"

I shook my head. "That was just a figure of speech. You just counted my operating budget. I've got a little more in the bank, but that's already spoken for. I need to find a client with a pulse."

Hichens looked at the wall opposite the desk as if there were a clock on it. "I'm going to make a few calls, starting with this lawyer Meldrum. If your story checks I'll kick you. Just so you know, I had to put two of my best men on unpaid leave for moonlighting as private stars. It didn't make me like you guys any better than always."

I didn't have anything for that. I let him take it on out.

Guests in evening dress had begun to seep into the Marriott lobby when I asked the clerk behind the desk if he had a

Morgenstern registered. He was a small-boned Mexican with a purple crucifix discreetly tattooed on the underside of one wrist.

"Yes, sir." He looked up from a drawerful of registration cards.

"J. Morgenstern?"

"Yes, sir."

I asked him to ring the room. He dialed and handed me the receiver.

"Yes?"

The voice was a mezzo-soprano with one of those sandy edges you can feel in the sole of your foot. It was just the sort of voice I would have invented for the cool redhead if she didn't already have it.

"Mr. Morgenstern, please."

"He's out. May I take a message?"

"When do you expect him back?"

"I can't say. He's attending a business meeting."

I looked at the clock on the wall behind the desk. "At six-thirty?"

"Mr. Morgenstern doesn't keep conventional hours. Who's calling, please?"

"Amos Walker. I'm a detective. I'd like to talk to him about an incident that took place this afternoon in the hotel."

"What sort of incident?"

"The murder sort. It's just routine."

"That doesn't sound like a ringing endorsement for the hotel." She sounded amused. I might have just told her something had changed in the room service menu.

"A guest on the third floor. I'm just calling around to find out if anyone saw anything."

"I'm sure if Mr. Morgenstern saw anything he'd have mentioned it to me."

"Are you his secretary?"

"I'm his companion."

I'd never heard it called that, but I didn't press it. "I have to ask the question anyway. I'd apprecite it if Mr. Morgenstern would call me." I gave her my number.

"What department are you with?"

"None. I'm private."

Something rattled against the receiver on her end; pink nails, to match her lipstick? "You left that out when you said you were a detective."

"Would you have stayed on the line if I didn't?"

"I'll tell Mr. Morgenstern you called."

I listened to the dial tone, then returned the receiver. I asked the clerk how long Mr. Morgenstern had been in residence.

"I'm sorry, sir. I can't give out that information."

I used the pay telephone by the restrooms to call Lawrence Meldrum, with Meldrum and Zinzser. I got a recording telling me to call during business hours.

A chain restaurant had opened up in what used to be a potato patch off an airport driveway christened for a county executive currently under investigation by the FBI for election fraud. My first meal of the day was beef tips and noodles, washed down by a cup of coffee filtered through a windsock. It was enough to make me miss the layup in the Wayne County Jail.

FOURTEEN

Meldrum and Zinzser occupied two floors of a downtown skyscraper with all the character of a washcloth. It stood on the site of a demolished umbrella factory and seemed to serve no architectural purpose other than to keep the Ford and Buhl buildings from colliding. The directory in the sterile lobby listed two other legal corporations above and below—a barrister sandwich—and a slew of single shingles throughout. I was at high risk for pinstripe poisoning.

Halfway through an article in *Hour* magazine about robotics, I got the nod from the receptionist, a tall black vision with gold rivets holding her ears to her head, and followed her down a hall lined with shriveled maps in frames and into a conference room. A slight man in gray double-breasted linen looked up from the stack of shiny red folders he was distributing around the table, a fifteen-foot slab of polished pearwood surrounded by U-shaped swivels upholstered in rhinoceros or something equally durable.

"Mr. Walker. I must say, you fulfill all my physical expectations." He went on dealing out folders.

"I wish everyone would stop saying that."

"Thank you, Judy." When the vision had faded, drawing the

door shut behind her, Lawrence Meldrum worked his way down the table and shook my hand. He was older than he appeared from a distance, hair more white than fair, and his skin looked as fragile as the vellum maps outside the room. His bluebottle eyes stuck out a little. "I haven't much time. I'm presiding at the marriage of two telephone companies in ninety minutes."

"I didn't bring a gift."

"I'm afraid I have a weakness for metaphors. Especially the matrimonial kind. In the dusty mists of memory, it was a toin-coss whether I attended business school or the seminary. Sometimes I'm not so sure I shouldn't have done both."

I watched him square a red folder with the corners of the table. "Isn't that a job for a legal secretary?"

"Normally. But I've steered this project through eighteen months of national emergency, the rotten economy, and suspicious government inspectors, and I don't want to jinx it in the last moment by letting the smallest detail out of my hands. By this time next year, you'll be able to place all your local and long-distance calls through one company."

"Isn't that how we started out?"

"It is, and what did change bring us? Two incomprehensible bills instead of one simple one, a different area code to memorize for each neighborhood, and a thousand tons of discarded competing telephone directories piling up annually in the nation's landfills. Who among us hasn't wished we'd left well enough alone?"

"So all this steering you've been doing is in reverse."

"Exactly. Throughout the twentieth century, 'progress' was the mantra of modern man. It built roads and factories, fed the hungry, cured plagues, and eradicated superstition—incidentally while placing ninety percent of the world's wealth in the hands of a group of men who could sit comfortably around this table. It also destroyed tradition and custom, polluted oceans, and drove Irving Berlin into bitter early retirement. One sage observer remarked that western civilization reached its highest point with the invention of the can opener; after that, there was nothing to do but add electricity. Now we're more interested in finding out where we took the wrong turn, which means retracing our steps. Have you noticed how often the word 'retro' occurs in today's advertising? It's used to sell everything from ballpoint pens to wings of hospitals. These days, backward is the new forward."

"Yeah, I say crap like that too when I want attention. I called to see you about the Garnet case."

"So you said. Your report arrived this morning. Everything seems to have concluded satisfactorily to all parties, deceased and quick." He resumed distributing folders.

"When I wrote it. Today the score is Deceased, two, Quick, Zero. Someone shot Delwayne Garnet to death in his room at the Airport Marriott yesterday afternoon."

A folder paused in mid-descent. "I'd heard there was a shooting. But the name wasn't Garnet."

"He'd been using a phony name for years. When the papers find out who he was, they'll play it up. A fugitive in a box is worth five in a cell."

"What was he doing at the Marriott?"

"He called and said he wanted to give me information he couldn't over the telephone. He wanted to hire me to find out who killed his father in nineteen forty-nine."

"Good God. Whatever for?"

"I didn't ask."

"Who killed him?"

"The father? I hadn't started looking."

"Not the father. I wasn't aware he had one until just now, and I certainly don't care what or who happened to him. Who killed Delwayne Garnet?"

"Who didn't? Vietnam made a lot of enemies on both sides, not counting any he might have made on his own in the meantime. I'll try to find out, if you pick up my day rate and expenses."

"And why should I do that? This firm's business with Garnet is finished." He fussed with the last folder. It had a monogram on the cover I couldn't read, with a lightning bolt through it.

"When the cops come around, you'll be able to say the incident is under internal investigation. It'll make you look better in the press."

"The press has always been cordial, insofar as we've had relations at all. It may surprise you to learn the police are capable of conducting a thorough investigation without help."

"More than capable. I never knock what the other guy is selling. One of the questions they'll ask is if you knew where Garnet has been keeping himself these past thirty-four years. A sheriff's investigator who wants to be sheriff can turn that into a case of harboring. If he doesn't, the FBI will. They need to shift the blame before someone on Capitol Hill thinks to ask them why they couldn't find him and you could. The media will want to know the same thing. Meldrum and Zinzser could be this year's Enron."

He straightened to his full height and faced me. His height wasn't all that full, but he was narrow and made the most of the illusion. It would impress juries. "Are you threatening extortion?"

"I'd be bluffing. I'm fresh out of merchandise. I told a county captain everything yesterday. I'm surprised you haven't heard from him before this, but I got the impression he thinks the manual is just a suggestion. All I'm after is a client."

"We'll take our chances. Would that be all right with you?"

"Hunky-dory. Someone comes up missing every day. Someone else will drop around eventually with a checkbook to ask me to look for him, and if he doesn't, I'll go to that second someone myself, just like I came to you today."

"In that case, if you'll excuse me." He looked at his watch, a thin gold oval with an ostrich band.

I didn't move. "There's another thing to consider, and you

can have it for free. I assume you're handling the rest of Beryl Garnet's estate, apart from her ashes."

"A number of institutions were named in the will, not that it's any of your affair. You'll get no details under this roof."

"She could leave it to Underwear for Animals as far as I'm concerned. I didn't ask. When homicide's involved, a lot of penny action draws more fire than it would ordinarily. IRS will be curious about whether she declared all her illegal income. Since she ran a cathouse for forty years, it would all be illegal. The tax boys won't care as long as they get their cut. An inquiry like that could tie up the estate until the Tigers win a pennant."

"We have an excellent tax attorney on staff."

"You'd better have a good PR guy, too. Otherwise you'll go on *Sixty Minutes* as the best-dressed collection of pimps in history."

He didn't throw himself down on the carpet and gnaw on a table leg. I hadn't expected him to. He did the next best thing, which was fold his hands behind his back. In that position he resembled the Duke of Wellington, when it still looked like Waterloo could go either way.

"And how do you, one man in one little office, propose to prevent that from happening?"

"It's a suite," I said. "One and a half rooms and a water closet. I can't prevent it. No one can. But with a professional investigator on retainer to get to the bottom of the Garnet mess, you might manage to look like a respectable corporation of counselors that got a little egg on its face and would like to know who threw it."

"Have you ever worked in public relations?"

"No. I do all my lying for free."

He unlocked one of his hands and stroked the slick surface of the folder in front of him. "My partners and I retain an agency to conduct our investigations. We only approached you in the matter just ended because the late Mrs. Garnet requested it. Why should we use you now?"

"There's every reason not to. Your partners will scream at you. I don't have any extra manpower unless I go outside, which is playing with fire when it comes to keeping things confidential, and what connections I have don't go far up. My references are no good, because if having top billing in a firm this size means anything, you already checked those out when Beryl mentioned me. I can't offer a thing your regular agency can't a couple of hundred times over with everything on it, except one."

"Good old-fashioned Yankee know-how?" His face broke into crossgrains when he lifted his lip.

"A running start."

I couldn't read his expression. He'd stood in front of too many juries. "You'll save us money on legwork? That's your offer?"

"Two or three thousand, minimum. Assuming your agency's minimum is my maximum."

"Two or three thousand. We spend that much every week on erasers."

"Your people make too many mistakes. You brought up money, not me. I'm saving you headlines. One local television station can air a hundred sound bites in one day. Multiply that by however many stations there are in this country. Don't even count the twenty-four-hour news networks, where the crawl never stops. Ask your partners where they stand on that."

"Are you actually saying you intend to solve this—murder?"

"I may solve two. No charge for the extra."

"The father? What the devil do I care who murdered him?"

"Garnet cared. Maybe someone else cared he cared. It's the long shot of long shots: fifty-three years and counting. But it has to be played."

"With my money."

"Yours and Zinzser's. Is there a Zinzser, by the way, or is he like Betty Crocker?"

"He's semi-retired. His always was the wiser head."

I heard the knock before he did. I didn't say anything. After a moment he shook himself like a lean old dog. "Yes?"

"A man to see you, Mr. Meldrum. He says he's with the sheriff's department." Even from the other side of a door, Judy sounded as exotic as she looked.

"I'll see him in my office." To me: "Wait in reception. If I send word to show you out, that will be my answer."

"I'll wait in my own stall. I know the way out of it."

"Please."

He got the word out with effort, as if it had been stuck between two teeth. Pleaders hate to do it for free.

"Okay. Your magazines are newer than mine, anyway."

"Thank you. I'll pay you for your time."

He held the door for me and locked it behind us. Captain Hichens towered over the receptionist in the hallway. I'd just about convinced myself he couldn't be as tall as I remembered. His bleak eyes showed no expression when he recognized me. Expressing plenty. He shook Meldrum's hand because it was in his way and pulled me aside by my sleeve. My arm was in the sleeve and I felt a bruise starting.

"Why the hell are you here?" He didn't shout. He didn't keep his voice low either. The other two people weren't there for him.

"Chipped a tooth opening a beer can. Meldrum says I've got a case against Stroh's. Or maybe it's a case of Stroh's. My Latin's rusty."

"Stay out of my murder."

"Okay if I investigate Curtis Smallwood's?"

"That what you're investigating?"

"You want to see the tooth? I wrapped it in evidence tape."

"Where's that gun I told you to bring around?"

I reached under my suitcoat and took it out of its holster. He gripped my hand when I offered him the butt. My fingers pressed fresh holes in the cylinder. "Not here, goddamn it. Bring it to the City-County Building." He looked around, appearing to notice for the first time we weren't alone.

Meldrum cleared out some phlegm. "My office is down on your left, Sheriff."

"Captain."

The lawyer sliced his way down the middle of the hall and turned through a door near the end. Judy had drifted away on a zephyr.

Hichens watched me put away the .38. "I had someone call the TV station. *The Letter* started at noon. The first gunshot on film took place two minutes and forty-two seconds into the broadcast. That checks with the hostess, who said West called just before twelve, asking you to meet him in his room; provided the killer turned on the set and timed his shots to coincide with the shots on the soundtrack. That's consistent with time of death as estimated by the coroner. In thirty years I've never had a more precise estimate."

"You sound disappointed."

"Life isn't Legos. I get nervous when all the pieces fit. Shooter could've done it as much as twenty minutes earlier, called downstairs pretending to be Garnet, then switched channels on the TV so we'd think he used the movie to cover the noise. Almost any other program could be cranked up loud enough to do the trick."

"I'm still covered. I got there a half-hour early. Ask my waiter. He's a light heavyweight named Joseph Sills."

"I talked to him. He said you were interested in someone else who ate in the restaurant, same time as you. Morgenstern was the name. First name Jeremiah."

"I didn't know that."

"He said he told you he heard someone address the man as Mr. Morgenstern."

"I didn't know Jeremiah was his first name. Did you talk to him?"

"I talked to a woman who said she was his companion; a redhead I wouldn't mind spending quality time with myself. She said he was in a meeting. She also said someone else had been asking about him. He even left his name and number."

"Guilty," I said. "If there's a law against it."

"There is when it gets in the way of an official investigation. What made him so interesting?"

"Mr. Morgenstern is the kind of person who calls attention to himself."

"Think he called attention to himself for a reason?"

"I didn't at the time. Maybe, if everything happened twenty minutes earlier. He was in a meeting when I called. If it was the same one, I hope for his sake he got a lot of work done. Who is he?"

"Venture capitalist, the redhead said. I don't know what that is, but whatever he does he does out of an office in Manhattan. His flight got in at eleven-twenty; plenty of time to do West and meet his party outside the restaurant for lunch. We're tracking down the party now. Of course, that would mean he slipped the gun through security at LaGuardia."

"Guy got a barbecue grill through the Seattle airport last week."

"This killer hedges his bet too much to count on that kind of break," Hichens said. "Seems to me you said something on the same order yesterday."

"What about prints?"

"We're still running 'em. Come next Christmas we should have a record of everyone who touched anything in that room over the past six weeks. FBI database matched West's with Delwayne Garnet's, by the way. A vacancy just opened up on the Ten Most Wanted list."

"Think I've got a chance?"

He wasn't listening. "We retrieved your prints from Lansing this morning. Not one set matched from that room."

"I said I didn't touch anything."

"That's what you said."

I blew air. "I took the job Garnet offered. When a client gets killed, I get curious."

"For free?"

"I'm working on that."

He gouged a hole in the air with his finger. "You're still my favorite. You could have shot him after you conned your way into his room. If I stumble over you again, I'll book you as a material. Chances are I will anyway, but why fuck with chance? Stay out of my murder."

He left me there and let himself into Meldrum's office without knocking. Fifteen minutes later he came into the reception room alone. He stopped when he saw me. He had on the same black-on-black suit he'd worn the day before or one just like it. He looked like an exclamation point. "Why are you still here?"

I put down my magazine and held out my wrists.

He told me where to put them and went out the main entrance. The pneumatic closer prevented the door from slamming.

Something purred on the receptionist's desk. Judy lifted a receiver, listened, and cradled it without a word. "Mr. Walker, Mr. Meldrum would like to see you in his office."

I got up. I lingered in front of the desk. "Do you date white guys?"

She sat back, showing the long line of her torso, and tapped a gold pencil against her teeth. They were nice teeth, small and even and sharp. "I don't date poor guys."

I tilted my head toward the inner sanctum. "I've got a rich client."

"I date the client."

I knew my luck couldn't hold. I went down the hall.

FIFTEEN

On a nice day in June it was a brisk walk from Meldrum and Zinzser to Walker and Nobody on West Grand. On an airless day like we were having, under a smut-colored sky screwed down to the rooftops, it was like crawling uphill through a dirty air duct. I stopped at my bank for a hit of conditioned air and to deposit Lawrence Meldrum's check, then resumed crawling. Back in the penthouse I hung my coat on a chair in front of the office fan, bathed from the waist up in the water closet sink, put on a fresh shirt from the supply I keep in the safe, and called the Airport Marriott. The telephone rang seven times in Morgenstern's room before the operator came back on to tell me no one was answering. I drew a question mark next to the Venture Capitalist's name on the desk pad. He was my obsession of the week. He tickled my throat like the first sign of a bad cold.

At the second number I tried, a computer-generated voice gave me a pager code. I dialed that, followed the instructions provided by another machine, and hung up to wait. It was getting to be possible to spend all day on the telephone and never hook up with the owner of a respiratory system.

The bell rang while I was going over my notes, the most I'd ever made on a case before I landed it.

"Where you been keeping yourself, super sleuth? I was beginning to think you'd tapped into a wealthy divorcee." Barry Stackpole's voice was a fresh breeze in my ear.

"Wealthy divorcees don't trade down; you know that. When'd you go on an electronic tether? I thought you took a vow."

"It's a loaner. I'm working a deal, and I've got competition."

"What's the deal?"

"Host of a reality-based crime series on CBS. Five grand a week to stand in front of a camera for twenty minutes."

Barry was an investigative journalist, currently and frequently without a journal; but never for long. He was a walking database on every left-hand operation that had taken place in Detroit since Chief Pontiac. The Pulitzer committee had tagged him twice and the mob once, with six sticks of dynamite and an artificial leg.

"I need about twelve hundred dollars' worth of your time," I said.

"Try me tomorrow. They're also taking meetings with a former attorney general and one of the guys from *Baywatch*."

"There were guys on *Baywatch?*"

"I have to keep the line open."

"Tomorrow's no good," I said. "I've got competition too. Its name is Captain Hichens."

"Wayne County Hichens? That's serious competition. He cracked the stewardess killing at the airport."

"I thought Forensics cracked that one."

"For the jury. Hichens collared the suspect a week after it went down. The guy walked for insufficient evidence. Modern science took eleven years to catch up with Hichens' hunch. After the arrest, the department reopened fourteen old cases and got eight indictments based on DNA testing, all against suspects who'd been interviewed and released. Hichens was investigating officer in all but one. That's how he made captain."

"He ought to be sheriff."

"Sheriffs are politicians. If you've met him, you may have guessed he's cuffed more hands than he's shaken."

"What makes him your hobby?"

"He threw me out of his office when I asked him how Frankie Acardo managed to board a nonstop flight to Phoenix the day he was subpoenaed to testify to a grand jury. I keep track of all my friends and enemies." He slurped something, probably a Coke. He was on the wagon since throwing a chair through a control booth window at WXYZ and thought bottled water was for French bicycle racers. "This have anything to do with the Marriott shooting?" he asked.

"Not if it's what it takes to get you that CBS gig."

"I'm ahead on favors, Maigret. Throw me a bone."

"Call you right after I call the cops."

"When the cops get it, so does everyone else. Call me before."

"I'll put you on speed dial."

"You mean I'm not already? What's the question?"

"Jeremiah Morgenstern."

"That's an answer, not a question. The question is, 'Who put the *M* back in Mafia?' "

I'd known there was something familiar about that tickle in my throat. "How come I never heard of him? I thought I knew all the players."

"That's because you're weak in German. Morgenstern in English is Morningstar."

"Oh, hell. I took Spanish. Ben Morningstar's kid?"

"Grandkid. Jerry made his bones when everyone else his age was marching on Washington. He went to New York to beat the heat, opened up a branch of the family business, and muscled in on the concession racket in the Broadway theaters. Short hop from there to costumes and set decoration, but all that was strictly for something to declare on his ten-forty. Jerry's a throwback. The mob spent fifty years trying to go legit, and all it bought them was congressional hearings up the yazoo and racketeering laws they couldn't kill or bribe their way around. He's spent the last twenty getting back to basics: labor, numbers, drugs, smuggling. He's got the corner on every carton of bootleg cigarettes that finds its way into high tax states like Michigan. I bet you're smoking one now."

I wasn't, but I got out the pack I was working on and looked at it. "Mine's got a stamp."

"That's the idea. When Lansing adopted it, it took all the profits away from the independents and put them back in the pockets of the boys who can afford the counterfeit presses. Give the seal a rub."

I scrubbed it with the ball of my thumb. "It didn't come off."

"The state's does. The printing contract went to the lowest bidder, just like it says in the charter. The Sicilians have more class. Those aren't cubic zirconiums winking on their pinkies."

"Morgenstern's Jewish. Or Morningstar was."

"Someone has to keep the books. Vegas and Havana were hemorrhaging greenbacks until Grandpa Ben got hold of the accounts."

"Sounds like an anti-Semitic slur."

"The mob never learned to spell ACLU. What makes the New York franchise your hobby?"

"He's in town. Morgenstern is."

"Detroit?"

"Metro. He's staying at the Marriott."

"He's not your boy. He's no Grandpa Ben but he's got too many smarts to stay under the same roof with one of his hits."

"Could be he's counting on the cops thinking the same thing."

"Uh-uh. You can't work the Statue of Liberty play with cops. They're too literal-minded. Anyway, he hasn't handled his own wet work for years. It's more his style to brown his toes at Far Rockaway and let his buttons munch on the pretzel sticks in Economy Class."

"Well, he's at the airport and so's a stiff. How come Hichens didn't know him?"

"County only gets a connected case when a chiseler shows up cold in a trunk in Long Term Parking. Then they kick it over to Lansing or the Federal Bureau of Incompetency. Even so, I bet Hichens knows who he is by now. The captain's the kind of cop who has his shield tattooed onto his chest in case he has to bust someone for picking pockets in the YMCA shower."

I rolled my eyes at the ceiling and saw something there. "Morgenstern's traveling with a redhead, a fox. Anything on her?"

"Nope. He married a Polish princess, black hair and breeder's hips. The redhead would be this year's travel model. You going to seduce her, make her spill her guilty secrets?"

"Yeah, I'm Jack Kennedy. Thanks, Barry. You saved me a morning with *Playboy's Illustrated History of Organized Crime*."

"That piece of—"

I never found out what it was a piece of, because I fumbled the receiver into the cradle without taking my eyes off the bowl fixture that hung from the ceiling—original to the building, not a hip nod to Lawrence Meldrum's theory of postmodern regression. A new shadow had joined the collection of flies and ladybird beetles mummified on the other side of the milky glass. I wouldn't have noticed it except it seemed to be suspended between the glass and the bulb, defying gravity. It might have been dangling from a strand of cobweb.

Well, the fixture was past due for cleaning. The crew that had the contract never worked higher than the doorknobs, and I had a swanky front to keep up. I planted the customer's chair in place of the wheeled swivel, climbed onto it, and unscrewed the bowl.

It didn't look like what it was, just a tiny cylinder no larger than a .22 short casing sealed in black plastic, perforated on the free end. Whoever installed it had connected it to the existing wiring. That made me mad. I don't mind being eavesdropped on so much as paying for it on my monthly bill.

SIXTEEN

I left the bug where it was, reinstalled the bowl, and went downstairs to talk to the superintendent. Rosecranz was older than sixty and younger than a hundred, and had evaded Cossacks and an NKVD hit squad in order to come to America, if he hadn't gotten all his stories out of the adventure pulps he used to teach himself English. I hoped he hadn't, because without them he was just a worn pair of overalls sitting in a little room filled with old-man fug and dusty shawls on every surface. He told me no one but the building cleaning crew was allowed inside the offices in the tenants' absence. Under cross-examination, he admitted doors were left open for indefinite periods while the workers went out to empty wastebaskets and borrow supplies from one another, and that the turnover in personnel provided a constant stream of unfamiliar faces. An unauthorized stranger wouldn't have had to train too hard to penetrate the inner sanctum.

"Something is missing?" he asked.

"No, something is added."

He thought about that. Then he blew his nose rattlingly into a blue bandanna handkerchief and shook his head. "I will never learn this language."

I told him I was struggling with it myself and asked to use his telephone for a long-distance call.

"How long?"

"Toronto. Take three or four minutes."

He demanded two dollars. I gave them to him and he pushed a black steel rotary with a ballerina waist across the desk. The mouthpiece smelled of boiled parsnips. I was pretty sure no electronic listening device could stand up to them, even if my office wasn't the only target. I made arrangements with the party on the wire, hung up, and left the old man to his tattered copy of *Soldier of Fortune*.

I drove to the City-County Building, unloaded the .38 Chief's Special, gave it to the guard by the metal detector to look over along with my permit, got them back, and traded the revolver to a distracted-looking clerk down the hall for a receipt. I asked if Captain Hichens was on the premises. He directed me to another clerk, just as distracted, who kept me waiting while he prowled a computer screen with a mouse, then picked up a telephone and asked. He told me Hichens had returned to the airport after checking in with the sheriff that morning.

I went to Records and signed out the public documents on the deaths of Stuart Pearman and Karl Anthony Mason, the anti-war activists who had paid the ultimate price for the cause when their explosive device detonated prematurely.

There was quite a bit that hadn't made it into the papers, but very little I could use. Both men were unmarried. Pearman was an orphan, without siblings or known associates apart from Mason and Delwayne Garnet. He'd left school in Ypsilanti at sixteen, and there was no one from his class who could say anything about him except that he kept to himself and didn't participate in sports or other extracurricular activities; not the warning signs in 1968 they would become in light of more recent criminal history. His foster parents were elderly, and aside from filing a missing persons report when he ran away from home—about the same time he'd dropped out—hadn't made any effort to establish contact with him for years, ditto him with them. His grades went up and down, apparently according to his level of motivation. He seemed bright enough when they were up, particularly in reading and social studies. Garnet had said he was the idea man in their little revolutionary society. Mason's story was as different as it gets: popular in high school and his freshman year at the University of Michigan, letter man in basketball and track, proficient in the sciences, chief among them chemistry, which had earned him a scholarship, forfeited when he left after two semesters. You can't ace the midterm and make bombs at the same time. Parents divorced when he was five; father deceased, mother remarried.

The mother held promise. Thirty-eight years old when interviewed, Regina Babbage blamed young Karl's dark turn on his late father's infidelities. Stepfather Winthrop was too gentle (read *weak*) to have exercised any influence, positive or otherwise, and so the boy had turned to others his own age in search of a male role model. She was especially vocal on the subject of Delwayne Garnet, but then she'd have to have been, Stuart Pearman being dead and beyond reach of her lash. She told the interviewing officer she wished Michigan had the death penalty so that she could attend the event after Garnet was captured, tried, and sentenced, and root for the electric current. She was singing with a band when she'd met the departed Mr. Mason, a drummer, and her statement was peppered with words she'd learned on the road and behind the bandstand. She was a big pile of steaming hate. She'd be seventy-two if her temper hadn't blown a plug in the meantime, aged well outside the demographic for revenge killers. But handguns aren't all that heavy. I added her name and vintage contact information to my notes.

I returned the material to the young woman at the desk, an arrested adolescent with candy-striped hair and a copper brad through both nostrils, and went back outside, where if anything the sky was lower and the air dirtier than they had been that morning. I ate lunch at a counter and asked the attendant for a metropolitan directory. He found it holding up a package of poppyseed buns, which as health code violations went didn't even dent the surface locally. Looking up the number was just something to do while I was waiting for the carcinogens to kick in. I didn't expect to find anything.

There was a W. S. Babbage listed in Royal Oak. I wrote the number on my napkin, made change for a ten, left a tip on top of the directory, and deposited the rest in the telephone by the door. Dialing the number was just something to do during digestion. I didn't expect anyone named Winthrop or Regina to pick up.

"Hello?" A woman's voice, cigarette-roughened at the edges.

"Mrs. Babbage?"

"This is Mrs. Babbage."

"Mrs. Winthrop Babbage?"

"That's correct."

"Regina Babbage."

"Who's asking, please?" Irritation had crept in.

I made a mental note to try the number on the lottery. "My name is Walker, Mrs. Babbage, calling from Detroit. I'm investigating an incident connected with the death of Karl Anthony Mason."

The pause was shorter than expected. "Did they finally arrest that son of a bitch Garnet?"

"I can't discuss details over the telephone. Is there a place we can meet?"

"How long will it take you to get up here?"

I said twenty minutes, if the lights were with me. She gave directions, which I shorthanded on the napkin under her telephone number. She broke contact without saying good-bye. This was going to be as much fun as poking grizzlies.

Woodward Avenue slices northwest from the Detroit River at a thirty-degree angle, passing the jeweled Fox and State theaters, the crater that was J.L. Hudson's Department Store, the library and art museum, and dozens of weedy empty lots before leaving the city. Several dimensions later it enters Royal Oak, a white-flight community of factory commuters and retired schoolteachers with a pocket-size downtown and housing developments that resemble architectural theme parks: false Tudor, faux Bavarian, Cold War ranch, and the ever-popular split-level, complete with step-down garage and a flight of redwood stairs to the ground floor. A lot of decent people live there, and they pay the city police a living wage to see it stays that way. If you pull into a school parking lot to change a tire, a cop will be along in two minutes with friendly advice and maybe a dope-sniffing dog. Every well-groomed town is a police state of some kind.

The neighborhood dozed in a cul-de-sac with a civilian patrol emblem mounted beneath the NO OUTLET sign, the one with Boris Badenov silhouetted in black to scare away prowlers. There were no Big Wheels or swing sets or basketball hoops, no cute two-seater convertibles, nothing to indicate that anyone under forty lived there or ever had. The vehicles in the driveways were large and sturdy, designed to ford the Amazon and scale K-2, and had probably never been driven above fifty even on the expressway. A very quiet place. I idled along at ten to hold down the rumble from my straight pipes. Even then I felt like a hospital visitor with squeaky soles.

Regina Babbage's address scrolled in wrought-iron script above the recessed door of a low stucco, connected by a dog-walk to a garage that was trying hard to look like a carriage house, with green shutters and zigzag crossplanks on the doors. It may have been, once; but only if Royal Oak had existed before the invention of the carburetor. I parked on a concrete pad and followed a flagstone border to the entryway. The lawn was fragrant from recent cutting, the terra-cotta tiles in front of the door swept and wearing a clean coconut mat. The place was scrubbed and plucked like an old lady who hadn't forgotten youth's first blush. It reminded me a little of Beryl Garnet.

The man who answered the doorbell was tall, with a ham face and ears that stuck out as if to keep his head from sinking any lower between his shoulders. He wore a gray sweater with a shawl collar over a white shirt buttoned to the neck. He had large hands and feet, the latter shod in scuffed leather loafers, and the knees of his trousers bagged like a miner's. If ever a man was born to bear the name Winthrop Babbage, this was it. We introduced ourselves without shaking hands and he let me into a living room with sleek leather sofas and loveseats in chrome frames and a fireplace with a black enamel mantel crowned with photographs in steel frames. The hearth didn't look as if it had ever contained a fire. You could have cleaned the whole room with a leaf-blower.

Regina Babbage stood in the center of the carpet as if she'd been waiting there for thirty-four years. She was a compact five-two and a hundred thirty pounds in a form-fitted blue shirt over black slacks with a crease that could cut glass. Her feet were small in cordovan slip-ons with brass buckles. She wore little makeup and her short hair was a plausible pale blonde.

"Thank you for coming, Mr. Walker. Is it mister, by the way? I don't recall your mentioning a rank."

"Mister's as good as it gets," I said. "I'm a private investigator, Mrs. Babbage. Thank you for seeing me."

Her face crumpled a little. She'd been holding it together through sheer will. "Does that mean Garnet isn't in custody?"

"He is and he isn't. That's what I came to talk to you about."

Her face collapsed the rest of the way. Winthrop glided to her side and cupped a hand under her elbow.

"Do you know how long I've waited to hear that bastard is behind bars?" she asked. "Thirty-four years, two months, and eleven days. He killed my son, and no one cares. Mr. Hoover cared, but he's as dead as Karl. They've become a joke, an anachronism, like *Laugh-In* and the Smothers Brothers. And I'm the one who's left with a hole through me."

I said, "Karl's prints were all over the bomb."

"What if they were? He wanted to draw attention to his beliefs. A handful of Bostoners wanted to dump English tea into the harbor to draw attention to their beliefs. They won, Karl lost. If it had gone a different direction, schoolchildren would be fighting to play him in the Fourth of July pageant."

"It was an anti-personnel bomb, Mrs. Babbage. That means it was meant to blow up people, not just a building. He stuffed it with nails and bits of bicycle chain."

"That was Garnet's influence. My boy had principles. Garnet twisted them around to his own ends. Then when things went wrong he ran away. You know what I wish? I wish he'd killed someone in Texas. That's one state where they know how to deal with a murderer. They let him sweat it out for years on Death Row, spending all his family assets on appeals. Then they wheel him into a room with glass walls and stick a needle in his arm."

Winthrop Babbage squeezed his wife's elbow. "Please have a seat, Mr. Walker. Can I get you something to drink?" His voice was a velvety rumble, with humorous undertones. A sense of the absurd would be the most well-worn tool in his survival kit. I put him around eighty.

I said a glass of water would be welcome. The pressure inside the house was nearly as high as outdoors, even disregarding the personality of the hostess. Air conditioners don't get much of a workout in the homes of old people.

Mrs. Babbage and I were sitting when he returned from the kitchen carrying a tall glass with ice cubes colliding inside. I could feel the sweat building up where my back rested against the leather cushions of my sofa. She seemed cool enough sitting in the center of the one opposite, her hands resting in her lap. Her nose had a predator's curve, with the skin stretched shiny across it and across her cheekbones; what feature writers call handsome and striking. Fifty years ago, her picture outside a ballroom would be enough to fill the place. Under a baby spot in a form-fitting gown, she wouldn't have had to carry a tune across the stage; the audience would meet her halfway.

She waited while I took a long sip and stood the glass on a mission table at my knee. "Who do you represent?"

"The legal firm administrating the estate of Beryl Garnet, Delwayne Garnet's guardian."

"I thought that whore was his mother."

"Not biologically or legally. I see you've made a study."

"The press dug up everything it could on everyone involved. Not from me, where Karl was concerned. I turned the hose on the vultures once. What they got was leaked by the police. They managed to twist even that. Garnet's background didn't surprise me. When you set out to raise a coward and a murderer, a brothel's just the place to do it. So she died finally. I didn't know prostitutes lived so long."

"Strictly speaking, she wasn't a prostitute," I said. "It might have occurred to you the press got that wrong too."

"Are you saying there's no difference between her and me?"

"He didn't say that, Reggie." Winthrop was poking tobacco into the bowl of a blackened brier. His leather club chair was the only piece of furniture in the room that didn't look as if it had been trucked in from a doctor's waiting room. In its corner you didn't notice it at first, like the man who sat in it. "A parent can do everything right and still fail. Look at Karl."

"Stay out of it, old man. If you'd been half the example a good stepfather is supposed to be, I wouldn't have to walk through an iron gate to visit my son."

"You've always blamed Ernest for that. Try to be consistent." He got the pipe going and dropped the clump of burned matches into a chrome tray on the coffee table. Clouds of smoke added another twenty pounds to the atmosphere.

"That whoremongering son of a bitch did his part every day of our marriage, and you didn't do anything to make up for it when it came your turn. I was outnumbered from the start."

"Delwayne Garnet's dead."

I was watching her closely when I said it. She didn't blink.

SEVENTEEN

inthrop took the stem out of his mouth. His ham face was gray. "How?"

"He was shot yesterday in a hotel room at the airport."

"*Which* airport?"

"Detroit Metropolitan. It was his first time back in the country in thirty-four years. He didn't last thirty-four minutes."

Regina Babbage closed her eyes then and looked all of seventy-two years old. She might have been praying, but I wouldn't have bet the collection plate on it. After ten seconds her eyes snapped open. "Who did it?"

"I don't know. Neither do the police. That's what I came here to talk to you about."

"Am I a suspect?"

"I didn't think so when I figured your age. Now that I've met you, I'd tag you for it on the first good evidence."

We locked glances for a bit. It was like a snake trying to hypnotize another snake.

"An honest one," she said then. "You were right, Winthrop."

I didn't ask what he'd been right about. "Where were you yesterday between eleven-thirty A.M. and twelve-fifteen P.M.?"

"Here at home with me," Winthrop said. "We're here every

day. We have no social life, no friends. We buried the last one two years ago."

"Is there anyone who can back that up? A husband's testimony doesn't draw much water with the cops."

"No. As I said, we have no—"

"For God's sake, Winthrop. We don't have to answer his questions, let alone volunteer information."

"It doesn't matter. We have nothing to conceal."

"She's giving you good advice," I said. "Even if you decided to confide in me, you'd have to do it all over again when the police come. They'll work their way around to you, probably before the day is out. Mrs. Babbage gave them every reason when her son died."

"When he was murdered," she said. "Euphemisms are opiates to silence survivors. Would you blame me if I killed Garnet?"

"Did you?"

She breathed in and out shallowly. "I almost wish I could confess, just to see the look on your face. On all their faces. No, I didn't kill him. I'd give my soul to have been the one who did. Shocked?"

"Paralyzed. Do you own a gun?"

"Certainly not," Winthrop said. "We're Democrats."

I kept looking at Regina.

"Do you want to see it?" she asked.

"Reggie!"

I said I would. She got up and went out, leaving me alone with Winthrop, drawing on his pipe with wrinkles stacked up to his bald crown.

She came back pointing a long-barreled revolver at my chest. I was drinking water. I froze with the glass against my teeth.

The old man had good reflexes. He scrambled to his feet. "Reggie, what are you doing with that?"

"I bought it a week after I lost Karl. I thought I might need it to keep the reporters away. I never did; the hose worked fine."

"For God's sake, stop waving it around!"

"Don't be so dramatic. Guns don't just go off, like in the movies. Mr. Walker knows that. Don't you, Mr. Walker?"

"Depends on the gun. *Hair-trigger* isn't just a colorful expression." I drank some water and made my throat work.

"I have a permit." She shifted it to her other hand then and held it out to me, gripping it awkwardly across the middle of the frame.

I set my glass down carefully, pried my fingers loose from it, and took hold of the butt. Her hand fell away and I felt the weight of the weapon. It was a Jet .22 with factory grips and an eight-and-a-half-inch barrel, a target piece. Remington hadn't made one in forty years. I thumbed the cylinder around, looking inside the chambers, checked the muzzle, and handed it back. Winthrop goggled.

"Garnet was shot with a larger caliber," I said. "Also that gun hasn't been fired in years. There's rust in the barrel and mold on the cartridges. You're supposed to clean and oil them every once in a while."

"I wouldn't know how. I've never fired one in my life." She let it dangle by her side.

"I've never lived in a house that contained a firearm," Winthrop said.

"You've been living in one most of your married life. You survived." She was looking at me. "Am I exonerated?"

"Not quite. It could be a prop you keep around for anyone who asks. I admit you hold it like an umbrella, which is hard to do once you know your way around a gun; like faking virginity. But you've proved you're smart."

"Such a cynical man."

"As long as you're around I'm just a talented amateur. Killing Garnet took planning. Whoever did it slipped the gun past airport security in the middle of a national emergency. Being a little old lady might help. Anyway you've had thirty-four years, two months, and eleven days to work it out."

"Thirty-four years ago there was no airport security," she said. It was a point. I wished she hadn't had it ready.

Winthrop said, "Are you working with the police?"

"I'm working in spite of them. Garnet was a client. Now Beryl Garnet's lawyer is. That's three jobs in one week, all involving the same family. I guess that makes me the faithful old retainer." I stood. "Thank you for seeing me. I'm sorry I raked up bad memories. It's that kind of case."

Regina's eyes followed me up. "What was he doing back in the United States?"

"We had an appointment. It didn't have anything to do with what happened in sixty-eight."

Winthrop took the pipe out of his mouth. He looked at it as if he didn't know what it was for. "How could my wife kill him if she didn't even know he was in the country?"

I paused. I tried to see a connection between the high-tech bug in my office and the rusty piece of machinery in the old woman's hand. I shook my head.

The old man reached down and closed his fingers around the revolver. She let him take it. All the gas seemed to have gone out of her.

"I'll see Mr. Walker out. Lie down, dear. Don't forget what the doctor said."

She nodded, and went on nodding as if she'd forgotten how to stop. She turned and went out through the same door she'd come through minutes before, holding a gun. Her feet dragged. It might have been part of the same act.

Winthrop put down his pipe, seemed to realize he was still holding the .22, and let it drop to the table with a thud. "Filthy things. The Chinese should have stuck with printing."

"People would just use rocks. You'd have to wait three days to buy one to border your garden."

"She could use a rock. I believe she could. Or her bare hands. I can't see her using a gun."

I said nothing.

You didn't notice his eyes were blue until you looked right into them. I doubted people did often. "I know it's your job to suspect people's motives," he said. "Hers is better than most. But she hasn't the strength to do anything about it. She can't even walk to the mailbox and back without help."

"Kind of thin. Picasso was making babies at ninety."

"Picasso didn't have Regina's pancreas."

I gave that some thought. I'd been expecting something like it ever since her string broke. "I'm sorry. If that's a doctor's opinion and not just Winthrop Babbage's."

"He gave her to the end of this year. The man is an optimist."

"Does she know?"

"We've never talked about it. We've never talked about Karl, either. Everything she's said she said to strangers." He nodded. "She knows. She's not the sort of woman you keep secrets from."

"Her son seems to have done a pretty good job."

It didn't seem to offend him, although I'd wanted it to. He was the sort of man who could be made to tell secrets if you could just crack his skin. "She was good at keeping them from herself back then. I suppose we both were."

"Who keeps the checkbook in your house, Mr. Babbage?"

That one went home. The ham face became opaque.

"I do, since she took ill. You're no kind of detective if you think she'd hire someone else and rob herself of the satisfaction of killing Garnet."

"That wouldn't stop you."

He drew himself up then, and I realized how big a man he was when he wasn't trying to fade into the furniture. "I don't think I like you, Mr. Walker. I doubt I would if we belonged to the same generation. The difference is I'd be in a position to do something about it." He went to the door and opened it.

I turned at the threshold. "What did your wife mean when she said you were right? It was just after she accused me of being honest."

He blinked. "Something I said once. She reminds me of it from time to time, usually to prove me wrong. I said if you live long enough, someday you'll ask someone a hard question and get the truth back, not just what you want to hear. It's not a virtue. It's a burden, like total recall."

I went out and he shut the door. The air in the open entryway was as heavy as ever, but I gulped it in as if I'd been holding my breath for an hour.

EIGHTEEN

L lewellyn Hale screwed the bowl back into place and stepped down from the customer's chair. I got up from the swivel in the corner, switched off the radio I'd put on to mask the noises, and followed him out through the little reception room into the hall.

The Canadian investigator ran his fingers through his pale hair, which had threatened to come untousled. Today he wore a Blue Jays jersey with the tails out over jeans as stiff and blue as the ones he'd had on when we'd met in the Loyal Dominion office. It might have been the same pair. The sneakers were different.

"It looks like a more advanced version of the latest gimmick in next year's catalogue," he said. " 'State of the art' doesn't cover it. Not for another six months anyway. This one could pick up half a decibel in a volume of air the size of a big top."

"You can tell that just by looking?"

"I'd have to take it apart and test it with instruments to be sure. You said leave it where it is."

I'd called him that morning from Rosecranz's desk, offering his day rate and travel to take a look at the new feature in my office, along with one or two other things. Electronic surveillance was a specialty at Loyal Dominion.

"The advantage shifts my way until whoever planted it finds out I know about it," I said. "Could it pick up both ends of a telephone conversation?"

"Did you check for taps?"

"I took apart the handset. Nothing."

"That means they went for versatility. If the party on the other end spoke loudly enough to be heard by someone else in the room, yeah. Easy. Let me know when you're ready to disconnect. Trade you my fee for it."

"Triple it. I may be technologically challenged, but I know the market. Would a private agency have access to anything like that?" I was thinking of the Babbages and how far they'd go to balance the account on Karl Anthony Mason.

"Pinkertons, maybe. Not even them, probably. Intelligence services always get first crack at the new toys."

"What about the mob?"

"That one I can't answer. We don't have organized crime in Canada."

I looked at him. His freckles joined in a flush.

"Okay. An experienced thief can lay hands on anything. Especially when there's a long history of cooperation between his employers and the various agencies. We *are* pickier about that up north; but then the security of the planet isn't our jurisdiction."

"You can have it anytime you ask. What about the other thing?"

He drew a miniature Etch-a-Sketch from his hip pocket and poked at the buttons with a stylus attached to it by a wire. "Lost Galleon Entertainment is a little more than just four guys, if you count a couple of wives and a girlfriend with a doting father and a little mad money. No wants or warrants, one misdemeanor conviction, possession of marijuana. That may be a job requirement. One bankruptcy, years back. Couple of passbook accounts dragging bottom, printers' bills in arrears to the tune of seventy-five hundred American. I spoke to the senior partner. He was high on Delwayne Garnet's scripting and artwork, not so high on his personality, as when was that ever a serious handicap for an artist. I don't think he killed him over it, but that's just my opinion."

"I wanted to take a crack at him myself. What else?"

"Junior partner's got a gambling problem. Casino Windsor barred him over a scuffle with a pit boss when he dropped the monthly distribution budget on a turn at blackjack."

"Run that down."

"I did. He pawned his wife's engagement ring to make good. Right now Lost Galleon is a comic book publisher with debts and no artist. Not exactly an inducement to murder their sole asset."

"What about insurance policies?"

"Can't swing the premiums. My opinion is you've got a homegrown homicide on your hands."

"You got all that today?"

"I got all that this morning. Part about the hocked ring came in over the on-board computer during the drive down. Your bill." He pocketed the gizmo, slid a folded sheet off his other hip, and stuck it out.

I snapped it open, read it, and put it in my inside breast pocket. "How many operatives you employ?"

"Two full-time. We're a second-rate power. We try harder."

"That famous inferiority complex of yours is just a blind for an ego as big as Newfoundland," I snarled. "You heading straight home?"

"I thought I'd make it a weekend, take in Henry Ford and the MGM Grand. I'm staying at the RenCen."

"Check your messages. I might have another errand or two since you're in town."

He produced a flip-phone from a slash pocket. "Number's on the bill."

"Where do you carry your wallet?"

"I get by on my boyish good looks." He grinned.

"You remind me of a reporter friend of mine. He thinks he's the lost Baldwin brother."

"I thought we already had one of those. I bet we wouldn't get along."

"Save your cash for the Grand." We shook hands. I hung on. "Ever hear of a boxer named Smallwood?"

"Sounds like a medical condition. Is it important?"

I let go of his hand. "I didn't think so until just now. When you found Delwayne Garnet so quick I didn't figure the job to set me back more than a day. I had to rewind better than thirty years. Now it looks like I'll have to go back further."

"How far?"

"All the way."

When he left I went back into the office and bought myself a drink from the honor bar in the desk; let whoever was on the listening end of my new sound system make what he wanted of the gurgles and clinks. I thought about Barry Stackpole, the local branch of the Llewellyn Hale chain of narcissistic professionals, and picked up the telephone. I needed all he could give me from the archives circa 1949 and the Curtis Smallwood case. It was beginning to look like Delwayne Garnet had inherited his father's enemies.

I was dialing when I remembered the bug all over again; like reaching for the light switch when you know the power's out. I called for the time instead, hung up, adjusted my watch, and left. At these prices even Bill Gates couldn't monitor every telephone in town.

A gray Jaguar prowled past as I was walking toward the booth in the next block. Since Ford bought the insignia they're as common as Starbucks, and I wouldn't have noticed except the car was doing half the speed limit, which in the Motor City is regarded as one of those quaint old laws like not leaving your milk wagon unattended between the hours of six and eight. I stepped in a doorway and pretended to light a cigarette while it took the corner, accelerating on the turn. Someone looking for an address. I lit up for real and continued walking. A few more cases like this one and I'd be hiring derelicts to start my car.

Near the corner a man walking my way stopped and asked if I knew the way to the Fisher Building. He was about my build, in his thirties, wearing an expensive brown suede jacket, poplin slacks with a razor crease, and Italian loafers that glistened like oiled mahogany. I'd seen him before recently, but I couldn't remember where. I didn't like that; but more than that I didn't like the fact he was wearing a jacket too warm for the weather. I told him I was a stranger myself and kept walking. There was no other traffic on the street, pedestrian or otherwise. He put a hand on my arm.

I spun with the pressure and brought my heel down hard on his instep. His other hand was inside the open zipper of his jacket. In the same movement I jabbed at his left eye with my cigarette. He got his shoulder up in time, but I followed through, mashing the cigarette against his shoulder and shoving him off balance. I broke into a run.

I cut the corner and ran flat out up the side street, which like the other was all parked cars and nothing else moving. My brain was working as fast as my feet. I remembered where I'd seen the man before: sitting across from Jeremiah Morgenstern at the noisy table in the dining room of the Airport Marriott.

At the same time I registered the presence of the gray Jaguar, stopped against the curb halfway down with the motor running. The curbside door popped open and a gun came out, hauling behind it another figure dressed all wrong for the season. It was that big of a gun; a full-length .44 magnum could have nested inside the L of its chromed frame. I made a dogleg between two parked bumpers, adjusting course toward the opposite side of the street.

A shot crashed. A chunk of asphalt jumped out of the street

three feet in front of me, leaving a sizable pothole. I stopped running then and put up my hands. Behind me I heard footsteps hurrying from the corner; uneven steps, accompanied by curses. I was going to pay for that broken foot.

NINETEEN

The Jaguar's rear seat was covered in graphite-colored leather, soft as heavy cream. It smelled like a saddlery, but that might have been the man in the suede jacket. He sat next to me with one shoe off and the stockinged foot propped on his knee, massaging it with his fingers as he wriggled his toes. He sucked air through his teeth. "Jesus."

"Busted?" The man who'd shot a hole in the street sat behind the wheel with an arm resting on the back of his seat and the barrel of the king-size gun lying across his forearm, pointing languidly at me. He seemed old for the work. His complexion, swarthy and whorled, made his hair look as white as a snow-cliff by comparison. Age didn't seem to have shackled him; he'd frisked and bundled me into the back seat without any unnecessary handling.

"How the hell should I know? I know it throbs like a son of a bitch. That a symptom?"

"If you can't get your shoe back on, that's how you tell. You ought to wear steel toes on this kind of job."

"It wasn't the toe he stomped on, you dumb fuck. Oh, *shit!*" He spotted something and tugged at his left jacket sleeve. I'd burned a hole through it with my cigarette when I'd tried to put out his eye.

I was ready for his elbow and rolled with it. My head smacked the window just the same. The interior of the car slid sideways, then righted itself like a ship heeling in the direction of its ballast.

"Hey, hey." Whitey sounded uninvolved. "The man said don't fold."

"This jacket set me back eight hundred bucks."

"You can get a decent suit for that, look like a mensch."

"How about you cut back on the fashion tips and drive the fucking car?"

Whitey opened his suitcoat, which had cost him considerably less than eight hundred dollars, and threaded the big revolver into an underarm holster as long as a rifle scabbard.

"Nice weapon," I said. "Pick up any satellite stations?"

Suede Jacket told me to shut up. He was busy trying to work his foot into its Italian loafer.

His partner looked at me. He had the kind of pale gray eyes that always look like they're swimming in tears. It's almost always an illusion. "Fifty magnum," he said. "New this year. Next size up comes with a navy man-of-war."

"How'd you get it on the plane?"

He thought about that. "Who says I flew?"

"My mistake. I saw your buddy eating with Morgenstern at the airport. Come to think of it, I didn't see you."

"I drove. Mr. Morgenstern don't like rental cars. Also it's easier transporting artillery. Flying's just too complicated for out-of-town work."

Both men had New York accents, neither as pronounced as Morgenstern's.

"I tried to get in touch with your boss," I said. "This how he returns calls?"

"You called the shot when you stepped on Nicky's foot. The

plan was just to give you a lift. You always make things this complicated?"

"I don't like guns. Especially other people's guns. Next time tell Nicky to dress for the climate. You can hide anything you want under gabardine."

"You too with the clothes?" The younger man slid a nine-millimeter Beretta out of his jacket. It looked like a tin whistle after the .50 magnum. "Why don't I punch a hole in that off-the-rack piece of shit to match the one in my sleeve?"

I laughed.

He almost dropped the gun. His knuckles whitened on the handle. "What."

"Here we are in the twenty-first century, up to our eyes in computers and wireless everything, and you everyday-low-price hoods are still running around talking like the Midnight Movie. I thought you'd all assimilated by now."

"Jesus. Some guys must want to die dumb. Jesus."

His partner said, "Nicky."

Nicky wasn't listening. Foam stained the corners of his mouth. It might have been his game face. They say Night Train Lane used to unhinge his jaw before scrimmages just to intimi-date the opposing line.

"How's the foot?" Whitey asked.

"What foot?" He waggled the gun. Trying to decide which end to use.

"What foot. Athlete's foot. Your foot, Jimmy Neutron. Get that shoe back on?"

That broke the spell. Nicky shuddered a little. He dragged the muzzle down my cheek and shook a finger in my face. Then he returned the pistol to its clip. "Yeah, I got it on. Stings like a son of a bitch."

I ungripped my thighs.

"Congratulations," Whitey said. "Take you dancing at the Arcade soon as we get home. This town rolls up the awnings at six. Nothing but coloreds after that." He buckled his seatbelt and started the motor bubbling.

After a few blocks we turned north. That wasn't the way to the airport, but Nicky was scowling again at the hole in his jacket and I didn't think it was a good time to ask. I'd risked my neck once to measure the length of his fuse. It might come in useful.

On Van Dyke we pulled into a triangular parking lot next to a cinderblock party store. Whitey took something off the passenger's seat in front and passed it over the back. It was a pink pasteboard cake box, one of the long ones designed for office parties.

Nicky didn't take it. "What about Mr. Blackwell here?"

"He's not going anywhere. He wants the meet. Anyway, we know where to find him."

"I bet they won't stop us. They haven't yet."

"Yeah, that sure means they won't. You want to share a cell with some raghead?" Whitey shook the box.

His partner took it, balanced it on his lap, and peeled out of the jacket. He unsnapped his gun harness and put it in the box along with the Beretta. He passed the box back to Whitey, who took off his suitcoat and did the same. The buffalo gun would only go in at an angle. He tied the box up with a string, put on his coat, and climbed out of the car.

He was inside the store less than a minute, and came out without the box. When he slid back behind the wheel I said, "This where Morgenstern unloads his butts?"

"Who're you now, the surgeon general?" Nicky said. "Cheap smokes are as American as Japanese cars."

"I just wondered if they carried my brand."

"I'd quit. If you think I'm going to let you burn holes in. Mr. Morgenstern's upholstery, you're as dumb as Shelly."

"I'm dumb," the white-haired man said. "I'm so dumb I almost shredded the package Mr. Morgenstern said not to fold. No, wait. That was you."

"This guy's heard that one already. Tell him about how you had Queens all sewed up. You gave out Caddies for party favors, the mayor dropped in to pay his respects at your twenty-fifth wedding anniversary. These days you pick up Mr. Morgenstern's shirts and take his dog out for a leak just for exercise."

"It was my thirtieth," Shelly said. He spun the car backward in a half-circle and chirped rubber pulling into the street. The eyes in the rearview mirror didn't look even a little bit teary.

Another piece of information to sock away for when it rained.

At the airport we were stopped at the gate to Short Term parking when a black sheriff's deputy stepped off the curb and made a cranking motion. Shelly rolled down the window.

"Good afternoon, sir. I need to ask you and your passengers to step out of the car and open the trunk."

We got out. Nicky crowded me close while his partner popped the trunk lock. The deputy peered inside, stepped back, nodded. "Thank you, gentlemen. Sorry for the inconvenience."

We climbed back in and rolled on. "Yeah, yeah," Nicky said. "You notice he didn't pat us down."

"He would if we were carrying. A good cop can smell it."

"Good cop's like a bad blow job. No such animal."

Shelly tripped the metal detector at the Marriott. He surrendered the pager on his belt, went through frisking and wanding, took off his shoes. His face wore a stoic expression he probably hadn't been born with. Nicky and I greased through without a peep. When we were out of security's earshot, Nicky asked his partner if he'd gotten off when the guard grabbed his balls.

The white-haired man lashed out a hand and lifted Nicky off his heels by his crotch. Nicky yelped. Shelly didn't say anything and his expression didn't change. After a beat he let go. Nicky adjusted himself and we continued walking. There was no conversation after that.

We rode the elevator to the top floor. Shelly rapped on the

door of one of the executive suites. The redhead opened it.

She was shorter than she'd looked in the restaurant, about five-three in braided silver sandals that showed the clear polish on her toes. She wore sky-blue slacks and a white drill top with a boat neck that exposed her collarbone, an erogenous zone often overlooked by designers. This one had gone to some trouble to fit it to her form. Her hair was a very deep red, close to cranberry, but whatever might have been added hadn't strayed far from the original, because her skin was an authentic redhead's, pale and almost blue. She wore her hair in a boyish cut. The lips today were clear gloss, and here was one female showpiece who didn't introduce any foreign material into them, or anywhere else so far as I could tell. She had large eyes, pale blue with a Tartar slant. They didn't spend any time on me at all.

"He wants you in there, both of you." She tilted her head toward a closed door near the entrance to the rest of the suite.

Nicky said, "The *bath*room?"

"It's your turn to scrub his back. My arm's tired."

"What about him?" He jerked a thumb at me.

She gave me some attention then; almost a tenth of a second. "I'll find him a magazine."

"Watch his feet."

Shelly sighed. "Let's go, for chrissake."

We stepped in from the hall and the two crossed the sitting room—Nicky still limping a little—and tapped on the closed door. I recognized the howl from the other side. They went inside and shut the door.

The woman turned her back to the hallway door and twisted the latch. She was leering like a bedroom lizard in an old-time melodrama. "Your feet?"

"I stepped on Nicky. He tried to lead."

"Yes, you look clumsy. You look—"

"Like a yoga instructor. I get that a lot."

"I'm Pet." She held out a hand.

She had a strong grip. Women do these days and it doesn't mean any more than a politician's. "Is that a name or a job description?"

She jerked free. "I told you on the phone I'm Mr. Morgenstern's companion. That means I go with him to the theater, arrange the seating at dinner parties, laugh at his stories—"

"Scrub his back?"

"Sometimes he scrubs mine. You act like you've never met a moll before."

"You guessed it. I never met a dip or a mug or a freebooter or a cutpurse either. You had to pick the lock on Grandma's diary for that one. What's your real name?"

"No. I don't like being laughed at."

"Mine's Amos. I never laugh at names."

"It's Petunia."

I laughed.

Her eyes sparked blue fire. "Maybe Nicky's not such a bad judge of character after all."

"Did they call you Petunia Pig in school?"

"Never the same person twice. I had three brothers, big Irish roughnecks with advanced degrees in mixing mortar. If you don't behave yourself I'll introduce you."

"Maybe after a drink. This room come with a bar?"

"No. Fortunately, Jeremiah does. What's your pleasure?"

I watched her drift to the kitchenette, where she opened a cupboard. Johnnie Walker Blue glittered among the bottles inside. I'd never really believed it existed. "Redheads first," I said. "Then Scotch."

"I'm afraid you'll have to take second best." She set up two Old Fashioned glasses and trickled two inches of Blue into each, without ice. She knew a thing or two about drinking premium brands. She carried them over to the little sitting area, set one down on a coffee table with an inlaid top, and curled up on the loveseat holding hers. I sat on the hard seat of the chair opposite and picked mine up. We clinked glasses.

"Death to the invaders." She threw back a solid inch.

"Which ones?"

"You pick. It's universal."

I sipped twenty-five dollars' worth. It tasted like distilled mist. "What's Morgenstern's business in Detroit?"

"I don't know."

"How long is he in town?"

"I don't know."

"Why'd he pick the Marriott?"

"I don't know."

"Who invented the cathode ray tube?"

"Philo T. Farnsworth." She drank another quarter-inch. "I'm his mistress, not his secretary. I never ask him about his business and he never volunteers anything. I've insisted on that from the start."

"That explains why you're not mixing mortar."

"It explains why I'm not swimming in it." She let a foot dangle off the edge of the loveseat. She had a tiny tattoo on her ankle. I couldn't make it out.

I dug the crumpled pack out of my shirt pocket and held it up.

"Go ahead. Try one of mine if you like. They're Turkish." She reached down and flipped back the lid of a plain deal box on the coffee table. Rows of cork-tipped cigarettes rested inside.

"Thanks. I've heard how the Turks cure tobacco." I lit one of mine and leaned forward to light the one she'd placed between her lips. She blew a plume and sat back, shrugging.

"You know what they say," she said. "Sooner or later you have to smoke your share of camel shit."

While I was leaning forward I squinted at the tattoo. Before I could focus she pulled it back out of sight.

I said, "Everyone around Morgenstern sounds as New York as takeout, except you. Boston Irish?"

"South Philly. I went to Columbia to study journalism. Now

I help Jeremiah reel in his dangling participles. He pays better than the *Times* and the work's more respectable."

"I know a fighter from Philly. Joseph Sills."

"I guess I missed him. You fight?"

"Only when I can't run. How about Curtis Smallwood?" I watched her closely.

"I missed him too." She finished her drink, looked at my glass. "You know, you don't have to pull your punches with this stuff. It doesn't bleed easy."

I took the hint. I drained my glass, stood, and carried mine and hers over to the kitchenette. "Two fingers?"

She started to answer. Someone was shouting on the other side of the bathroom door. I couldn't make out the words but I knew that bray. She paled a little. It made her skin almost translucent.

"Throw in a thumb," she said.

"He ever holler at you like that?" I poured. The stuff had been aging for fifty years when I was born and it didn't look as if it was going to survive the day.

She dragged on her cigarette, ran that hand through her short hair. "His bite's worse than his bark."

A moment later Shelly and Nicky came out of the bathroom. The younger man's face was almost yellow and the white-haired man's mouth was set in a grim line. Their clothes were wet through, a mystery. They walked between us without a word and let themselves out of the suite.

I was handing Pet her drink when Morgenstern bellowed again. She set it down, got up, splashed some Blue into another glass, and carried it into the bathroom without knocking. I got a good look at the tattoo on her ankle then: a hummingbird in flight. I didn't get it.

TWENTY

While she was gone I investigated the bedroom, which didn't look as if it belonged to the same hotel Delwayne Garnet had died in, or even the same world. There was a TV with a screen as thick as a cookie sheet, another sitting area upholstered in burgundy leather, and a king bed with a gold satin headboard, freshly made. A laptop computer sat open on an executive desk with all the ports necessary to take over British Petroleum. The window looked out on I-94, opposite the roar of the runways. Matchbox cars and trucks crowded the interchange, heading home. Pet's pink suit shared the closet with cocktail dresses, an evening gown cut to the equator, and men's business wear with the same Central Park West address on all the tailor's labels. Morgenstern traveled with nearly as many pairs of shoes as his mistress, complete with cedar trees.

I took a closer look at the computer. It was a more advanced model than I'd ever seen, with a built-in microphone for voice commands. Anyone who could own it could afford to bug my office with better-than-state-of-the-art equipment.

"Don't bother," Pet said. "You need a password to access the password, and even then it's all in code. His tech guy used to work at the Pentagon."

I turned and put my hands in my pockets. She was leaning against the doorjamb, holding her glass. I said, "Not on my account. I don't know a CD-ROM from a slippery elm. I thought you two never discussed business."

"We don't. But I know Jeremiah, and I can guess the rest. He's ready for you."

"I'm no good at scrubbing backs. Is he out of the tub?"

"Not for another ten minutes. He always soaks for an hour, like Napoleon. I'd accept the invitation. We have a seven o'clock reservation at the Blue Heron." She drank. Something about the way she handled the glass told me she'd come there by way of the kitchenette.

"You might want to start pulling your punches with that stuff," I said. "A five hundred-dollar hangover's just as bad as the other kind."

She smiled. She drifted over, tacking a little in no wind at all, and slid a hand down my arm. Then she backhanded me across the face. It stung like a willow branch.

"I don't take advice from men who go around sniffing bicycle seats," she said. "Stay out of my things."

I stroked my cheek. I felt the heat on my palm. "You can't walk out of the room and expect the cat not to jump up on the table."

Sparks came to her eyes again. The hand holding the glass jerked. I caught her wrist. "Save it for someone's face who's worth throwing it in. It's a day's pay for me."

She smiled then. "I forgot. I've been spending too much time lately with Nicky. He keeps me company when Jeremiah's in meetings."

"It should be Shelly. I wouldn't trust Nicky to feed my goldfish."

"Shelly'd refuse. He only bends so far. He used to be an important man."

"The mayor came to his anniversary party. I heard. Where'd he slip up?"

"I'd tell you to ask him, only he wouldn't answer. Whenever anyone forgets and starts talking shop I put my hands over my ears and yodel." She pursed her lips and raised her fingers to my cheek; withdrew them when I flinched. "That's going to show. Don't tell him I'm the one who hit you. He'll think you gave me a reason."

"I did."

"He'll think it's a different reason."

"I'll say I fell out of bed."

"You'd better sell it. I wasn't kidding about his bite. He's third generation."

"I knew the first. I don't like gangsters whatever their pedigree, but I'd rather take my chances with Jerry Morgenstern than Ben Morningstar."

"God, don't call him Jerry to his face. He was born Jerry Morningstar. He had it legally changed. He likes his roots."

"I bet it's the first thing he's done legal since his bar mitzvah."

"Please go in. He'll take it out on me if you don't."

I grinned. "I bet you made those three dumb Micks dance the polka."

I left her standing in the bedroom and knocked on the bathroom door.

"Enter!"

The room was all mirrors and chrome and white tile and sweating like the Brazilian rainforest. Moisture fogged the mirrors and made pools in the grouting. That cleared up the mystery of the soaking-wet stooges. In a deep square tub reclined a skeletal naked man with rhinestones of perspiration glittering in his curly black hair. He was sipping from a glass that was almost too heavy for his wrist. Soothing noises simpered from a mood tape playing somewhere in the room: whales mating, or possibly tuneup time at a French horn recital.

He peered at me through the billowing steam without moving his head. "Nicky admitted he roughed you over. He didn't say anything about your face."

"Razor burn. You didn't have to send Siegfried and Roy. I left a number with Petunia."

"You called her that? No wonder she hauled off and smacked you. What brand you smoke? I'll send over a carton."

"I'll pay the tax."

He chuckled. It sounded like a machine gun firing a test round. "Ben said you were a pain in the ass. I never thought I'd get the chance to see it for myself. I figured you'd be retired by now."

"That was twenty years ago and change. I didn't know I'd left that big an impression."

"You came through on the job. He remembered that kind of thing."

"The way I hear it, he remembered when it went the other way too. He went through more blow torches than Chrysler."

"Toward the end he didn't know who he was talking to one minute to the next, but he could tell you what kind of car he drove for six months in nineteen thirty-two. He even knew the mileage. The brain's funny that way."

"Hilarious. Is this going to take long? I'm done on this side."

"That part's up to you. You're the one wanted to see me." He took another sip, made a face, and set the glass on the edge of the tub. The Scotch must have been close to boiling. "Second switch on the right goes to the exhaust fan."

I found it and flipped it up. The motor whirred behind a vent. The fog began to clear, which wasn't entirely a good thing. There were no bubbles in the water. He'd been circumcised.

"You were in the hotel when Delwayne Garnet was killed."

"I already talked to a cop about that, beanpole named Hickok. I never knew nobody named Garnet."

"Hichens. Your grandfather knew the woman who raised Garnet. He used to make his payoffs through the hookshop she ran downtown."

"Before my time."

"If he told you what kind of car he drove under Herbert

Hoover he probably told you about her. There's another connection. A fighter named Curtis Smallwood."

He seemed prepared for that too. Hichens had been thorough. "That *shvarze* cost Ben plenty. A quarter million in pro-
motion and trainers' fees went down the shitter when he got
himself clocked. That was money then. The cops kind of overlooked that when they named Ben a suspect."

"Rumor had it the fix was in on the Joe Candy fight. Smallwood bet against himself."

"All the more reason to let the fight happen. You don't fix a
bout from the winning side. The loser's people bet the opponent and clean up. Throw me a towel."

I scooped a folded one off the rack and tossed it. He caught
it and hoisted himself out of the water. His ribs stuck out and he
didn't have enough meat on him to support a tapeworm.

"There wasn't any fix," he said, rubbing himself dry. "That
was a story cooked up by some cop who didn't get his cut.
There wasn't any need. The game was golden. TV didn't have
the equipment to shoot football or baseball; couldn't get it on
account of the movie studios was boycotting the whole industry. But all you need is two cameras to show a couple of goril-
las beating each other's brains out in the ring. Viewers ate it up.
The networks were pissing money at palookas that couldn't
punch a clock, just to fill out the hour. Ben said he made more
money legit off the Friday night fights than he pulled down
selling bathtub gin all through Prohibition. A good-looking kid
like Smallwood, with a dynamite left, was worth what he
tipped the scale in long green. Only a wrong gee with a death
wish would take the chance of blowing a sweet deal like that
with a crooked match."

I knew then where Nicky got his dialogue. Barry Stackpole
had said Morgenstern was a throwback. The act was strictly for
the cheap seats and I didn't buy it for a second. But what he'd
said made sense.

"Smallwood was going out with a white woman, a movie

actress," I said. "He got her pregnant. That was bad press in forty-nine. Networks canceled contracts for less."

"It wasn't anything you couldn't paint over, and if you couldn't, you could always can the son of a bitch and take the loss, deduct it from your ten-forty just like a solid citizen. If it's bad press you're worried about, you can't get worse than a killing. Smallwood liked his quail pale, by the way. The Hollywood chippie was just a piece of ass in the crowd. If I was you I'd tag her for it. Or one of the others. Women was spilling blood for love a million years before there was a Cosa Nostra." He stepped out of the tub, sat down on the edge, and mopped his feet. His toenails were neatly pruned. I wondered if pedicures were one of Pet's responsibilities. I was in a rotten mood.

"I never heard about any other women."

"Ben did. He kept tabs on his investments. He got chatty near the end. We had to be careful about who heard him. Anyway there was a band singer and a department-store model and I think a couple of cigarette girls. In those days there was always a bunch of dollies hanging around outside dressing rooms, sniffing around the dark meat. They liked it dangerous. I guess you couldn't blame Smallwood for caving in, a kid from the ghetto suddenly surrounded by all that wet white pussy."

I was getting my fill of Jeremiah Morgenstern, but I fought it. Lack of charm is a weapon too.

"We're wandering astray of Delwayne Garnet," I said. "He hired me to find out who killed his father. I don't have to tell you who he was."

"I heard stories. Ben never spent much time on gossip, even when his brains turned to shit."

"When a hood like you—"

"Venture capitalist."

"What's the difference? When a venture capitalist whose grandfather came over on a rumrunner's yacht checks into a hotel the same day a stiff turns up under the same roof—a stiff with a history all tangled up with the venture capitalist's—it opens a whole new world of investigation. What's your business in Detroit?"

"I can't talk about that."

"Pretend you trust me, Jerry, just for a minute. I didn't give Ben to the cops when it would buy me a get-out-of-jail card."

"The name's Jeremiah, you dumb fuck." He unslung a silk dressing gown from the hook on the door and belted himself into it. It gave him a little gravity. "You want to know why I keep guys like Nicky around? If I tell them to dump someone down an elevator shaft, all they ask is which floor do they start from."

"I saw that one last week on E-Bay," I said. "I wondered who'd bought it. When are you chimps going to start scripting your own material?"

The skin of his face shrank tight to the skull. There hadn't been much airspace there to start. Suddenly he laughed. His mouth dumped open and the hee-haw rang off the tiles and scampered straight up my spine.

"I'm going to start calling you Dangerfield. You got it all up here and you hop around like Open Mike Night at the Improv. You don't even use notes. Let's go out and cripple the bar." He stuck his feet into a pair of black velvet slippers with birds of paradise embroidered on the toes and opened the door. Conditioned air gushed in.

In the sitting room his gaze went from Pet sitting curled up on the sofa with her glass to the bottle of Scotch, whose level had dropped below the blue label. "Christ, we just broke the seal this morning. That ain't Crown Royal."

Pet sipped and said nothing. She held the glass in both hands like a shipwreck victim clinging to flotsam. I might have bought the act if she weren't working so hard to sell it.

Morgenstern took down two fresh glasses, tonged ice into them from a chrome bucket, and poured liquor over the cubes. "You're supposed to drink this stuff straight up, but I'm already sweating like a fish. You, too, I bet."

"So take cold showers. Too-hot baths make you sterile."

"Thank Christ. I got two kids. Ain't a day goes by I don't think about tying 'em up in a sack with rocks and dumping it in the Hudson." He handed me a glass and led the way into the bedroom. He closed the door. "I don't talk about work in front of Pet," he said. "Thing like that can get complicated."

"I thought it was her idea."

"She's smart. Ivy-league girl. She tell you how we met?" He sat in one of the leather armchairs and crossed his hairless legs.

I took the one facing his. I didn't like it. It reminded me of the Jaguar's back seat. I shook my head.

"She called me cold to ask for an interview. I don't even know now how she got the number. She said she'd use the piece to angle a job on a city paper. She caught me in a good mood; I said sure. Halfway through the interview I made her a better offer."

"She's smart." I drank. "Why the Marriott? The newer hotels in town are more comfortable and you don't get the noise from the jets."

"I didn't choose it. I'm meeting with some people who like the convenience of catching a plane right after without going through security. They get that out of the way before. Makes for a more relaxing negotiation."

"Negotiating what?"

He took a tiny sip. He was a careful man for all the volume. Then he grinned. Since it made him look more like Shock Theater than usual I let the question wither on the vine.

"Would these people be the same people I saw you having lunch with yesterday?"

"So that's how you found out I was here. Those were my people. Pet and Nicky you met. I never leave town without my lawyer and my personal assistant, who has his own personal assistant. If I was a rock star I guess you'd call them my entourage, only we don't trash hotel rooms."

"Just P.I.'s."

He frowned. "I told those lunks to use company manners."

"Whatever deal you're working, a new connection to an old murder wouldn't improve your bargaining position."

"I didn't know Garnet was raking it up when I came here."

"I left my lie detector in my other suit. If I'd thought to bring it, I'd be leaving now. If I thought you passed."

"If I wanted you to leave I wouldn't need it."

It was my turn to grin. "Nicky?"

"Nicky keeps Shelly's blood circulating. Shelly's the one with the experience. Don't let that cannon he carries fool you. It draws attention from his white hair."

"If he stumbled badly enough to get knocked down from *capo* to common strongarm, how come it wasn't bad enough to demote him to corpse?"

"I don't retire people I can still use. I'll tell you what happened, since you're the curious type and don't shoo. Shelly vouched for someone he didn't know like he thought. A lot of key people went to jail. Some people learn from their mistakes. A good businessman takes that under advisement."

"He doesn't strike me as the kind of person who would make a mistake like that."

"He was blinded by blood. The someone was his son."

"So who tied the son in a sack and dumped him in the Hudson?"

He swirled his ice cubes and said nothing.

After a beat I got it. I was slow that year.

"So that's why Shelly's still around," I said. "He made a trade."

"He learned from his mistake." Morgenstern shook his head. "Can't help you, Dangerfield. If I knew Garnet was here and I wanted to pop him, I could've done it without leaving Manhattan."

"That's the conventional approach in your line. Being in the same building at the same time as the murder is just as good, if you make enough noise to alibi yourself while it's going down."

I didn't say Garnet might have been killed as much as twenty minutes before the party sat down to lunch. I wanted to see how far he'd go to help me out. Killers can be over-accommodating.

"That's rookie shit. Flash like that can get you life."

"Maybe. Shelly wasn't at your table. Garnet wasn't shot with anything as big as a fifty magnum, but he's smart enough not to sign his work."

"He was on the road with the Jag all day yesterday." He took another careful sip. I remembered my own drink and took a careless gulp. Liquor clears my head, up to a point. He said, "I'd be on the same block with those other mugs if I thought a fresh kill wouldn't box me in worse than a hit that went down before I was born. Just sharing space with it could screw the deal." He spat the words, as if he'd just realized their truth. He wasn't that dull; he'd only reminded himself. "I didn't know Garnet was in the country. I barely knew who he was, and I ain't thought about him in years."

"Somebody knew. He bugged my office to find out."

I got a reaction, not the one I was looking for. His face went dumb as a bottle cap. Then he laughed; the raucous, braying laugh that stood my skin on end.

"Brother," he said when he found his breath, "you're still playing with pick-up sticks. I been bugged and tapped so many times I don't even bother to sweep no more. It costs a bundle, and then when it happens again I have to start looking all over again from scratch. I ain't used a phone in years except to make a dinner reservation, and I don't talk business anyplace I pay rent. I don't know nobody that does. If you're idiot enough to open a hot conversation anywhere but out in the open where you can see who's listening, you need to wear a helmet."

"Okay. Thanks." I took a last slow pull at my Scotch. I wasn't likely to taste another like it for a long time. He hadn't offered to send over a case of that.

"Thanks for what? I'm a born liar. You practically said it to my face."

"I'll say it, then. It used to be considered an insult. You're a liar, but you're nobody's idea of an actor. You almost dropped a stitch when I accused you of planting that bug. That's what I came here to see. You're off the hook with me." I got up. "And thanks for the booze. You're a lot more generous than your grandfather."

He set down his glass and rose. "He'd be glad to hear you say that. He couldn't believe what I paid for a hot dog. He thought they should still be a nickel."

He didn't offer his hand. He was smart enough to know I wouldn't take it. Part of being a made guy is avoiding disrespect.

TWENTY-ONE

Pet was still on the sofa in the sitting room. Her glass stood empty on the inlaid coffee table and a glance at the bottle told me the tide hadn't gone out anymore. She'd hit the wall. She sat with her head back against the cushion and her eyes closed, hanging on to the seat with both hands. Her bluish pallor wore a tinge of green.

"It's better with your eyes open," I said. "You may not be tall enough for this ride."

She started and they opened. They found focus, then lost it. "I thought you'd gone."

"Which way, the window? Jerry's not in my weight class."

"Did you get what you wanted?"

"Did you?"

Focus snapped back. "What the hell is that supposed to mean?"

"Probably nothing. I'm a little sloshed. I'm going to catch a bite downstairs before I hit the road. Hungry?"

"What time is it?"

I looked at my watch. "Five-thirty."

"I have to get ready." She didn't move.

"The Blue Heron. I forgot. You'd better grab something

from room service before you go. You might miss the elevator."

"I've drunk before," she said. "Who made you my alcoholic angel?"

"So sorry. Thanks for the hospitality." I went to the door.

"Don't leave in a boil on my account," she said. "I get this way whenever I meet someone from outside. Jane was probably okay with Tarzan for months and months. Then the great white hunters came to call, and all she had to greet them in was a tiger skin."

"Lion. Tigers aren't native to Africa. And those skins I saw hanging in your closet would tame Hemingway."

She smiled a sad Blue Label smile. "I forgot you're a detective. Your cheek looks better. Not so red. Did he ask about it?"

"He thinks you objected to being called by your real name. I let him." I touched the cheek with the back of a hand. It was still warm. "I was hoping to keep it alive a little longer. You didn't give me a rose to press in my memory book."

"Don't mush it up. You didn't make that big an impression."

"That's me, footprints in sand. Why a hummingbird?"

Her brows drew together. Then she remembered the tattoo on her ankle. "I got it last year. Do you know anything about them?"

"I know one weighs about as much as a playing card, and they're the only birds that can fly backwards."

"They migrate all the way to South America. Little things like that." She stretched out her leg, turning the ankle so she could see it. "What do you suppose they do down there?"

"Same as up here, probably. Drink nectar and make little hummingbirds. Maybe Sundays they flock outside the church and bombard the bishop's Buick. I have an idea they're Protestants."

"I hope you're wrong. I'd hate to think they made it all that way just to fall into the same bad habits."

"Why not fly down and see for yourself? The international terminal's that way. Northwest has a flight to Caracas leaving every Thursday at eight A.M. Change planes in Miami."

"How do you know that?"

"It's the work. You'd be surprised how many missing book-keepers wind up in cabanas. Or maybe not. You can't cover your ears and yodel all the time. It would annoy Jerry."

I couldn't tell if she'd heard. She was staring at the tattoo. Then Morgenstern bellowed from the bedroom, asking about cufflinks. She unfolded herself from the sofa, swayed on her feet. "Whoa."

"Cheese is good," I said. "The protein soaks up the alcohol. Order Stilton if they have it. It goes best with an expensive buzz."

"You're just a little Heloise, aren't you? What do they serve on the flight to Caracas?"

"I don't know. I only follow them as far as the airport. The rest I farm out."

"I guess you're no hummingbird."

"Just a city pigeon." I said good-bye and left just as Morgenstern shouted again.

The dining room was filling for dinner. The female linebacker was on duty at the reservation desk. She looked at her book and said the smoking section was full. That's how things are in Detroit. We also chew the stuff and spit it into a Folger's can between our feet. I said nonsmoking would be all right and asked if Joseph Sills was available. I didn't have any fresh questions for the boxing waiter from Philadelphia. I just wanted a familiar face. She told me it was his night off.

She seated me near the kitchen. The waitress who came eventually took my order for coffee and veal and I watched the servers bumping in and out through the swinging doors until the food arrived. I ate and drank without tasting—I hadn't had anything all day, but the Happy Hour upstairs had made me drowsy and I didn't want to take a cab all the way home and leave my car on the street near my building overnight. Although it didn't look like much from the outside, the engine would pay the rent on a chop shop for a month. I was paying the bill when Captain Hichens came to light on the chair facing me. His gaunt frame in the black suit looked like a carrion bird perched on a branch. But then I had birds on the brain.

I blinked. Then I sat back holding my cup of lukewarm coffee. "The monitors by the metal detector. I should've known you review the videotapes."

"Better. I have monitors in my office. Not the one where we talked; that's just a dummy. I was busy, didn't get the chance to follow it up till a little while ago. I caught Morgenstern and his squeeze on their way out to dinner. I got his side of your conversation. You want to give me your half, see if they match?"

I gave him the works, interrupting the flow only when the waitress came for the check. She asked Hichens if he wanted anything. He shook his head. When she left with her tip I told him the rest. I didn't hold anything back. I didn't know how much Morgenstern had told him.

Silence fell while he concentrated on the paper airplane he was making out of a napkin. He spent a lot of time on the flaps. All those years at the airport had taught him a thing or two about aerodynamic engineering.

"Morgenstern told me about the bug. It would've been nice if I heard it from you first."

"I only found out about it this morning."

"Think he planted it?"

"It made sense when I came. Now not. I'm pretty sure it came as a surprise to him."

"Yeah, these wise guys have no experience faking innocence." He tore out a notch and smoothed the ragged edges with a thumb.

"They never bother to fake it. They expect to be suspected, so they lie and count on there not being evidence to convict. You didn't see his face when I sprang it on him. He might've taken out the twin towers, but he's clean on this one. Since there's no other way he could have known Garnet was here wanting to solve the Smallwood murder, it follows he's clean on that too."

He folded a wing. "So it's his sore luck he picked the time he picked to check in here. He ought to check his horoscope before he leaves home."

"He said someone else picked the spot for his meeting. He wouldn't say what it was about. Maybe he was set up."

"That smells better. Not like lilacs. Who?"

"If I knew that, I'd be on my way off this case."

"Who says you're not?"

"Three guys: Meldrum, Zinzser, and me."

"That's a lot of guys."

"I didn't mention the guys who drew up the state constitution. I haven't given you a legal reason to take me off it."

"I don't have to use legal means to do it."

"Think it'll fly?"

He looked up at me. Then he finished folding and sat back, propping the airplane between his forefingers. It was a pretty thing, balanced and sharp. He pushed his palms together and crumpled it into a ball. "Who else you talk to?"

I told him about Winthrop and Regina Babbage. He rolled the ball of paper between his palms all the time I was talking. When I finished he tossed it onto the table. It bounced, rolled, and came to a stop against my saucer.

"I'm headed up there tonight," he said. "I made the appointment with Winthrop over the phone. He mentioned you. I wanted to see if you'd volunteer it."

I didn't show relief. I didn't feel it. I said, "I like Regina for it better than I ever did Morgenstern; or Winthrop, if she's as sick as he says she is. The motive's fresher, and nobody can do you a hate like somebody's mother. It's the only thing holding her together."

"You think the Babbages bugged your office?"

"They could have hired that part, but they'd have to know I had some connection with Garnet first. Beryl sure wouldn't have told them. If the lawyers leaked it, I'd need to know why, and that would take time I'd rather put into this end. Anyway I don't see either of them slipping a gun through airport security. That wasn't dumb luck. Garnet took planning. You can't count on some guard looking at his thumb while you smuggle in hardware. You wouldn't mistake this couple for Mr. and Mrs. James Bond."

"They could have hired that part too."

"Wait till you meet Regina. Given any choice she'd pull the trigger herself."

"She's sick, you said."

I let him have that one.

He said, "I'd like to see that bug."

"Later. As long as whoever's listening doesn't know I know about it, I'm out in front. I don't know just yet what I'll do with the lead, but I'm not giving it up without a warrant."

He thought about that idea. Then he crumpled it too. "Speaking of guns, you can pick yours up at the City-County Building. I had them run it through ballistics at Thirteen Hundred. Garnet was shot with a thirty-eight revolver, unjacketed slugs, just like yours; but not with your gun. I thought you'd be happy to hear that."

I thanked him dryly. Thirteen Hundred Beaubien is the address of Detroit Police Headquarters, and it was a sign of the changing times that the authorities there were willing to help out Wayne County. There'd been sour blood between them for a long time after sheriff's deputies shot it out with undercover cops during a bungled sting operation in the seventies, and the relationship hadn't improved during twenty years with a paranoiac in the mayor's office who was convinced everyone outside the city limits was out to get him. No one ever did, for the record. Emphysema and the devil got him in the end.

"Am I still a suspect?"

"I'd grill the pope if he prowled around Garnet's room before he was even room temperature. For a guy who says he knows the state constitution, you sure pissed all over it up there. But you didn't kill Garnet."

"The constitution's only forty years old," I said. "They'll just draw up a fresh one."

"You still investigating this from the Smallwood end?"

"I'm starting to think that isn't the reason he was killed. But I can't shake the feeling it wouldn't have happened if someone hadn't killed Smallwood. Who said genius is the ability to hold two conflicting thoughts in your head at the same time?"

"Sybil. I got another one for you. No sense only one of us going home fluttering his lips with his finger."

I tensed. I watched him smooth out the crumpled airplane, examining it with all the attention of an FAA consultant trying to reconstruct a crash. Finally he pushed it away.

"You've got instincts," he said. "If I didn't have a few myself I'd think you'd been holding out on me. After you told me about Curtis Smallwood, I requisitioned the evidence from Oakland County. I had Detroit Ballistics compare the slugs that killed Garnet to the one the county coroner dug out of Smallwood's brain. Father and son were both killed by the same gun, fifty-three years apart."

TWENTY-TWO

studied Hichens, the bleak eyes in the unremarkable face cut off abruptly at the top by the straight black hairline, like a Greek mask. All around us crockery rattled, flatware jingled, busboys and servers murmured among themselves as they stripped the tables between onslaughts. White noise from an improbable future, buzzing disconnectedly below and behind the solid reality of December 31, 1949.

"Dead certain?" I said.

Hichens chuckled joylessly.

"Dead and certain. I looked through the eyepieces myself. Right-hand twist, identical wear patterns in the striations. At the risk of sawing off the limb I live on, I'd say the gun was never fired between the two killings. Not enough anyway to wear down the grooves any further."

"So where's it been all these years?"

"If I knew that, I'd know where it is now. My guess on the last would be the bottom of the Detroit River, with all the rest of the ordnance."

"What kind of killer kills a man, waits for the victim's son to grow up, then kills him too?"

"The kind I'd like to clap in solitary for however many years he's got left. I don't care if he needs a walker to make it to the end of the cell block."

"You know that won't happen."

"Juries are soft. They'd acquit Hitler if he showed up at his trial wearing a hearing aid. But that's not my job." He retrieved the creased napkin, then pushed it back. "You said the Babbage woman blamed Garnet for her son getting himself blown up. That's a long time to carry a grudge. Maybe she had practice from before."

"It's a theory," I said. "That's all it is, unless you can put her in that roadhouse parking lot the night Smallwood bought it."

"If she's as bitter as you say, it might not take much leverage. You want to come with? I'll let you be good cop."

"Why so generous?"

"You've got a history with the case. My official partner wants to be sheriff. That doesn't mean he's a lousy cop, necessarily."

"He just won't dive for grounders."

"I've still got gravel in my palm from the first time."

I shook my head. "Thanks but no thanks. One day with the Babbages gets me a pass through purgatory. I'm not looking for a halo."

"Suit yourself." He got up, reminding me all over again how tall he was. "Morgenstern said he sent a car for you. I guess it didn't occur to him to offer you a ride back. Where's your buggy?"

"West Grand. It's a little out of your way if you're headed up to Royal Oak."

"County pays for the gas."

"I'll take a cab, thanks. Drivers never ask questions you have to answer."

"We'll pretend I'm off duty."

I hesitated. When a cop offers a favor, you get suspicious. Then curious. I said okay.

He got his blue Chrysler out of the restricted lot and picked me up in front of the hotel. He drove with both feet, like a trucker, and did most of his shifting ahead of the computer.

"I thought I'd have to fight the feds for this case." He kept his eyes on the semi highballing in front of him. "I expected Garnet's explosive past to set them panting. All they did was ask for copies of the paperwork. I don't understand how these flag boys operate."

"They don't either, yet. The jurisdictions are so new all the lines are marked off in chalk."

"If he wore a turban I'd be busy rubber-stamping towing contracts right now. Who you talking to next?"

"I'm pretending I'm deaf," I said. "Just like I'm pretending you're off duty."

"Shop talk. Cop to cop."

"I'm not a cop, as you cops keep reminding me."

He said nothing, a powerful argument. I was still curious.

"I don't know what's next," I said. "Most of the witnesses are dead or so far out of the loop they might as well be. Witnesses and evidence are all you need to make a case. You can make it with one or the other if you play it right and you're lucky. I'm tapped out on both."

He passed the semi finally. It had slowed down for an exit, the first time it had dipped below eighty.

"What's the coldest case you ever broke?" he asked.

"Forty-three years."

"Bullshit."

"On the level. Cops made the arrest in a nursing home."

"Bet the jury voted to acquit."

"It never went to trial. The defendant had Alzheimer's."

"This time they may have to open a grave."

It was a conversation killer. Neither of us spoke again until it came time to direct him to where my car was parked. He slid in behind it next to a plug. "Your building's around here, isn't it?"

"That's it down the block. The one where they shot *Monty Python and the Holy Grail*. I'm on the top floor."

"Big-time troubleshooter like you ought to have an office in every country in the world, like Red Adair."

"He puts out fires. I spit on 'em and run." I left the door handle alone. I wondered if he was working up the courage to kiss me goodnight.

"Go on up," he said. "I'll meet you there in five minutes."

"It was a lovely evening, Captain. Let's not spoil it."

"Five minutes," he growled.

"Better make it ten. There's no elevator."

He flipped down his visor with its official seal and we got out. The dusk was charged with nitrogen; we had a thunderstorm coming, the kind that flooded underpasses and snapped power lines. Turning into the foyer of my building, I saw Hichens wrestling something out of the trunk of the Chrysler.

Eight minutes later—I hadn't factored in his long legs—he mounted the top landing carrying a square fiberboard carton that had once contained a two-drawer file cabinet. I held open the door to the outer office and he carried it inside and dropped it on the floor with a thud. A cloud of dust and bits of decayed paper puffed out between the top flaps.

"My compliments to your trunk," I said.

"I had to take the spare tire out of the well." He kept his voice low, remembering the bug in the inner office. "It's the physical evidence in the Smallwood case."

"I thought maybe it was your partner."

He wasn't listening. "You can't keep it or take it out of the building. I signed for it. Evidence is evidence, and this just got hot again, like a pile of old greasy rags. Good thing you don't have any plans tonight."

I hadn't told him a damn thing about my plans. As if it mattered.

"When you coming back for it?"

"That depends on the Babbages. Whenever it is, you'll be here, awake and waiting."

"Yes, Captain."

"Fuck that. I get enough of the rank from Joe Candidate. You see anything in that junk I didn't, I see it too. Otherwise I'll yank your bond. A private license isn't worth shit without it."

"Why the boost?"

"It took a couple of outside eggheads to break the biggest case I ever had, and I had to wait eleven years for it. I'd like to break this one before I retire."

"That stewardess got under your skin."

"I don't like killers on my watch," he said. "It's an insult. I'm not some ham-footed hotel dick with a pint in his hip pocket."

"Nothing in this box would convict anyone for yesterday. I can tell you that much without opening it."

"I'm not running for sheriff. Oakland can have the collar, if it breaks at that end. Which murder isn't important. You can only serve one life sentence, even if two separate juries manage to bring their balls into the courtroom. If the same hand fired that piece both times, I want it in a steel cuff."

"Thanks." I actually meant it.

"I'm not doing it for you. Nobody does anything in-house anymore; not the *News* or the *Free Press* or even General fucking Motors. It's called outsourcing. Anyway, you won't find anything, and for the next few hours at least I know I won't be tripping over you."

"I've never seen the evidence room in Oakland. It must be the size of Tiger Stadium."

"It isn't. When they close a case they hang onto the stuff till the appeals run out; then they destroy it. The rest goes into private storage. Watch out for spiders. I got a hell of a bite first time I pawed through it. I'm expecting my super powers any minute."

After he left, I lifted a flap and peeked inside the box. The first thing I saw was a gray wool felt hat, crushed and moth-pitted, with a torn silk band. The last time I'd seen it was in a newspaper photo of Curtis Smallwood, taken outside a downtown hotspot with Fausta West at his side. Hichens hadn't been kidding about greasy old rags; the box smelled like the back room of a Red Shield store, with the dry musk of mouse droppings added to taste. It felt like Christmas.

TWENTY-THREE

New Year's Eve, 1949.

I have on a peach-colored silk shirt, a $200 suit built piece by piece to my measurements at Clayton's, brown-and-white spectators, a thirty-dollar borsalino hat, and a Harris Tweed topcoat that wraps around and ties with a sash just like a bathrobe, no padding in the shoulders; I don't need it. I weighed in this morning at one thirty-eight, six pounds down from the Castillo fight (which I won on points in front of ten million people watching from their living rooms), and all of it muscle. Enough of it anyway to swing around the floor of the Oriole Ballroom all night, sleep two hours, eat breakfast, and do four hours of windsprints and an hour apiece with the light and heavy bags and then report to Sportree's for an evening of wringing hands and slapping backs, without losing steam. I'm not muscle-bound like Marciano or that lump Carnera, or for that matter any of those heavyweight battlewagons slogging around the canvas, throwing two halfass punches and then going into a clinch, boos all around. No wonder the networks prefer middle-and lightweights. Stripped to my trunks I'm smooth and supple like a swimmer, no unsightly knots or bulges. I'm golden as long as I lay off the potatoes and go easy on the hooch, which can bloat you up and ruin your good looks.

And the looks are good, the rearview reminds me: no scar tissue, nose unbroken, hatbrim cocked precisely over the right eyebrow. A little too delicate, maybe, which is why the Clark Gable moustache, a wisp of a thing that needs barbering daily, but it stops the rumors before they start. If I were white they'd bill me as Pretty Boy, or maybe even Baby Face. But The Black Mamba's not bad. George Raft's friends call him Snake. The ladies don't seem to object, in his case or mine.

But if looking pretty were all I had, I'd be wearing a white coat and serving boilermakers to some auto-money hag up on Lake Shore Drive, and maybe something else upstairs when the old guy's in a board meeting. Not this fella. I can deliver a combination like a B-24 payload, and I've got a clipping from a big-time magazine in my wallet comparing my footwork to Gene Kelly's. I've stood twenty-three times with my glove in the air. Next week will make twenty-four, with nothing standing between me and Sugar Ray Robinson but open road.

That's next week. The hot destination tonight is the Lucky Tiger, a pole-barn roadhouse on an asphalt lot scooped out of solid woods on a lonely twisting two-lane blacktop twenty minutes from downtown; less if I open up the eight cylinders under the Alfa-Romeo's hood, gunmetal-colored and rounded like the bowl of a spoon. I caught yellow hell over that purchase from Archie, who says by the time I pay it off I'll need a wheelchair to come out of my corner; but managers are old ladies, convinced they'll starve if you stiff them on one towel fee. I can feel the motor grumbling through the sole of my foot all the way up to my groin. The dotted lines dart past like laser blasts in a Flash Gordon chapter, the meaty whitewalls wail on the turns but grip the pavement like flypaper. Anyone who tells you it ain't good to be twenty-two and nice-looking, with a roll in your pocket and a shift-knob in your hand, is a dirty commie.

I pull into the parking lot, cut the motor, and with one foot on the ground I can feel the throbbing of the band in full stampede.

The local version of Woody Herman's Thundering Herd is blasting "Satin Doll" loud enough to stagger the rhythm of the neon sign flashing on the roof. The air outside is flinty, the windows frosted over, but the heat inside is apparent from this distance. The crowd's fed up with the forties, war and rationing and production quotas. The prospect of 1950 shines like a new dime on a dirty sidewalk. No more suspicion or fear.

The lot's filled with Fords, Chevies, Buicks, Oldsmobiles, Hudsons, Studebakers, DeSotos; most pre-war, some fresh from the line, operating back at capacity after all the retooling from defense. I don't mind the hike. I'm used to parking away out to avoid dings and scratches. Long-legging it up the aisle with my collar up and my fists deep in my pockets, striding through the vapor of my own spent breath, I don't notice I'm not alone until someone calls my name from behind. I turn, ready to sign an autograph or block a sucker punch from some country palooka out to impress his girlfriend. I don't even see the muzzle flash. . . .

Thunder broke with the harsh sulfur-edged crack of a pistol shot and I jumped awake. I had a crick in my neck, courtesy of the maple rail along the back of the upholstered bench in my outer office. The dream lingered for a minute, as the worst ones will; it had been vivid enough that I looked down at my hands for signs of dark skin and the calluses on the knuckles that come from throwing rights and lefts that connect with bone and immersing them in brine to thicken the skin, a popular practice in the fight game before others took its place.

The floor at my feet and the bench on both sides of where I was sitting were littered with the contents of the box Captain Hichens had left. I looked at my watch. I'd been out about ten minutes, time enough for the fusty smell of fabric stored too long under non-climate-controlled conditions, of moldy shoes and old paper, to penetrate to my subconscious and put me in Curtis Smallwood's place for the last moments of his life.

Or my idea of his place, based on the evidence. It suggested he was alone and that his assailant was crouched between parked cars; position of the body was consistent with turning away from the roadhouse, perhaps in response to someone calling his name, just before the slug went through his eye. The rest was guesswork. For all I knew, Smallwood was modest about his appearance and his skill in the ring. Dressing like a dandy, driving too much automobile, and carrying a laudatory press clipping in one's wallet proves nothing. But it's a rare youngster who can accept so much attention without wanting to prance. He'd certainly liked the night life, according to the columns. Then there were his affairs, which he took few pains to conceal. In a time when they were still lynching Negroes in the South for whistling at white women, that was nearly suicidal bravado.

A volume of water the size of an Olympic swimming pool struck the roof all at once, roaring off the stucco and tarpaper and gurgling out of the rainspouts. I stood and stretched, bones crackling, and returned the unhelpful stuff to the carton, including the clothes Smallwood had been wearing when he was killed; quality stuff despite the ruination of years, bearing the labels of defunct tailors. Apparently he'd left no known next of kin to claim his personal effects after the investigators were through with them. Silverfish and rot had shredded the silk shirt, a wan pink that might once have been a vibrant shade of peach. The necktie, rayon with a Deco design, two fields of thin diagonal stripes set at opposing angles, was wrinkled but in relatively good shape, and was even back in style. Too bad he'd bled onto it. I threw it into the box.

The .38 bullet, flattened slightly when it came to rest against the back of the dead man's skull, interested me not at all. I had no reason not to believe it was the cause of death, or that it matched the two that had killed Delwayne Garnet, and so I left it in the modern Ziploc bag Hichens had put it in after he was through with it.

That left two glassine bags, one containing Smallwood's jewelry, the other the items he'd had in his pockets. I'd had it all out once but I looked again. The jewelry was gold: a Curvex watch with a pigskin band, a tie bar with a Deco design that complemented the tie, cufflinks with musical clefs engraved on the facings. I opened the other bag and took out a wallet—pigskin to match his watchband—forty-six cents in change, two twenty-dollar bills and a five that some deputy had removed from the wallet and bound together with a paperclip. Carefully I unfolded a square of paper that from its rubbed condition had ridden around for a while inside the wallet. It was a page torn from a magazine that had once been slick, now worn dull and tissue-thin, tattered at the folds. A legend at the bottom identified it as a tearsheet from *Gloves & Laces,* one of a flock of national magazines devoted to the sport of boxing at the height of its popularity. I'd skimmed it before, but now I reread the first paragraph:

> The canvas arena has known its share of celebrated warriors, from the legendary John L. to Dempsey and the Raging Bull, but few if any have combined movie-star good looks with athletic grace and power. Curtis Smallwood, poised at present on the apron of national fame, is a handsome dusky lad from Detroit's urban jungle with an astonishing record of 22 fights and 22 victories, who on appearance alone could hold his own in the Negro cinema, colored entertainment's answer to Tyrone Power. . . .

Someone, presumably Smallwood himself, had scribbled "23" in ink in the margin, updating the record. A squib at the end of the article described its author, Edie Van Eyck, as a staff reporter with the *Detroit Free Press.* I'd seen her byline on two of the follow-up stories published in the *Free Press* in the wake of Smallwood's murder; she'd interviewed Paul Wellstone, the producer at MGM accused of threatening the fighter with mayhem unless he stopped seeing Fausta West, and Ben Morningstar, who'd been equally unforthcoming. She seemed to have made a hobby of The Black Mamba. (Another conquest?) I refolded the sheet and put it away.

A yellowed inventory sheet that had come with the box also listed a set of keys in a pigskin case and three hundred in twenties in a roll held together with a rubber band. I found the key case—empty but for what looked like a key to a house or apartment—but not the cash. The finance company would have claimed the car keys when it took possession of the Alfa-Romeo. As for the money, at any given time there are several hundred thousand dollars in currency and merchandise in a police evidence room, and attrition is a sad fact of the human condition. It was a wonder the jewelry had survived.

I glanced at Smallwood's Social Security card and his picture on his Michigan driver's license. His face wore a smirk. The bureaucrat behind the camera hadn't succeeded in washing out the fine features. Van Eyck had been right about those. He must have had a terrific defense to preserve them from eager fists. I had to get a look at him in action, if any footage existed.

Personal effects. While you're alive, they're called your possessions. One minute you're distributing them among your various pockets, getting tarted up to see in a new year filled with fat purses and popping flashbulbs. The next, someone's shoving them into a box while a bored sergeant describes them for a deputy with a steno pad. "One wallet, brown. One wristwatch, yellow metal. Band brown."

I tipped a second pair of cufflinks out of the second bag and cupped them in my palm. A careful man-about-town, Curtis Smallwood; carrying a spare set in case he lost one of the ones he was wearing. These were gold like the others, with a design machined into them.

I held one up and looked at it for a long time. Something

sprouted in a damp corner of my skull and grew rapidly. Soon there was barely room for anything else.

From the bag containing jewelry I pulled the tie bar and one of the musical-clef cufflinks, dumped the old magazines off the coffee table, and laid the pieces side by side, placing one of the other cufflinks next to them. Then I got up again and rooted inside the box. My hand closed on something long and narrow. I drew out Smallwood's belt, a sporty gusseted job with a small gold buckle. Changing temperatures and humidities had dried it out and cracked the pigskin. It was brown, like his watchband and wallet and key case and shoes, except for the white caps on the toes; but I'd seen it before and I knew that. It wasn't the belt I was after.

The necktie had slithered to the bottom of the box. I shoved aside the moth-ravaged tweed topcoat, the wreck of a suit, pulled out the tie, fished one of the cufflinks he'd been wearing from its glassine bag, and held it up against the tie. Then I laid the tie on the coffee table between the link and one of those from his pocket. I placed the tie bar on the tie and stood back to look.

Fifty-three years. Someone ought to have noticed.

Maybe someone had, and no one had listened. Hard science was sacred then as now, in forensics as in boxing. The sluggers, the intuitive types, were considered obsolete. Prewar. Or maybe it hadn't panned out.

A minute of that and then I let myself into the inner office, switched on the overhead light, and got the bottle and two glasses from my desk. I splashed some into one and held it up in a mock toast to the electronic bug in the light fixture before pouring it down my throat. It wasn't Johnnie Walker Blue. It killed the nerves in my tongue like Novocaine and plowed a smoking furrow all the way to the floor of my stomach.

Lightning strobed outside the window.

"Nice touch." I didn't care who heard me.

When Hichens came in from the hall, a few minutes after

eleven, he found me sitting on the upholstered bench drinking. The bottle and the other glass stood on the coffee table among Smallwood's things. The rain had stopped gushing and had settled in for a long steady pour.

He took it all in. His hair and shoulders were soaked and he looked worn through. "I miss the party?"

"You're just in time to help me see in the new year. How'd you get on with Winthrop and Regina?"

"He's a passive pain in the ass. He never killed anybody. She'd kill Bambi's mother if she gave her half a reason. How about you? Figure out who killed the fighter?"

"Not yet," I said. "But I know who didn't."

TWENTY-FOUR

U h-huh," he said. "You got a bathroom in this establishment?"

I jerked a thumb in the direction of the private office and
he went that way. Five minutes later he came back with his hair
combed and glistening. I wondered if he carried a tube of
slickum in his pocket. He cast a questioning glance toward the
ceiling of the inner office.

I shook my head. "I don't think it can pick up anything in
here. Then there's the rain."

He cleared some homicide evidence off the other end of the
upholstered bench, sat down, and stretched out his long legs.
He waited.

I asked him if he knew anything about fashion. He made a
noise with his lips.

"I dress like an undertaker on purpose. Life's simpler when
you don't have to fuck around with what goes with what. This
got anything to do with the haberdashery?" He straightened a
finger at the display on the coffee table.

"Smallwood was a sharp dresser. That was important then,
especially if you didn't always have money and suddenly promoters were throwing it at you in buckets. It didn't matter that

most of it went back to his manager. A roll of bills is hard to see around when you're young."

"That hasn't changed. I busted a kid last month for possession for sale. He had six hundred bucks on his feet. He was too short for basketball."

"Someone gave Smallwood tips on how to dress, maybe Fausta West. In those days the studios kept an army of couturiers and former Russian royalty on staff to teach their contract players which fork to use and when to wear diamonds. Anyway he was wearing a thousand in tailoring and jewelry the night he was killed, and all his accessories matched, including his wallet and belt. Except for one item; two, actually." I picked up the necktie and tie bar and handed them to Hichens.

He held them up, the bar against the tie. "They look pretty close to me."

"They are. Those aren't the items I was talking about. The match isn't exact, but that's just for uniforms. They're both Art Deco. That's—"

"I know what Deco is," he snarled. "I'm married."

I retrieved one of the cufflinks and stuck it out. He took it in the hand holding the tie bar and held them both against the pattern on the necktie.

"I'd call it a match," he said. "Two sets of lines going both directions. He must've had the links made for the tie. Or maybe the other way around. I'm not following."

"This is one of the links he was wearing." I scooped up one with a musical clef engraved on it.

He had to put down the tie bar and the other link to take it. He held it up against the tie. "Well, I wouldn't arrest him for it. But if he had a pair on him that matched—" He dropped his hands to his lap, their contents forgotten. His eyes got a little less bleak.

"I wondered the same thing," I said.

"Maybe they mixed 'em up in Oakland. Put the wrong links in the wrong bags."

"Doubtful. They listed everything in separate categories in the inventory. It checked."

"I thought maybe he took along an emergency pair."

"Me, too, at first. Then I had to ask why he kept the pair that went with the outfit in reserve and wore the pair that didn't."

"He had on the right pair when he went out." He said it as if he'd been there; he was that certain. "He took 'em off and put them in his pocket and put on the others before he went to the roadhouse."

"Why?"

"The musical ones were a gift."

I slumped back, exhausted now that I knew I wasn't alone. "He put them on to please the person who gave them to him."

"A dame."

I grinned out of habit. He was as bad as I was. Surrounded by 1940s artifacts, discussing a half-century-old murder as if it had happened last week, it was hard not to talk like Roscoe Karns.

"He wasn't alone that night," I said.

"It doesn't have to be a woman, though. Maybe it was his manager."

"Not him. Archie McGraw was on the list of suspects because he'd been riding Smallwood about his spending habits. He wouldn't have given him gold cufflinks. Anyway, men didn't give men jewelry then. Even if they did, it's more likely Smallwood would stop off to see a woman on his way to celebrate the new year. She was his date. She gave him the gift when he picked her up."

"It isn't evidence."

"It might have been, if someone had thought to trace those cufflinks to a jeweler. Now there's no telling where they were bought or who bought them."

"I can't believe everyone overlooked it."

"Too many cooks, probably," I said. "It was a high-profile case at the time. Oakland brought in Detroit and Lansing to help. A lot of investigators trying not to step on one another's toes and a herd of reporters can trample all over a little thing like intuition. They were so busy looking at fingerprints and treadmarks they missed the one thing that might have led them to the murderer."

"Or a witness."

"If she saw it, why didn't she come forward?"

"Fausta West had two good reasons not to. She was seeing a black man, and she had a morals clause in her picture contract."

"She was already on the griddle for getting her picture taken with Smallwood outside the Oriole Ballroom. She'd have been committing career suicide to go with him to a New Year's Eve party."

"I never heard she was smart."

"If she wasn't any smarter than that, she wouldn't have been able to read her lines."

Hichens looked at the items in his hands. "You said Morgenstern told you Smallwood had a harem of white women. Any one of them could have seen it and kept her mouth shut."

"You're not thinking like the killer. Why take the chance? The three biggest suspects were McGraw, Wellstone, and Ben Morningstar. Of all of them, McGraw was the only one who might have done the job himself, and he was hosting a private party that night at home, in full view of eleven witnesses. He might have hired the job—certainly the others would have; they were above street work. A pro would've taken out an eyewitness right along with the target. There would have been two bodies in that parking lot."

"If it was a pro."

"That brings us back to the woman. Or another player."

He shook his head. "That's a dead end. If one of his dollies killed him, she needed a motive. How do you go from giving someone a gift to taking his life the same night?"

"It happens. Sometimes for the same reason. She would have had the cufflinks and the gun together in the same purse.

Maybe it *was* Fausta. She was single and pregnant. I'd hate to face those odds in her time and place."

"You think she proposed and he turned her down?"

"That's a jump. We don't even know it was her."

We listened to the rain whirring on the roof. He leaned forward, put down the tie and cufflink, poured two fingers of whiskey into the empty glass, and drank. He pulled a face. "So that's what you meant when you said you knew who didn't do it. On the female side we can rule out Bess Truman. Unless she was in town."

"Don't forget Sarah Bernhardt. She was dead." I worked my neck. The crick was still there. "I've seen the physical evidence and I've read the official reports. I know what the papers had to say. The usual next step is to talk to people. Only they're all dead."

"Not all of them." He picked up the Ziploc bag and held it by the top, with the ugly lump of lead weighing down a bottom corner. "Someone lived long enough to fire another of these from the same gun. Or to give it to someone who did."

"That's your end."

He turned his bleak gaze on me.

"I've done everything I could on Garnet," I said. "It wasn't much but it was all I had. You can subpoena witnesses and evidence. You work that end."

"So good of you to give me permission." He turned back and took another drink. "Where do you buy this piss?"

"It's honest liquor. You can tell by the taste. Guys like Morgenstern drink the premium brands. If there's anything to Sunday school he'll boil in it in hell." I drank, rolled it around my mouth, and spat it back into the glass. "You're right, it's piss."

"You get used to it after a little."

He finished his, got up, and started scooping the stuff on the coffee table into their bags and the bags into the big carton. Then he hoisted it and looked down at me. "You going to spend a little of your client's money on a ouija board or what?"

"I have a friend who's a historian. Not the kind that studies ancient civilizations; more like the aging uncivilized. If he can't help me I may have to sneak into Mount Elliott Cemetery with a shovel."

TWENTY-FIVE

I drove home through clear gelatin, wipers beating out of dull habit, with the occasional bracer of mud slung off the tires of trucks passing in the opposite direction. I left my sodden clothes in a heap on the bedroom floor and crawled between the sheets feeling as crisp as a cigarette butt drifting in a mug of cold coffee. If I dreamed I didn't remember it when I woke up, which was fine because my account was overdrawn on Curtis Smallwood until the next business day.

The telephone caught me toweling off from the shower at 8:00 A.M. I wrapped the towel around my waist and answered in the living room. It was Judy, the gatekeeper at Meldrum and Zinzser, asking me to hold for her employer.

The coffeemaker in the kitchen had finished gurgling. I set down the receiver and went in to pour a cup. Lawrence Meldrum was barking down the line when I sat in the armchair and picked up.

"I'm here, Mr. Meldrum. The teapot was whistling."

"I'm waiting for a progress report," he said. "I expected to hear from you before this. Now that the police have traced Garnet to this firm—thanks to you—it's only a matter of a day or so before the media find out. I need answers for their questions. If you'll recall, that was your selling point."

I swallowed coffee and set the cup in the ring reserved for it on the little table. I admired his proper plural use of the word *media.* "Your patience is appreciated. I've been out pounding the earth. The method is the opposite of legal procedure. The paperwork comes after."

"An oral report will be satisfactory at this juncture."

He even knew the difference between *oral* and *verbal.* He hadn't always been a lawyer. "I interviewed a woman with a strong motive for murder. She blames Garnet for her son's death."

"Is she in custody?"

"No. I don't have to tell you motive alone isn't enough to make an arrest stick. Also she doesn't fit with one or two other aspects of the investigation." I didn't mention the bug in my office. A lot depended on whoever had put it there not knowing I was aware of it, and you never can gauge the range of word-of-mouth. "There's been a development on the murder weapon," I said, before he could ask about aspects. "The sheriff's department in Wayne County has connected it to the gun used in the Curtis Smallwood killing."

"Who in blazes is Curtis Smallwood?"

I didn't know anyone used "blazes" anymore; but I let it glide. "Garnet's father. I told you he'd hired me to look into it."

"This firm isn't paying you to play archaeologist. If you expect us to bankroll your private obsession, I'll fire you and bring suit to recover your retainer."

"How'd the wedding go?"

It caught him in mid-seizure. "Wedding?"

"Last time we talked you were getting ready to play parson for two telephone companies. Can I count on one source for all my local and long-distance needs?"

"Oh. It's not public yet, but I can tell you the meeting ended most cordially. What has that to do with what we were talking about?"

"It means you can afford to carry me a few more days. Court costs being what they are, you might as well let me run up the amount you can collect damages on. It's a screwy case, Mr. Meldrum. It's the blind men and the elephant. The trunk and the tail don't match and it's going to take some time to come up with the body that goes in between."

Air stirred on his end. The windows in his corner office would be triple-glazed to seal out traffic noise from the street. "I hope for your sake you're not stringing this firm along, Walker. For both our sakes. It takes me days to recover after I destroy someone's career."

I picked up my cup and drank. "Feel better?"

"I do, as a matter of fact." His tone changed. "Do you really drink tea? I do myself, when I have the time. It forces one to pause."

"I was just kidding you, Mr. Meldrum. But if you let me see this thing out I'll have you over and brew some camomile. I'll make scones."

"That won't be necessary. Just keep receipts of all your expenses. I have to justify this whole adventure to my partners." He told me good-bye.

Over a second cup of coffee I made two calls. I got Barry Stackpole's pager number again and dialed that. Then I spoke to a contact at the Detroit Institute of Arts and arranged for a check to find out if there was anything in its extensive video archives from Curtis Smallwood's fight with Manuel Castillo, which was televised by NBC on September 30, 1949. I still had some goodwill with that establishment after recovering a priceless document that had disappeared from its vaults. He informed me, with granite in his voice, that he was in the middle of translating a cuneiform tablet and that it would be a while before he had a chance to consult the fight card at Madison Square Garden. I said I got that excuse all the time and I'd be grateful if he could get back to me on it at the office. Goodwill appeared to be losing value against the Euro. I'd just cradled the receiver when the bell rang. It was Barry. I asked him if he got the reality TV gig.

"They offered me six weeks with an option for thirteen," he said. "Even if they didn't renew they had to use me somewhere, maybe to put the drops in the CBS eye. It came with a car, an apartment in Bel-Air, and a salary that read like the population of Grand Rapids."

"Why'd you turn it down?"

"Who said I turned it down?"

"You did. You're too good a writer to abuse the past tense."

"I turned it down. They wanted me to wear a trenchcoat."

"You don't have a trenchcoat."

"I could always borrow yours."

"I don't have a trenchcoat."

"No shit? What do you wear to those foggy assignations on the waterfront?"

"Kevlar. Why'd you turn it down?"

"The apartment in Bel-Air. I told them up front I wouldn't negotiate unless they agreed to shoot in Detroit. I've got unions to support. I didn't get here alone."

"Unemployed?"

"Did you know you can't smoke in a bar anywhere in that state?"

"You don't smoke."

"And I've been comfortable all these years with that being my idea. What's on your mind this A.M.?"

"I just got chewed out by a hieroglyphics expert."

"In English or Sanskrit?"

"It's not important. I just thought it worth mentioning. I called you about a fighter."

"Curtis Smallwood."

I took a hit from the cup. "Did you bug my office?"

He thought I was kidding. "Eavesdropping's for people with no imagination. Last time we spoke you said Jeremiah Morgenstern was at the Airport Marriott. Imagine my shock when I turned on the radio fifteen minutes later and found out a party named Lance West had just been shot there. The name rang a bell. I entered it in my software and came up with Delwayne Garnet. Delwayne Garnet gave me Smallwood. Turns out getting squiffed runs in the family. I made a bet with myself on how long it'd take you to get around to asking me about The Black Mamba."

"You're a witch, Barry."

"Spread that around. If it gets out I'm a good reporter, they'll burn me at the stake. What do you need, before I start overworking my hard drive?"

"I'm short on live witnesses."

"So were the cops in forty-nine."

"I don't mean eyewitnesses. I mean people who knew some of the principals. If you've got the police reports and the press coverage, you've got their names. If you can raise any of them without a seance, I'll be ever so grateful."

"You know the terms. In on the kill before anyone else gets the story."

"I have a client to report to first," I said. "Okay after that. This may be Sunday feature stuff, Barry. Cracking Smallwood won't necessarily crack Garnet."

"It ought to. They were both shot with the same gun."

I set my cup very carefully in its ring. "I only got that last night. Where did you?"

"I'm a witch, remember?"

"You didn't cast a spell over Captain Hichens."

"If Hichens were drowning in Lake St. Clair and I was the only one within earshot, 'No comment' would be all I'd get from him."

"His partner's a better catch. He wants to be sheriff."

"Face time, kid. It's what put the *P* in politics."

"Better you than *Twenty Twenty*. What's Jerry Morgenstern doing in Detroit?"

"You mean besides Detroit itself?"

"Don't be a tease. I could hear your keyboard rattling as soon as I got off the telephone."

"Some things can't be done on a computer. Snitches don't thumb their way down the information superhighway. I'm not complaining; there's nothing like greasing a couple of dirty palms in a couple of blind pigs to remind you you're not working at a travel agency."

I waited out the dramatic pause. While I was waiting I sloshed some coffee around my mouth, strictly for the caffeine, and washed it back into the cup. It had grown cold.

"Casinos," he said. "What else? Word is he's out to deal himself a silent partnership in a second Indian casino going up in Greektown."

"It's been tried," I said. "If the gaming commission gets a whiff, they'll run him out of town on a rocket."

"Word is he's got a go-between with connections in Washington."

"How good's the word?"

"It didn't come cheap, and I'm a good horse trader. Do what you like with that." He sounded offended.

"Any names?"

"Sure. Website, too: W.W.W. Fuck You Dot Com. What the hell, Amos? You throw me a bone, I bring you back a steak, you ask for a side of beef."

"Let's not fight. I had to ask. It's good information. Morgenstern said the meeting was set up on this end. That would be the go-between. A gambling concession in Greektown would be big enough to bring him back to Detroit."

"We endeavor to give satisfaction." He sounded mollified.

"The only thing that would make me happier is if he had anything to do with the case I'm working. He eliminated himself yesterday with one dumb look."

The silence on his end was eloquent. "Thanks for the heads-up. I could've put the bribe money down on a Corvette."

"If I had, you would've spent it just the way you did. The

story you got is bigger than two murders. When can I call back on the other thing?"

"Say two o'clock. Seeing as how I'm once again out of work."

The telephone rang again while I was wiping shaving cream off my face. It was Llewellyn Hale, Canada's polite answer to Boston Blackie, calling from his hotel room at the Renaissance Center. I asked him how he'd made out at the Grand.

"I didn't go. I went to the Henry Ford instead. They have the chair Lincoln was shot in and the limousine Kennedy was shot in. What is this American fascination with death by violence?"

"You're too hard to beat at hockey. What can I do for you?"

"You can put me to work. I don't feel like driving back home yet, and I've seen the sight. I'm bored."

I thought. I hate turning down offers of help. If you make a habit of that sort of thing, the time will come when you need it and no one's offering: cat in the cradle.

"Pick up a city map," I said. "One that shows the suburbs too. You'll probably find one in the hotel gift shop. Take it to your car and drive till you get lost. That won't take long; the streets around here change names as often as rap stars, and sometimes you have to turn north in order to go south. Then get yourself found. Do that ten or twelve times. After that you shouldn't need the map."

"Is this busy work?" He sounded wary.

"Maybe. About the only thing I need to double-team is a vehicular tail. That means two in a car, in case the mark finds a parking space and you don't."

"Do tell."

"Okay, so you know that. You also need to know your way around. Then it's more than just busy work."

"Any neighborhoods I need to look out for?"

"There's a block on Monroe, between Brush and Beaubien."

He paused long enough to write it down. "Wrong'un, eh?"

"Not at all. It's where you run to get away from all the others."

"Are you joking?"

"Only a little. But it's the only stretch in the city where you can walk at two in the morning with your gun in its holster. Police headquarters is there, also a casino and family restaurants open late. A mugger might take his chances with the cops, but not with an angry foreigner in an apron with a cleaver in his hand."

"I don't own a firearm."

"Hang on. I'll give you an address where you can get one."

"Don't bother. I'll buy the map."

"I'll quiz you on it when I need you." I hung up, grinning. Hazing out-of-towners is fun as well as useful. If he was going to be any use to me at all he'd still be in town when I called him back.

TWENTY-SIX

On my way into the office I stopped by the City-County Building to claim my revolver. A grandmotherly clerk with eyes screaming to get out stamped the claim slip signed by Captain Hichens, handed me a receipt to sign, and slid the weapon across the counter in a manila envelope. In the car I reloaded the cylinder from the box I kept in the glove compartment and snapped it into its clip in the hatch, next to the unregistered Luger, a speed-loader, and the extra magazine for the automatic. I was back in business.

A gray Jaguar with New York plates was parked in a loading zone half a block from my building. Shelly sat behind the wheel, presenting an unhappy profile to Nicky, who was carping about something with both hands in motion. I didn't know if they knew my car by sight, but I rotated the sun visor to cover my face as I drove past in the opposite direction and around the corner. I turned around in the driveway to the lot where I usually parked, went back the way I'd come, and slid into the curb behind the Jag. At the last second I stamped on the pedal and rapped the rear bumper hard.

Both models were built sturdy. The jolt was just enough to crease sheet metal and rattle a pair of street soldiers. They were still reacting when I jumped out with the .38 in hand. Shelly buzzed down the driver's window with one hand and fumbled with the portable twelve-pounder under his arm with the other. The lining of his suitcoat tore with a noise like a knife gutting a fish, and he had only about three feet of shining steel free when I jammed the squat barrel of the Chief's Special into the soft flesh under the corner of his jaw. He froze.

"There's a reason they tell you not to shoot elephants from inside a vehicle," I said. "Next time try something lighter."

"Drop it *now!*" Nicky shouted, close enough to his partner's ear to make him jump. His Beretta was pointed at me.

"Oh, put it up." Shelly sounded done in. "He can't miss."

The younger man's face ran its full emotional range, ending in a pout. He lowered the pistol to his lap.

I withdrew the muzzle from Shelly's neck. He worked out the kinks, twisted the big magnum's barrel free of his suitcoat lining, and resettled it in its holster. "I hope you got plenty of insurance. Mr. Morgenstern had this car built from the ground up."

"Then you shouldn't leave it on the street. Especially my street."

Nicky said, "You should of used that popgun when you had the chance."

Shelly was looking at me. "They ran *Reservoir Dogs* on the hotel TV last night. Nicky took notes."

"I stepped on him once. Every time I see you guys I have to raise the ante. What more do I have to do to keep you out of my Zip code?"

"Not everything's about you, golden boy," Shelly said. "We're waiting on a passenger. You got a customer upstairs."

"Morgenstern?"

"Go on up and see for yourself."

A string of cars cruised past. I turned my body to mask the revolver. The older man looked at his partner. "Put it up, I said. People can see in from the windows."

"What about him?"

I grinned and stuck the .38 under my belt. Nicky swallowed the insult, swallowed it hard. He popped open the glove compartment and laid the Beretta inside. He left the lid open.

Shelly rubbed at the spot where I'd poked him. "I'm getting old. I should be home watching golf."

"You're just overqualified for the job," I said. "There's a parking lot around the corner. Cops enforce the ordinances on this street."

"Thanks." He started the motor.

"The hell with that. If Nicky drills a meter maid in this neighborhood I'll lose the little off-the-street trade I've got left."

"Some loss," he said. "You're the first pedestrian we've seen since we got here."

"Yeah. King Tut called. He wants his tomb back." His partner barked a laugh that sounded just like Morgenstern's.

Shelly put the car in gear. "Shut up, Nicky."

I smelled her from the landing.

The scent was fragile, and she hadn't sprayed it on with a fire hose. Old buildings, like old dogs, have an odor all their own, of moldy plaster and dry rot and tobacco chewed by teeth that had been grinning at coffin linings since the Bank Holiday, and anything fresher than this morning is bound to smell like the British Botanical Gardens. The last time I'd been in contact with this particular perfume, I hadn't taken much notice because it was laced generously with Scotch. I took my hand off the gun under my belt and let myself into the outer office. The door wasn't locked.

Pet was standing with her arms folded loosely, reading the fine print on the original *Casablanca* poster in its frame, the room's only decoration apart from the plastic plant in its bed of molded Styrofoam. She was dressed for the street, if the street were Fifth Avenue instead of West Grand, in a frost-green blazer over a black top and a black skirt that ran out of fabric six inches above her knees. They were nice knees, and all of a piece with her legs, sheathed in sheer hose. She had on three-inch heels, frost-green like the blazer, with open toes. She was turned three-quarters away from the door to the hallway. I admired the way her deep red hair grew up from a *V* at the nape of her neck without a single black root.

"Did you know this poster is worth a fortune?" she asked without turning. "Jeremiah trades in them. He bought out an entire estate at Sotheby's last year. A few more thousand and he could have owned the building. You ought to keep it behind lock and key."

"Funny, I thought I did." I closed the door behind me.

"Your super let me in. I think he has a soft spot for red-heads."

"He wouldn't admit it. To hear him tell it, he poisoned Stalin and blew up Sputnik."

"I heard of Stalin. I didn't know he was poisoned. I don't know who Sputnik was."

"Nobody's that young," I growled. "Shelly moved the car to a lot around the corner."

She faced me. She had amber rings under her eyes behind the powder. "You saw him?"

"I ran into him downstairs. I only told you because you don't want to stand on the street looking for your ride."

"You think I'd be arrested for soliciting?"

"In this town we only arrest the johns. We import hookers by the busload just to keep a steady supply. This isn't the best neighborhood for a woman alone."

"Are men out of season?"

I didn't have anything for that. I lifted my chin. "You shouldn't drink so much. On you it shows."

She touched her face. "I don't, usually. I was bored yesterday. Do you give out beauty tips to all the women you meet, or am I a special case?"

"Are you a case?"

"I get it. Small talk's over. Jeremiah sent me to hire you."

"He wasted your time."

"He said you might say something like that. He said to remind you you weren't always so picky."

"I don't mind working for gangsters, if it's legal and they're not just using me for bait. I don't even mind working for people I don't like. Gangsters I don't like are something else. I need a certain amount of hostility to deal with some of the people I have to in the course of an investigation. When I've wasted most of it on the client, it puts me at a serious disadvantage."

"If I put it to him that way, you'll be a lot more than just disadvantaged."

"Put it to him any way you like. Tell him it's outside my specialty."

"You don't even know what it is."

"I'll guess. He wants me to find out if the person he came to Detroit to meet lured him here to set him up for Delwayne Garnet's murder."

Her eyes widened a little. They were too blue for the room. "You're a good guesser."

"I've been a detective a long time. Not all the way back to Sputnik, but what would be a very long time by your calendar. I tried to make him mad all the time we were talking. The only time it worked was when he realized that just being in the same hotel where a murder took place had probably queered the deal he was working. It's not much of a hike from there to the notion he'd been set up."

"I suppose you know what the deal was."

"That wasn't much of a hike either. If it makes him feel any better, you can tell him it wouldn't have panned out anyway. Greektown already has one Indian casino. It won't support two even if the gaming commission gave it thumbs up. This town only has so much money to piss away at the tables. It doesn't draw any from outside."

She shook her head. "I can't begin to tell you how many ways he underestimated you."

"That's the idea, Petunia. Nobody has to tell a private detective anything if he doesn't want to, and any real cop fresh out of a cadet's uniform can pop him for withholding whatever information he manages to get. Privileged communication is only for priests and lawyers, and we all know what they are. Being underestimated is the only weapon I've got."

"Please don't call me Petunia. I can barely tolerate Pet."

"What's your last name?"

She hesitated. "Duffy."

I grinned.

"My great-grandfather came from County Kildare," she said.

"Okay, Duffy. How come I'm talking to you instead of to Jerry?"

"He can't be seen outside the hotel. There may be some people on the gaming commission who can put two and two together as well as you."

"Uh-huh. He could've sent Shelly. Which he did."

"He was going to. I convinced him I made a better first impression."

"You didn't say that. If you did, Shelly and Nicky would be up here with you."

She smiled. "I can steer Jeremiah up to a point. I'm a trained communicator, remember?"

"Uh-huh. Who's Jerry's contact in Detroit?"

"He didn't trust me with that."

"Then I've got no place to start. But you don't care if he runs a casino in Detroit or the marbles concession on Long Island."

She stopped smiling. "What makes you so sure of that?"

"Up till tonight, you've done everything to avoid Jerry's affairs but avoid Jerry. I've got a nice head of hair and one of those crooked grins that breaks hearts like potato chips. Only not yours. So it's not Jerry's business and it's not monkey business. What business is it?"

She picked up a purse the size of an eyeglass case from the coffee table. "Can we go inside? I don't feel like submitting to a complete physical in the waiting room."

"This week it's more private out here."

"There really is a bug in there?" She glanced toward the inner door. "Jeremiah couldn't keep his face straight talking about it. I thought he was kidding."

"No reason you shouldn't have. It's been a joke ever since Watergate. Except you can put sixty of the kind they're using now into one of those and pick up six hundred times as much." I opened the door to the hallway.

"Where are you going?"

"My neighbor next door is a mail-order tycoon. He only uses the place for a drop slot. We can talk in there."

"Do you have a key?"

"Why bother with a key when we've got Rosecranz?" I went down to get him.

TWENTY-SEVEN

The room was a twelve-by-twelve box with an old-fashioned pull-down shade over the window and all the ambience of a janitor's supply closet. The bulb in the ceiling fixture had been burned out since Dred Scott, leaving only the razor edge of light around the shade to illuminate the bare walls and linoleum floor. A pile of letters and packages toppled over when I pushed open the door, which was pierced only by a skeleton keyhole and a slot with a hinged brass hatch. The mail was addressed in large, moronic handwriting. There wasn't much of it and most of it wore a fine skin of dust. The operation was a front of some kind but I didn't know for what.

A charmless desk with a gray composition top on a steel frame stood against the wall under the window with a chair made of plywood and bent tubing shoved into the kneehole. I drew out the chair, wiped off the dust with my handkerchief, and tugged out the desk's only drawer. It contained two paperclips and a gnawed stump of orange pencil.

"No liquor, sorry. I won't insult you with my brand. It comes in a fifty-five-gallon drum."

"That's all right," Pet said. "I'm taking the pledge. My looks are all I've got."

I gave her the deadpan. "You need a license to fish in this state."

"I wasn't fishing for compliments. But thank you for not taking the bait. May I have one of those?"

I'd perched on a corner of the desk and lit a cigarette. I tapped another one out of the pack and held it out. She plucked it free inexpertly and managed to put the right end between her lips. She leaned forward to let me light it.

"First one this life?" I shook out the match and dropped it on the linoleum.

"Not really. I maintain a two-a-year habit. They help settle my nerves."

"I wouldn't think life with Jerry Morgenstern would be so peaceful."

"He's kind of sweet, actually. The belligerence is just an act for the office. Mostly it's boring. I tried writing a book."

"I was wondering when the next mob memoir was coming out. It's been a couple of weeks."

"It was a novel. A romance." She moved a shoulder. "It never got beyond fifty pages. I have a delicate gag reflex. I went to night classes in journalism, keeping my hand in. That didn't last. Night was the only time Jeremiah had for me. I tried shopping, but I don't like the stores in New York. The prices are a joke and the salesgirls all look like drag queens. Everyone there is acting some sort of part. Me, too. I'm the moll with a college education, too good for the role she's stuck in."

She stopped talking, tore the cigarette out of her mouth. She looked around for a place to dispose of it.

"Try the floor." I flicked ash on the linoleum.

She dropped it and stepped on it. "I'd hoped to do this in better surroundings."

"Do what?"

"Cast my feminine spell."

"Don't let that stop you. I've been seduced in worse places."

She smiled, ran a hand up and down her arm as if she were cold. "Well, the moment's sort of passed. You're not supposed to talk about it before you do it."

I took a drag, blew out a chuckling stream. "It's a wonder you got as far as fifty pages. Let's try it without sex. You want out."

"I want out."

"So get out."

"It isn't that easy. Why do you think he sent Shelly and Nicky with me? It isn't that he's afraid I won't come back. He's afraid of where I'll go and what I'll say."

"Back at the hotel you seemed to have it all figured out. What happened to covering your ears and yodeling?"

"That doesn't always work. Some things filter through. Everyone else gets the chance to retire, even racketeers. The golden age home for burned-out mob mistresses is a cemetery on Long Island."

"Ever hear of WitPro?"

"Witness Protection is for witnesses. I don't intend to testify against Jeremiah. He doesn't have that coming. It isn't his fault I'm bored out of my mind. Anyway, if I went that route, I'd just be swapping shackles. Someone else would decide where I live and what I do. I didn't come here to wind up teaching freshman English in Nebraska."

"You should have that hummingbird removed from your ankle. It's gone to your brain."

She looked at me a long time. Then she opened the little pocketbook and took out a brick of currency bound with a rubber band. It made a thump when she tossed it on the desk.

I left it there. "That looks like a lot of smuggled butts. How long before he notices it's gone?"

"It's mine. I wasn't barefoot in rags when I met him. You'd be surprised how a money market account can grow when you don't have to dip into it from day to day."

I picked it up, riffled through it with a thumb. It was all Benjamin Franklin. "Where to, lady?"

"Does Northwest still have that eight A.M. to Caracas?"

She had a cell telephone the size of a ticket stub in a pocket of her blazer, part of Morgenstern's leash. I borrowed it and pecked out the number of Llewellyn Hale's cell from my notebook. He answered from inside a wind tunnel.

"Walker," I said. "Where are you?"

"I got lost, like you said." He was shouting. "Where's Auburn Hills and why do I have to drive through a drainage ditch to get there?"

"You're on I-75. Get off at fifty-nine and double back."

"More busy work?"

"Taxi service." I told him where to meet us. I flipped the telephone shut and gave it back to Pet. "You need a place to stay tonight. What about clothes?"

"I thought I'd buy what I need when I get down there. I didn't clean out the store," she said when I looked down at the bills in my hand. "I've got credit cards, and I checked on doing an electronic transfer."

"The credit cards are history, or will be when Morgenstern figures out you took a powder. Make the transfer as soon as you get away from here. Hoods like him collect bankers like china." I tugged five bills out of the pack and held out the rest. "The fee's five hundred a day, same for molls and sisters of charity. The gentleman I just called is on retainer in another matter."

She started to say something. I held up a hand, shutting her off. Two sets of feet were squeaking their way up the third flight of stairs outside.

I slid off the corner of the desk, took her purse, and stuck the money inside. I gave back the purse and went to the door. The feet were in the hallway now. I waited until they passed the door, then opened it a crack. Shelly and Nicky had stopped in front of the door to my outer office. Pet had been gone twice as long as she needed to put Morgenstern's proposition to me. Nicky tried the knob, found out it wasn't locked, and drew his Beretta. Shelly hauled the big fifty out into the open and they went inside fast, clapping the door shut behind them.

There wasn't time for conversation. I took hold of Pet's wrist and pulled her out into the hallway and toward the stairs. We were on the second flight going down when I heard a door slam above. I wasn't holding her wrist now. We picked up the pace and hit the foyer on the run.

The car was where I'd left it after I rammed the Jaguar. I put her in the passenger's side and started the motor just as the two men boiled out onto the sidewalk. The guns came up when they saw us. I laid twin black streaks all the way around the corner. The roar of the big 455 drowned out any revolver reports. I didn't figure there were any; Shelly at least was smart enough not to open fire with the boss's girl in the car.

I eased back a little when we joined the heavier traffic on Livernois. I gave the Wrong brothers three minutes minimum to get to the Jag and pry it out of the parking lot, and I didn't want to give up the advantage by attracting a scout car. They'd just heave to and pick us up when we resumed rolling. In a little while I made my way down to Fort and First, where I pulled around behind a white glazed-brick building and eased between a pickup with a mangled right fender and a Dodge Charger missing its engine, where the battered body of my old Cutlass blended in like chalk on whitewash.

Pet worked the door handle on her side. I reached across her and yanked the door shut.

"We're a little early," I said. "Just sit back and soak up some history."

"What history would that be?" Her voice shook. She was looking at the homely old building, with its outside doors marked MEN and WOMEN.

"The oldest drive-in gas station in the world. Also the first, and still in operation. Before that, whenever you needed to fill up, you went inside and bought it by the jug."

"What is it with this town and cars? Isn't just building them enough? Do you have to have invented the parking meter, too?"

"As a matter of fact, we did."

Last night's storm had swept away the clouds. The sun hammered the asphalt, drawing ribbons of heat from it like molten glass. A seagull off course from the river perched atop the ALL OTHERS WILL BE TOWED sign and spread its wings, drying its armpits. I turned on the ignition and used the air conditioner. We'd been sitting there ten minutes when a red Malibu turned off Fort, hesitated as it rounded the building, and parked on the grass on the other side of the gutted Charger. Llewellyn Hale got out and walked around to my side. The sun brought out his freckles.

I cranked down the window and made introductions. He bent down and smiled at Pet. "Hi."

"Hi. You're standing on sacred ground."

"Is that so?" He glanced at the seagull for explanation. It shrugged and fluttered off.

"Yeah. Father Marquette stopped here to gas up the canoe."

I said, "How's your room at the RenCen?"

"It's a room," he said.

"How many beds?"

"Just one, a queen. You moving in?"

"Not me. See if you can get another room on the same floor. Next door with a connecting would be best. You've got a neighbor for tonight."

He smiled at Pet again. "Hello, neighbor."

"She's got a morning flight tomorrow from Metro. Set your clock for five-thirty and don't let her out of your sight until she goes to her gate. After that you can head back to Toronto and send me a bill."

"Bad husband?" he asked her.

"Is there any other kind?"

"Ask my wife. We work together."

I remembered the receptionist at Loyal Dominion, with Hale draped across the station talking to her. I'd thought he was on the make. I reached across Pet's lap, worked the catch under the glove compartment, and snapped the Luger free. I inspected the load and stuck the pistol out the window, butt-first.

Hale didn't take it. "Sorry. I never saw the use."

"You will if two guys named Shelly and Nicky show up. Shelly's gun came with training wheels." I waggled the Luger.

He took it, found the release, examined the magazine for himself, and rammed it back into the handle. I looked at him. He stuck the pistol under his belt. "I didn't say I didn't know how to handle one. You Yanks weren't alone in Desert Storm."

"Put it in an envelope with my name on it and leave it at the desk when you check out. They're doing random checks at the airport."

"I guess I don't get to know what this is about."

"That part's up to your passenger. I'm under the seal of the confessional. If you spot a gray Jaguar with New York plates, beat it downtown. You won't be able to stay ahead of it on the open road." I grinned at his reaction. "You asked for work, don't forget. You were bored."

"There's a lot of that going around." Pet was looking at me. "What about you?"

"I've never been less bored in my life."

"You know what I mean. Jeremiah flies off the handle when he loses a cufflink."

"I'll try not to hurt him. You got a passport?"

She took a navy folder stamped in gold out of her blazer and showed me the eagle. "I've kept it on me ever since it came through. He doesn't know I have it."

"How's your Spanish?"

"I know, 'Where's the bathroom?' and 'I have money.' "

"Hire a tutor."

"Do they come with long sideburns and tight pants?"

"Better get an old fat one with boils. You'll need to concentrate. You may not be able to come back next year with the hummingbirds."

"There are newspapers in Venezuela. Someone has to write the obituaries." She returned the passport to her pocket. "You got a passport?"

I shook my head. "I'm too old to learn any new languages."

Suddenly she leaned against me and gave me a kiss I felt in the back seat. Hale turned away and admired the pickup with the crippled fender.

When we came apart she said, "You notice I never asked why. There are easier ways to make five hundred dollars."

"Send me a list." I reached out the window and swatted Hale's arm. He turned back, saw my hand, and shook it.

I said, "Anytime you want to join the States."

"Anytime you want to turn Tory."

I looked at Pet. "You still here?"

She beamed, piled out of the car. When she looked back in I raised a hand.

"So long, Duffy."

After the Malibu turned into the street I got out and stood on the corner, watching until it vanished. No tail.

I felt a little lonely. Cars pulled up to and away from the pumps, clanging the bell as they drove over the black hose on the pavement. The station had been self-service for thirty years and no one was answering.

If Shelly and Nicky earned what Morgenstern paid them, they'd be waiting for me back at my building. I used the pay telephone outside the station to call my service. My contact at the DIA had called. He'd found the videotape of Curtis Smallwood's only televised fight. I was back on the clock.

TWENTY-EIGHT

He was a flawed poem, a plot with a hole in it, a showpiece bridge with a design defect; a thing made to impress, but that would collapse the first time pressure was applied to the right spot. That first time might be years in coming; it might come in the next minute. You couldn't keep your eyes off him for fear of missing it.

Even in the shimmery, overexposed black-and-white Kinescope filmed directly off a TV screen, then transferred from film to videotape, Smallwood's speed and ferocity shone. He moved in on his opponent smoothly and swiftly as if mounted on rollers, no holding back, and scissored at him, left, right, left, right, left-left, step, left again, following through boldly with each blow, no concern about missing and spinning himself around into harm's way. He lived in the moment. Whoever tagged him The Black Mamba had known a little about the snake's work ethic. He was fast, he was focused, but most important, he was young, and therefore immortal. The other man, Manuel Castillo, was three years older, smart and in good shape, but somewhere in those thirty-six months he'd lost that last bit of iron that makes all the difference between reckless confidence and cautious percentages. He was trying to beat a tiger on points. It can't be done.

But when the first flush faded, when you got past Smallwood's speed and the oiled machinery of the lean, hard, dark body in the black-and-white trunks, particularly if you'd spent three minutes in the ring, any ring, you saw that he put too much effort into protecting his face. He'd bought into that "colored entertainment's answer to Tyrone Power" offal the flacks were shoveling, at the expense of covering his midsection. He bent low enough moving in, but when he threw his right, he opened a window to his solar plexus. An opponent with patience and a sense of timing would wait for that next right, then duck in under his arm with a left hook and fold him like a Christmas card. Smallwood would probably recover—he hadn't gone 23 and 0 without someone laying a glove on him somewhere painful—but his faith would be shaken. From then on he would divide his defense. That was where experience gained points over animal instinct. When he went down, he would go down on his face and stay there like poured cement.

Not this time, however. Smallwood battled Castillo to a lopsided decision at the end of ten rounds, annihilating the competition on the basis of a knockdown in the sixth, an episode on the ropes in the ninth, with the older fighter covering up before a fusillade broken up by the referee, and cosmetics. At key points the victor managed to appear calm and in control while the more experienced man looked panicky, even when delivering combinations that under normal circumstances would raise his stock. This was politics. Archie McGraw, or someone if not Smallwood's manager, had understood that spectator sport is a beauty contest at bottom and that judges are influenced as much by a show of grace under pressure as by an exhibition of skill.

The fight was Smallwood's all the way. Nothing less than a KO would have pulled things out for Castillo, and three or four rounds in it was clear he wouldn't get it without support from infantry. I wondered what had become of the loser. In 1948, there wouldn't have been much in front of him beyond selling used cars in local commercial spots and an endless stretch of would-be comeback bouts with one-time fellow contenders and farmhands who trained by lifting harrows and stunning Angus bulls with short-handled sledges behind the barn. If he caught a break he might have wound up as a stunt double for George Reeves on *Superman*. If his English was good, some producer might give him a speaking part as a *bandido* on *Hopalong Cassidy*. Likely he went back to Mexico or Guatemala and found work pumping gas and reliving his best fights for starry-eyed youths in a back room smelling of Valvoline and scorched fan belts.

Sitting in the viewing room at the Detroit Institute of Arts, alone on a metal folding chair in front of a sixteen-inch monitor on a cart, I watched the tape through twice. I muted the sound the second time, to eliminate the distraction of the irritating blow-by-blow by the announcer; then as now, they never seemed to be watching the same fight I was, and were always puzzled by anything less pat than a knockout.

It was pure self-indulgence on my part. Nothing about the fighting form of a man who'd been in his grave fifty-two years would tell me who put him there and why. Reading about Smallwood had aroused my nostalgia for a game that had become silly and irrelevant in later years, debased by loudmouth promoters, circus matches with professional wrestlers, and psychotic apes. It was crooked and brutal, always had been, but somewhere between the tank bouts and the greased palms of the officials you got to see a couple of youngsters with good reflexes literally battling themselves up out of the gutter. For all I knew, the racket may have taken a different direction if Smallwood had given the roadhouse a pass that chill winter night.

Probably not, though. Boxing would always belong to the sharpers, the hoods in sharkskin suits and the media musicians in their shock hairdoes. Any kid dumb enough to stick his face into a buzz saw for money would never learn how to split a buck into ten parts and keep eleven.

The camera work was bare-bones primitive. The Hollywood embargo against television had restricted the industry to equipment ancient even by the standards of Poverty Row, and the men who operated it were unemployable anywhere else. From the bawling introductions ("Ladeeeeeez and gentulmennnn") to the manic clangor of the bell at the end of Round Ten, the lenses remained on the ring, with the exception of a broad sweep around the audience when the program came back from commercial ("Mabel, Black Label"). That may have been an accident, a miscue from the floor manager that caught the technician looking, followed by a hasty swipe and frantic grope for focus on the men standing on the canvas. I'd seen it the first time, of course, but hadn't paid much attention for wanting to get back to the fight. Now I'd seen the fight.

The arena was Madison Square Garden, that drafty echoing airplane hangar where champions and presidents had been made and broken since Buffalo Bill. The place was packed tight and everyone except the fighters was dressed up, including pearls, homburgs, and cummerbunds. This was the same crowd that turned out for a first night on Broadway. Even the fighters looked groomed and glossy.

I got up and stopped the tape.

I rewound to the commercial, then played the sequence again. It was too brief to confirm what I thought I'd seen. I looked for a frame-by-frame feature, but the TV/VCR didn't have one. I went back again, crouched in front of the screen, and hit Pause. I missed it again, rewound again, and this time I punched the button just ahead of the shot that had caught my eye. The picture froze on a handful of faces in the audience at ringside.

I went back to my chair and perched on the edge, leaning

forward with my hands braced on my knees. The show wasn't in the ring. It had been in the seats all along.

A pretty blonde in what looked like an expensive fur stole sat in the lower lefthand corner of the screen, eyes wide, nostrils flared, a predator's smile on her painted lips; the action that followed showed Smallwood charging out of his corner at the bell that began the round, which was enough to bring out the aggression in a confirmed Quaker. I was disappointed at first. I'd thought it was Fausta West. There was a strong resemblance, and she was seated in the front row, traditionally reserved for VIPs, splenetic boxing commissioners, and leeches in the combatants' entourage. But she was younger than the actress had been at the time. This one was nineteen or twenty, her hair more frizzy than flowing, probably the result of a home bleach job, and her features were narrower. That still put her in Smallwood's wheelhouse, if he liked women of a certain type. She had on a cloth hat of the pillbox variety, pinned almost to the side of her head, with a butterfly clip crusted with stones that even in monochrome looked like cheap costume jewelry. Probably nothing else she wore would come close to costing as much as the fur. That made it either a splurge from savings or a gift from an admirer. It looked like the fighter's taste.

That was as much as I could get from a split-second shot, two generations removed from the present. At that it was probably more than was there. You can get too clever, in prizefighting and sleuthing. I found myself losing interest in the blonde. Not so the young man sitting next to her.

He was a boy really, a husky sixteen or seventeen. His suit fit him like a piano shawl and might have been made from a bolt of burlap. It might have come with his first pair of long pants. He had a square face and a stubborn cowlick that looked as if his mother wasn't through training it. The woman in the next seat had a stranglehold on his upper arm and he was looking at her with the expression of someone whose prized poodle had just wet the neighbor's new carpet.

That was definitely too much to get out of an expression. When I hit Play it was gone, and it hadn't been there for as long as a heartbeat. I was more interested in the face that had worn it. I recognized it, sort of. Half a century is as hard on hunches as it is on faces.

TWENTY-NINE

I made some arrangements with my DIA contact, who had some things to say about them in plain modern English, but said he'd see what he could do. His attitude was a clear indication I'd overdrawn my account there at last. That was okay. It had been burning a hole in my pocket for years.

From the lobby I called Barry, who said he had a name for me.

"So do the cops," I said, "but I'm not sensitive. Does this name belong to Jeremiah Morgenstern's grease man in Detroit?"

His computer squawked in the background, one of those sound bites you program in to tell you a message is incoming. It was Edward G. Robinson explaining to someone how he can dish it out but he can't take it.

"A couple of hours ago you declared Morgenstern a dead ball," Barry said then. "You practically cleared him of killing Garnet."

"I haven't changed my mind. He sent someone to hire me to find out who set him up for it."

"Business must suck. You never turned finger before."

"I didn't this time. The job didn't come with the name of his contact, so I turned it down. The contact set up the time and place of the meet with Morgenstern. If he didn't rig the frame, he knows who did."

"Jerry ought to be able to figure that out."

"Jerry has people to answer to in New York. He can't drop a piano on anyone without proof, and he can't strong-arm the evidence he needs this far off his turf without drawing the kind of fire he needs to avoid. I'm the only semi-legit character he knows in town who can find his nose with his thumb."

"Which you proceeded to do. And they call *me* gonzo."

"Brother," I said, "you don't know the half of it."

I could hear his slow smile spreading. "What did you do?"

"Played Sir Walter Raleigh. Not an Oscar-quality performance; you need a cloak to do it up right. Anyway it isn't for publication. Listen. Whoever tried to pin Jerry to Garnet killed Garnet, or knows who did. An out-of-work journalist I know could peddle a story like that into a full-time job."

"He could also finish up with a matched set of prosthetic legs."

My fingers pinched a cigarette out of the pack in my shirt pocket, thinking for themselves. A security guard padding the lobby aimed a scowl at me. I parked the cigarette behind an ear. He nodded and prowled on. "I didn't know you took inventory on that sort of thing," I told Barry.

"I keep count. I just like to be the one who decides how far I stick my neck out. You asked for the name of someone who knew Curtis Smallwood and lives to tell the tale. That's all I'm peddling today."

I wrote down the number, but not the name. I'd been reading it in bylines since the start of the case and didn't think I'd forget it. It was Edie Van Eyck, the *Free Press* reporter who'd interviewed Smallwood for *Gloves & Laces* and followed the investigation of his murder all the way to Hollywood and back to its grave in the open files of the Oakland County Sheriff's Department.

"Yes?"

She'd answered on the first ring, one of those granite-edged homesteader accents you hardly ever hear anymore.

"Ms. Van Eyck?" I asked.

"Yes?"

"*Edie* Van Eyck?" The voice sounded strong for someone who had to be hovering around eighty. It might have belonged to a daughter or niece.

"Yes."

I told her who I was and said I'd gotten her name from Barry Stackpole, a colleague of hers. I said I was investigating the Curtis Smallwood murder.

"Yes?" She sounded interested for the first time.

"It just got hot again," I said. "Is there a convenient time when I can see you?"

"Yes."

The address she gave me—the only time she answered more than "yes" to any of my questions—was in Dearborn. I took Warren, and got five blocks before I passed a gray Jaguar headed in the opposite direction.

I figured they'd grown tired of staking out my building and gone trolling.

I was tucked between a semi carrying the U.S. mail and an SUV two stories high, but any hope I'd had that they hadn't seen me went out the exhaust pipe when I saw them pulling a U-turn in the middle of my rearview mirror.

I turned right on Rosa Parks, crossed the line to pass a city bus, and got back just in time to avoid running over a new-style VW beetle coming my way. The beetle bleated and the bus whomped its air horn, a surround-sound effect. I goosed the accelerator, knocked a piece off the corner of Hudson, and made a left on Commonwealth. I blew out some carbon there, making for Holden.

Grand was coming up. If they didn't see me turn, I might decoy them into thinking I was running to ground. Meanwhile I'd be burning asphalt in the other direction.

Shelly was too good a driver for that. The Jag swung in

behind me, bumping over the curb and skinning shoe polish off a pedestrian starting to cross. I doglegged back to Parks and went the wrong way for a block, turning onto Antoinette nine feet short of a head-on with a minivan going the legal way. That should have lost them, but I picked them up again in the mirror when I heeled onto Sixteenth Street. For a disgraced mob boss, Shelly—if it was Shelly behind the wheel—drove like a getaway artist.

The Grand Trunk crossed dead ahead. The trains don't run as often as they used to, not nearly often enough to count on one to cut off a tail. But approaching the slumbering guardrails I got an idea.

I slowed down.

The Jag came up quickly. Shelly had to touch the brakes to keep from ramming me; he was still chary about the boss's car. I slumped down a little, in case one of them—Nicky, of course—decided to risk a shot in broad daylight, and bumped up onto the tracks, shaving very close to the edge of the pavement where it had been built up for automobile traffic, doing about fifteen. From my tires the berm dropped off sharply to the cinderbed.

I was tempting prey. Nicky would have gone for it in a New York minute, but Nicky wasn't driving; a glance at the white head on the left side confirmed that. The older man had more experience and better judgment. But I'd humiliated him twice in close order. I was counting heavily on the blindness of fury.

At first I thought I'd lost the gamble. He entered the crossing cautiously. Then he accelerated and wheeled right, drawing abreast. Nicky aimed his Beretta at me through the open window on his side.

I spun the wheel his way. Metal screeched. The jolt jarred his trigger finger. The bullet struck my left front fender and tunneled under the paint, making a mound like a gopher. I tore the wheel the other way.

Shelly was still reacting from the collision. He swung left

and plunged the Jaguar off the edge of the asphalt on his side. Two tires blew. I flinched, even though I knew the reports hadn't come from Nicky's gun. I opened the carburetor wide and powered away from there.

I felt a little sorry for Shelly. He wouldn't have let his partner shoot. That wouldn't have been in the orders, at least until they found out what I'd done with Pet. He'd failed at the executive level, and thanks to me he'd flopped as a stooge. No Mafia in the world would hire him now.

To hell with him. He'd put a hole in his own son and dumped him in the Hudson to buy himself back into Morgenstern's good graces. The march of years was making me mellow. In a little while I'd be offering CPR to tarantulas.

Dearborn is Ford country, built from the axles up by the same people who gave us the Model T and the modern American labor movement. The local Ozymandias is everywhere represented: in its schools, its medical facilities, its public institutions, and its street names. Henry Ford Museum, Henry Ford Community College, Henry Ford Hospital, and the Ford Motor Company's global headquarters are all there, a piston-rod's throw from Ford Road and the Edsel Ford Freeway. The old crab's angular figure stands in bronze, marble, granite, and cream cheese throughout the city, and with excellent reason. If not for him the place would still be a farm village, the mighty River Rouge plant a mosquito-infested swamp, and the whole not worth the effort of collecting taxes.

Dearborn is also thirty percent Arab, the unofficial capital of the largest concentration of Muslims and Chaldeans outside the Middle East. Loudspeakers wail Islamic prayers, beards and turbans abound, and women glide down the corridors of the Fairlane Shopping Center, examining the merchandise through the slits in their burqas. They're just one more contribution to the local ethnic cocktail.

Edie Van Eyck lived in a historic structure of a specific type.

It was one of those narrow-fronted, steep-roofed frame houses built by Ford's engineers for the use of Ford workers employed at the Ford plant, in a neighborhood that had once been filled with similar buildings but now had gone over almost entirely to split-levels. It looked a little like its famous architect, tall and gaunt and poised squarely between two centuries. It wore a fresh coat of paint, and green-and-white-striped awnings made puptents above the windows on the south side.

I parked on a bed of fresh limestone, climbed the little front porch, and pushed a gutta-percha button next to the doorframe. A buzzer coughed toward the back of the house.

The front door stood open on a warm summer day. Through the screen door I saw a dim living room with the rounded square of an old TV glimmering silver in a corner; company for the aged. Then a shadow blocked it out.

"Yes?"

There was that hardscrabble twang, and behind it the Liberty Bell shape of a woman in a billowy summer dress with penguins printed on it. Her face was a blur behind the heavy nylon mesh.

For answer I took out one of my cards and flattened it against the screen. She leaned forward to peer at it, then reached up and tinkled a hook out of an eye. I took a step back, and she pushed the door open against the grinding complaint of its spring.

"Ms. Van Eyck?"

"Yes." She had a bulldog face framed by a page-boy cut, the bangs cut square across the broad forehead. Her hair was iron-gray, streaked with rust, and she had sharp little eyes with space between them for plenty of brain. She looked like Gertrude Stein, if Stein had ever gone out for the shot put. She made room for me, holding the door open. I stepped inside and she let it bang shut.

I hesitated on the square of rug placed for additional foot-wiping. What looked like a pistol in her left hand was actually a long black remote control shaped like a bedroom slipper. She pointed it at the TV and flicked the Power button. Just before the screen blipped and went dark I saw the hydrocephalic head of a space alien. A crescent-shaped gizmo studded with buttons lay on a tray table set up in front of the set. She'd been playing a video game.

"I was headed up to the next level," she said with a sigh. "But I've been there before. Can I get you a beer?"

I said a beer would be fine. She told me to make myself comfortable and went through a square arch into a bright kitchen, dragging one foot slightly in its scuffed white sneaker.

The living room was like a mineshaft after the sunny front yard. I found a switch that turned on a pair of lamps with pleated paper shades. The walls were paneled in blonde laminate with a duck-hunting scene in a cherrywood frame and diplomas sealed in clear Lucite. She would have journalism degrees. I didn't know if she would hunt ducks. An orange carpet with black flecks covered the floor wall to wall. There was a sofa and some chairs and a coffee table stacked to the corners with paperback mysteries, rectangles of paper sticking out like tongues from between their pages. She looked to have eight or ten of them going at the same time. I wondered how she kept track of the clues.

On a wall opposite the hunting print hung a rectangular arrangement of stamped metal strips in a steel frame held together with thumbscrews. Random squares that might have been tintypes broke up the rows; zinc photoengraving plates from a hot-metal printing operation, locked in a steel chase among the rows of type. The letters were all backwards, but I read the names KENNEDY and CAVANAUGH in the bolder heads. It was the front page of an eight-column broadsheet newspaper set in lead alloy. The masthead was done in Old English letters: *The Detroit Times*.

"I see you found the monstrosity. It's not exactly a theme you can decorate around."

I turned. She was standing inside the square arch with a Stroh's longneck in each hand.

"I thought you wrote for the *Free Press.*"

"I did, until Mr. Hearst offered me twice as much to write for the *Times*. He used money like a blackjack. I've made worse mistakes. He died the next year. The chain rattled on without him, but the paper ceased publication in nineteen sixty. That's the front page of the last issue you were looking at. Everyone else was stealing office supplies."

"Was that your last newspaper job?"

She nodded, double-stacked some books to clear space on the coffee table, and set down the beers. "It's a wonder I lasted that long. Mr. Hearst made me fashion editor. I dressed the same way I do now."

"You look comfortable."

"I'm not. I'm recovering from a stroke, and I've got a uri-nary tract infection that would cripple a bull elk. Diabetes, polyps on my colon—growing old is a serious health risk, Mr. Walker. You shouldn't consider it without a note from a physi-cian."

"I'll keep it in mind."

"I can't think why. It isn't as if knowing it will make a damn bit of difference." She dropped heavily onto the sofa and snatched up one of the beers. "These things are best drunk ice cold. Stroh's went to hell when they dynamited the plant on Jefferson."

I picked up the other bottle and sat on a platform rocker with as much play in it as an eight-week-old puppy. She'd replaced the furniture recently. Indentations in the carpet showed where a monster davenport and what had probably been a matched pair of recliners had stood. The place wasn't any cleaner than it had to be, without appearing slovenly. She didn't strike me as a bad housekeeper so much as an indifferent one. I liked her so far. But it was early in the visit.

"When the paper folded I still had some contacts I'd made

on the Coast when I covered Smallwood," she continued. "I rented out this house, took a place in Malibu, and wrote script continuity for ten years. Continuity, that's what they call it when you plug the holes left by the writers they pay two thousand a week. I worked on *Cleopatra,* but then who didn't? Couple of Jeff Chandler vehicles, one line in *Lawrence of Arabia,* which was the only thing they cut. Then the youth cult rolled in and I was retired at the ripe old age of fifty-three. I wrote a memoir. You can read it, if you like. It's holding up the short leg of the nightstand in my bedroom."

"What did Mr. Van Eyck do?" I drank. She was probably right about the brand, but the bottle was sweating and pleasantly cold to the touch.

"Mr. Van Eyck was my father. He gave up farming for five dollars a day at Rouge and blew an artery working in the glass plant in nineteen twenty-seven. He was forty. I never met a man who measured up."

She leaned back suddenly and dug in a dress pocket. I thought she was going for medication, but she pulled out a salt shaker and shook it into her beer. She offered me the shaker. I said no thanks and she stood it on the table. She could have strangled a poodle with one of her big, heavy-veined hands. "How do you know Barry?"

"He fell on me in a shell hole," I said. "He didn't say he knew you."

"He might not remember. We shared a table at the press club once; they let us fossils in every time one of the rags hits the century mark. He was busy trying to nail the waitress."

"I think he'd remember you."

"I'm a fascinating old gargoyle," she averred. "The last twitching remnant of the venerable and abused sorority of sob sisters. Give us two columns and a seat in the gallery at the murder trial of an auto heiress and we could squeeze tears out of a shotgun." She lifted her bottle, toasting herself, and drank it down to the label.

"Speaking of murder," I said.

"What murder?" She licked a crust of salt off her upper lip.

"That little pug committed suicide."

I stopped in mid-swallow.

"Suicide by blonde," she said. "Peroxide's poison."

THIRTY

opened my throat and let the beer do its work. "You snagged me by the gills there," I said. "I thought you were being literal."

"I was. Men are dumb. There's a skull and crossbones on the bottle, plain for all to see. But they always lead with their dicks."

"Jack Johnson liked blondes. It didn't get him killed."

"It didn't make him Gene Tunney either. Anyway, we're not discussing race."

"Sure we are. That's what sent you to Hollywood. Fausta West's producer would never have threatened his life if he were white."

"Wellstone didn't kill Smallwood. He didn't pay to have it done either."

"He told you that?"

"He didn't have to. Back then, reporters were paid to think as well as report, not like now. Now, when people ask me how I spent my tender youth, I tell them I was in prison. Who needs the stigma?" She tipped up her bottle.

"What convinced you he was innocent?"

She shook her head, like a bulldog shaking a rat in its jaws.

"Suppose you tell me why Smallwood's suddenly current."

"That's fair. The other day a man named Delwayne Garnet was shot to death at Metro Airport, with the same gun that was used to kill Curtis Smallwood. There's more. Garnet was Smallwood's son by Fausta West."

"I read about the Marriott shooting," she said after a moment. "The cops must be sitting on the rest. How'd the gun get past security?"

"We'll ask the killer when we find him."

"Who's *we*?"

"Me and the Wayne County Sheriff's Department."

"Your card says *private*."

"I've had three clients on this case so far. At present I represent the legal firm retained by Garnet's late mother."

"Beryl." She nodded. "I wondered why the name was familiar."

"Did you know her?"

"Not personally. The Freep frowned on its lady employees hanging out at hookshops and gin mills, at least during working hours. Beryl Garnet's place was like a clearinghouse for leads. Male reporters went there daily to hang their ears out. Schlongs too, probably." She shook her bottle, drained it off, stood. "Ready for a second round?"

"Not yet." Mine was still half full.

"Don't count on getting me drunk. I cut my teeth on Kansas City shine."

I'd have guessed Kansas. The more she drank, the more hardrock came out in her speech.

When she came back with a fresh longneck I said, "You were going to tell me why you don't think Wellstone killed Smallwood."

"Was I?" She sat down. Then she smiled. Her teeth were worn down by eighty-plus years of chewing her consonants. "Okay, my turn. Wellstone was a pansy. He was terrified of the publicity he was getting in connection with a murder. It was okay to be a fruit in Hollywood even then, so long as it didn't get into the papers. He'd survived one witch hunt already, naming names to the FBI to avoid appearing before the House Un-American Activities Committee. He never said that. That was homework. The other thing, the faggot thing, was an open topic everywhere in L.A. Howard Hawks threw him off the *Red River* set for servicing Montgomery Clift in his trailer."

"A smart prosecutor could use that against him."

"Even if it didn't convict him, it would wash him up," she said. "He was too smart to put himself in that position for the sake of a minor contract player. Oh, he threatened Smallwood, I'm sure of that; the goons were just getting their hooks into the studios then, and intimidation was already part of the negotiating process. Believe me, if I thought for one moment he'd carried it out, the front page would've led with it the next day. The libel laws were just suggestions then."

"Then."

She let that one sail past. She'd already taken her swipe at the postmodern press. "So I took in some sun, met Lana Turner and Clark Gable, and took the train back home with enough feature stuff to fill the section. Gable had false teeth and bad breath, and he was still sexier than the milk-babies who fill theaters today. Or I'm told they do. I haven't seen a picture on the big screen since they turned the Michigan into a parking garage."

"What about Lana Turner?"

"Stoned to the eyeballs. Some things about the town never change." She drank, eyes twinkling. "Incidentally, it wasn't her daughter who stabbed that thug Turner was sleeping around with; that one was all Mama's. Years later I collaborated with the screenwriter who wrote that little scenario for the boys in PR."

"Let's concentrate on one crime at a time," I said. "Who killed Smallwood?"

"If I knew that I wouldn't have squandered my God-given talent on that puff I filed."

"How well did you know him?"

"I didn't. I only met him once, when I interviewed him for a piece I sold to a national magazine. You wouldn't have heard of it. It folded after twelve issues, along with three-quarters of the ring magazines that sprang up after the war. They glutted a narrow market."

"*Gloves and Laces.*"

She lifted her eyebrows above her bottle. "It appears I have a fan."

"Smallwood was one. He had the article folded up in his wallet the night he was killed."

"That's no testament to me. His father was a barber in the old Black Bottom. Before Curtis put on his first pair of gloves, the closest that family came to fame was straightening Billy Eckstine's hair when he was in town. Curtis was one of the lucky ones. For every one of him, there were ten colored boys who climbed into a ring to get out of the ghetto and left their brains on the canvas."

She took a swig, swallowed fast, and thumped down the bottle. She'd remembered something. "That interview was an exclusive, a scoop. He'd won the Castillo fight and was on his way home from New York. Every reporter in town had a copy of his train schedule. When that oilburner pulled into the Michigan Central, you couldn't swing a cat without knocking the hat off of one of them. I left my cat at home, borrowed the society editor's Auburn, and broke every law between here and Monroe; also a headlight when I clipped a mile marker passing a haywagon on an inside curve. Monroe was the last stop before Detroit. I boarded there and bribed a porter for the number of Smallwood's compartment. That skunk Archie McGraw tried to have me thrown off the train, but Smallwood was still high from the win, and maybe from something else. Maybe he thought I was a blonde. Anyway he agreed to the interview. I had it all down in my pad by the time the rest of the pack crowded in. I'll never forget the look on H.G. Salsinger's face when I stepped down from Smallwood's car. He was cock-of-the-walk in the sports section of the *News* for fifty years. But not that night."

"It's a wonder they didn't run you out of the business."

"I filed the interview with the *Free Press*," she said. "That was the job, and the bonus I got allowed me to replace that broken headlight. The thinkpiece I freelanced to the magazine paid me enough to put something down on a car of my own. Not an Auburn. Topping a hundred on those roads put me off speed for life."

"Speaking of speed. What was Smallwood high on besides beating Castillo?"

"Nothing, maybe. I didn't know him; maybe he was born giggling. If I had to guess, it would be cocaine. Ben Morningstar had that racket buttoned up tight in this town."

"Morningstar was high on the suspect list."

"He lived there. Next came Tony and Vito Giacalone, and then Sam Lucy. To read the papers, you'd think they started the eighteen oh-five fire. I don't buy Morningstar for Smallwood. He had too much invested. We used to say you could do anything to Specs: screw his wife, spit in his face, call him a pimp in public, and all he'd do was shake his head and laugh. But steal one goddamn nickel from him, and he'd crucify you."

"What about Fausta West? Did you ask Smallwood about their relationship?"

"No, and I wouldn't have if it had been public knowledge then. 'Thou shalt not piss off the subject.' That's one commandment we all lived by. Anyway that was before they had their picture taken together. I didn't ask him about the girls I knew he was seeing either. It was a piece on boxing."

She looked annoyed. I wondered why.

"I heard there was a band singer and a department-store model and a cigarette girl or two."

"You cast a long line." She tilted the bottle, but she didn't drink. She lowered it. "Nobody's mentioned the model in fifty years. Who broke silence?"

"Morningstar's grandson. He calls himself Morgenstern. He said Ben rambled toward the end." I chipped at the label on my bottle with a thumbnail. I didn't want her to see my eyes. "What about the model?"

"I saw her on the train. She was leaving the compartment as I was heading toward it. I recognized her from Hudson's. I had to buy a black dress to cover Henry Ford's funeral at St. Paul's."

"What was her name?"

"How should I know? I just wanted to throw money at a dress and get out. I told you I wasn't a clothes horse."

I looked up from the torn label. "You never asked; and Smallwood never mopped the canvas with Manny Castillo. The ref and the New York Boxing Commission and ten million viewers got it all wrong. And you found me in a basket in the rushes."

"You need another beer," she snapped. "That one's weaned."

By the time she hit her stride, there was a forest of empty beer bottles standing on the coffee table and I was feeling bloated and balloon-headed. Edie seemed unaffected, apart from the occasional Homeric belch just as her story was heating up.

After her return from California, the *Free Press* lost interest in the Curtis Smallwood murder investigation. The paper had run out of new ways to report that the police were following up on promising developments, and more provocative events had intervened in Washington and Korea and Briggs Stadium, where lights had been installed. The sordid murder of a black boxer just didn't measure up, particularly as the details had grown stale. But she had the bit in her teeth and conducted her own inquiry.

The mystery model angle was golden. A slant like that could

keep a story running for weeks on the fumes alone, longer if there were pictures. But if it broke too early it would stampede the Detroit press corps and trample Edie under a hundred wingtips, size eleven triple-E. Good timing had put her in possession of a fact even the police didn't have. She was a better reporter than she was a citizen and kept it to herself until she could gather enough to fill a lead column.

"I pumped the girls in ladies' wear at Hudson's," she said. "They changed them with the window displays. I only found one who recognized her from the description; brainless little brunette with big knockers. She thought the girl I wanted had quit a day or two after Miss Knockers came on the job. But she had a name for me. I took it down to personnel. It cost me fifty bucks to look at her file."

The young woman's name was Opal Benton. She was twenty-two, a 1946 graduate of Central High School, parents deceased. She was a petite blonde with a nice figure, too short for runway modeling, but pretty enough to have attracted the attention of the captain of the high school football squad, who married her the day after commencement. The marriage lasted three months, was annulled, and after her parents died she sold foundation garments behind a counter at Hudson's to support herself until someone noticed the way she filled out her clothes and promoted her out of girdles.

"You got all that from her personnel file?" I asked.

"Just her age and education and her first job in the store. The rest came later." She twisted the top off the last soldier in a six-pack. "I never tracked down how or when she hooked up with Smallwood. I found out she rode on his train to New York and registered at his hotel. She took a room down the hall. Nice room. It would've set her back a week if she was paying for it. I don't figure she was. I assume she attended the fight.

"I figure the trip was Smallwood's way of saying toodle-oo. That picture of him with Fausta West outside the Oriole Ballroom was taken a week after the Castillo fight. She was in town to promote some flash Esther Williams musical that had maybe ninety seconds of Fausta, in a one-piece bathing suit. I guess she was a fight fan."

"He could've been two-timing them both."

She speared me with her sharp little eyes. "Who's writing this piece?"

"Sorry."

"I know a little bit about men. That's why I never married. When they trade up, they don't look back. Bagging a mannequin might get you some respect down on Twelfth Street. A movie queen makes you Nat King Cole."

"I wouldn't call Fausta a movie queen."

"After Opal she would seem like Rita Hayworth." She burped into a massive fist. "Pardon. The idea was to scrape up as much skinny as I could before I talked to her. It helps to catch someone in a lie right off the bat so you don't have to worry about it later."

"It's the same in my work. Only you have to worry about it later, too."

"Sometimes, but by then you know the tells. She had an apartment on Fielding, crumb palace without a working elevator; what the Chamber of Commerce calls a historic building. I decided to brace her at home. I brought along a photographer, a natty little guy named Shansky. He died on Pork Chop Hill. I parked him on the landing. I needed to soften her up before I brought in the heavy armor. When she didn't answer her door I grabbed Shansky and we went back downstairs to find the super. He asked us if we were with the police."

I ran a finger up the side of my bottle, drawing a channel through the beads of moisture. The cold surface of the glass chilled me to the shoulder. Something nasty was coming.

"We were six weeks too late," she said. "I've missed my share of scoops, but that was a record. Morning after Christmas, Opal's downstairs neighbors got the super out of bed to complain about flooding. She didn't answer his knock, so he let himself in with his passkey. He found her stretched out in her bathtub with the faucet running. The water had washed away nearly all of the blood."

I stopped playing with the bottle. Two corpses had seemed more than sufficient.

"Suicide?"

"Botched abortion. The coroner said she was two months along."

THIRTY-ONE

Finally, Edie Van Eyck had had her fill of beer. We took turns using the bathroom and I helped her collect the bottles and take them into the kitchen, where the pantry contained separate receptacles for paper, glass, cans, and deposit bottles. Stroh's empties rounded up a pair of industrial-size trash cans. We found niches for the fresh casualties. It was like building a house of cards.

"Who was the father?" I asked.

"The fetus' blood type didn't rule out Smallwood. But they weren't looking for Smallwood. I read the police report, talked to the investigating officers. Opal didn't have any friends she confided in, and no one they interviewed could tell them anything about her social life. Her only surviving family was a kid brother, but he'd been away at school since the car crash that killed their parents; he knew less about her than the girls she worked with. Remember, this was way, way before DNA testing. Had they found the father, he might have told them the name of the butcher who performed the operation. Apparently he kicked her loose still bleeding and she went home and soaked in a tub to ease the pain. The hot water would have just sped up the hemorrhaging. There was some evidence she'd struggled to get out, probably to call for help. But by then she was too weak. She passed out and just floated away."

A heavy rig downshifted on Ford Road, the rumble of its wheels jittering the panes in the windows.

"Too bad she didn't work for Fausta West's studio," I said. "They could have sent her on location for seven months."

Edie backed up to a white enamel sink, leaned her rear bumper against it, and folded her arms. She looked like Mr. Clean in a Prince Valiant wig. "She got a line or two in the late editions when the body was found. I never saw it, and neither did anyone else."

"Who claimed the body?"

"The brother, I guess. I never saw him. Why bother? She was dead almost a week before the murder. And my story with her."

"Bummer, ain't it?"

"You too, huh?"

"Someone was with Smallwood the night he was killed, a woman. She saw something. I had a theory it was the woman you say was Opal Benton. But theories are like kids. Sooner or later they grow up and disappoint you."

"I wouldn't know. About kids, I mean. I'm an expert on busted theories. Mine was she killed him. Being dead is a tough alibi to crack."

I said nothing. Reporters aren't detectives, no matter how much they like to think they're related. The tactics are similar but the strategy's different. I was already drawing up a new plan of battle.

"It wasn't long after that I went to work for Mr. Hearst," she said. "I'd ducked too many assignments at the Freep and had nothing to show for it, not even a picture to prove a connection between Opal and Smallwood. When the puzzle editor quit and they asked me to fill his slot, I gave them my two weeks."

I took a square of glossy paper from my inside pocket and showed it to her.

She unfolded her arms and leaned forward to squint at it. There was nothing wrong with her eyesight; no glasses had ever pinched the thick bridge of her nose. "That's her. She had on that same fur aboard the train." She leaned back again, a scowl pulling down her heavy jowls. "If you had that all along, why'd you act like you never heard of her?"

"It wasn't an act. All I had was the face. I needed a name to go with it. I had someone at the DIA shoot this off the screen while a tape was playing of Smallwood's fight at the Garden. It was the only time the network crew didn't focus on what was going on in the ring. My guy used a digital camera and processed it on his printer. Quite a century we're living in."

"I'll tell the world. Everyone in Detroit watched that fight on TV, but there isn't one who could've seen what you did. Back then they only broadcast it once. There was no chance to go back for a second look, let alone freeze a shot that took one second to air. To think I spent hours with a loop in my hand, going over all the shots Shansky took of Smallwood getting off the train, trying to catch a glimpse of Opal. She must've stepped off the other side."

I put away the picture. "You wouldn't still have those shots."

She winked. "You saw that thing on my living room wall. You ought to have guessed I never throw anything away."

She went upstairs to rummage while I prowled the ground floor, strictly in the interests of architecture and to clear my beery head. The place ran a thousand square feet, tops. It would have sheltered a family of four comfortably, taking turns in the little bathroom, crowding into the dining room for meals, listening to *Lum 'n' Abner* and Lowell Thomas in the living room, and doing most of their congregating in the kitchen, which was the biggest room on that level, and probably in the house. They'd been born too early to know you need a family room and a home theater and four bathrooms and a hot tub to function, also two incomes and eight credit-card accounts to keep the bank circling the firelight.

I heard bumping and opened the door to the stairwell. Edie had both arms wrapped around a load of dusty shoeboxes and a photo album the size of a Gutenberg Bible. She had cobwebs in her hair.

"I thought I'd have to kick it down," she said. "What were you doing, sniffing my undies?"

I needed that on top of a bellyful of hops. Without answering I relieved her of part of her burden and we carried it into the kitchen and dumped it on the stainless-steel table. We sat down and spent the next hour sorting through pictures. Most were black-and-white snapshots: strangers posing in front of bulbous automobiles, grinning on the beach in baggy swimsuits, playing euchre around folding card tables with bottles of beer at their elbows and cigarettes lisping smoke from piled ashtrays. A younger, not-as-hefty Edie, always in print dresses and white cotton gloves, seemed never to be without a brown bottle close at hand. Older Edie didn't remember half the names of the people who shared the pictures and I didn't know any of them, although I thought I recognized a callow Walter Reuther with his arm crooked awkwardly around her waist, smiling in front of a fraternal banner in some hotel ballroom or other, set up for a dinner.

These things got a cursory glance at best. We reserved more time for the professional contact sheets and grainy press blowups, all of them stamped PROPERTY OF THE DETROIT FREE PRESS on the backs, some with faded crop marks and penciled codes for the boys in the composing room. Here and nowhere else, the Ford Rotunda still stood, throngs of men and women in hats streamed through the doors of the Union and Michigan Central stations, and politicos with Irish noses and skimmers on the backs of their heads shook hands with men in coveralls carrying lunchpails. Rudy Vallee, gullwing hair disheveled and bow tie askew, feigned a punch to the shoulder of a pop-eyed Eddie Cantor at some wartime benefit crowded with young men and female nurses in military uniform. It would have made nostalgic grazing through a Detroit I'd never known if we weren't looking for something specific. We browsed a hole right through a fine summer afternoon and when dusk sifted in I got up and switched on the overhead light.

We found what we were after between the black construction-paper pages of the big photo album-turned scrapbook, mounted with more snapshots in cardboard corners and saffron clippings pasted in of articles bearing Edie's byline. It was in a shabby manila envelope bound with string, which came apart as she was untwisting it: a sheaf of four-by-five shots taken with a Speed Graphic camera, printed on cheap grainy stock for the approval of a photo editor, who would select those he wanted for processing on zinc plates and discard the rest. The rejects would go into a morgue file for possible later use, and probably disposal in the trash when no such use materialized; the glass negatives would be stored in separate files. Edie had taken the test prints home without permission and with a clear con-science, knowing how small the chances were that someone would ask about them later.

They'd been snapped at the busy Michigan Central. Curtis Smallwood survived here in still life, his hatbrim shunted to its trademark jaunty angle, houndstooth overcoat draped over his tailored shoulders like the mantle of a victorious Roman emperor. The teeth beneath the Errol Flynn moustache shone, his hands in each shot were poised in gesticulation; in or out of the ring, the fighter had never lived who could be trained to keep them at his sides. Even the Band-Aid slanting over his right eye, where Castillo had managed to open a small cut, looked like a combat ribbon.

Behind him stretched the rounded windows and gleaming combed steel of the streamliner that had borne him from Grand Central Terminal. Beside him stood a rat-faced charac-ter in checked lapels, floppy bow tie, and a moustache that slashed straight across his upper lip like a strip of electrical tape. Edie identified him as Archie McGraw, Smallwood's manager, but I'd guessed that. Around them were gathered the guardians of the press in their stove-in fedoras and cloches, hunched gnomelike over their steno pads and folds of newsprint; contemporize their wardrobe, substitute radio microphones for their stubby pencils, and they could have stood in for a modern television crew, right down to the room-to-let expression on their faces.

I wasn't interested in any of this. I knew what Smallwood looked like, and the rest was just scenery. I spread the prints in front of me like solitaire and accepted a heavy magnifying glass with a bone handle from Edie, who said if I was looking for Opal Benton I was wasting my time. "Anyway, you've got the evidence in your pocket, for whatever it's worth now."

"I'm not looking for Opal."

She didn't ask any questions after that. I decided she was a better journalist than either the *Times* or the *Free Press* had given her credit for.

I took out the digital photo from the DIA, laid it beside the press shots, and slid the lens over the faces in the crowd at the train station. Newspaper photography had lost an artist when Shansky died in Korea. Even disregarding those he hadn't bothered to print, any of the ones he'd submitted would have been striking enough for the front page of any daily in the United States. Despite the obstructions and distractions of passengers and their parties flowing to and from the tracks, reporters trying to elbow their way closer to the catch of the day, and photographers from rival newspapers jockeying for position, he'd managed an even dozen prospects. Most of his colleagues in those competitive days would have been happy to settle for one.

The peripheral images alone were suitable for framing. In the backgrounds, a handsome black porter in his trim tunic and cap assisted a middle-aged woman in seamed stockings down from the car with a white-gloved hand on her elbow; a small boy in a Cub Scout uniform sprinted toward a grandfatherly type in white handlebars lugging a two-suiter; a hulk in a mackinaw bent to inspect a wheel, one cheek pregnant with tobacco. There was a honey of a shot of a fat slob dressed in the rumpled standard issue of the Fourth Estate taking a picture of the inside of his own hat, knocked off his head by the corner of a trunk passing by on a baggage cart; printed, most likely, for the amusement of Shansky's editor. All were in sharp focus, and any one could have been blown up and hung in a museum of Americana. I wasn't interested in any of them either.

I missed what I wanted the first time. My eyes were watering from the close work, crying pure beer, and I slid the lens right past it. I'd seen it; it just hadn't registered, because I was already thinking ahead to the next photograph. When I finished with the last print, I rubbed my eyes and started again.

"Good luck with that," Edie said. "That's one weekend I'll never get back. It's a wonder I never needed bifocals. Sometimes I think—"

I shushed her.

It was barely in the frame and almost out of focus. One hand was in motion and blurred. I blinked away the ghosts, bent closer, and centered the image in the lens. The face leapt forward.

He looked older in traveling clothes, carrying a coat over one arm and a scuffed satchel and wearing a grown-up hat with a braided band. The good-looking porter was reaching up to help him down, but the blurred hand was waving him back; he already had one foot on the platform, a lad in a hurry. Husky build, with some babyfat still showing on his face. Time would render it down. He already had the square jaw.

I looked from it to the digital photo and back. My eyes swept past Opal to the boy whose arm she was grasping in the seat next to hers. Then I turned both prints around and slid them toward Edie, tucking Opal's face out of sight beneath the newspaper shot. That put her male companion into center frame. I handed Edie the lens and pointed at the boy stepping down from the train. She looked at both images.

She sat back. "Same young fella. Who is he?"

"Opal's kid brother," I said. "The one who was away at school when she died."

THIRTY-TWO

ow do you know that?" Edie asked. "You didn't even know who she was when you came here."

"I could be wrong. Maybe she picked up a newsboy in New York and he followed her home. Anyway, I know who he is. Fifty years can change a lot of things about a person, but not his bone structure. Benton was Opal's married name, wasn't it?"

"I think so. I lost most of my notes in the move to Malibu. I'm not sure I ever knew her family name. It wasn't important to the story. Do you think he killed Smallwood?"

"He had a hell of a motive, if he thought Smallwood was responsible for her pregnancy. It cost her her life. I'm still short a witness."

"You're pushing your luck. The last five years went through my friends like grapeshot. I've outlived most of my pallbearers."

"Isn't that the idea?"

"Up to a point. A grave looks pretty bleak without flowers."

"What kind do you like?"

"What kind do you?"

"Good point." I stood and shook circulation back into my

legs. "Thanks for the day. I'll let you know where it goes."

"You'd better."

I asked if she needed a hand putting the stuff away. She shook her head. She'd gathered the prints and curled snapshots into a pile, and now she plucked one off the top. "You can get me a beer while you're up."

I did that, and left her sorting through dead friends.

I was still a little woozy. I stopped at a Middle Eastern place, ate shredded lamb and rice, dry as pencil shavings, settled it with milk, and drove home. There was a bare chance Shelly and Nicky were staking out the place, but I was too tired to care. I'd been Walter Raleigh and Bulldog Drummond and the Roadrunner and Uriah Heep, all since breakfast; Salman Rushdie would have to wait until tomorrow. In any case there were no strange cars in the neighborhood.

I felt musty; when I caught a whiff of myself I smelled like old magazines. I took a shower, put on a robe, and drank part of a glass of Scotch watching amateur singers fracturing old Whitney Houston tunes on TV for a panel of judges. Both the drink and the singers were flat. I switched off the set and dumped out the ice and went to bed.

There was a band singer and a department-store model and I think a couple of cigarette girls.

Jeremiah Morgenstern's klaghorn voice was the last thing I wanted to jerk me out of the first shallow swells of sleep after an hour spent rolling the lumps out of my mattress. Enough alcohol in your system can make you drowsy; one drink too many can hold off sleep like a chorus of jackhammers. I was finally sinking under when I remembered what he'd said in his suite at the Airport Marriott.

Smallwood liked his quail pale, by the way. The Hollywood chippie was just a piece of ass in the crowd.

A band singer and a department-store model and a couple of cigarette girls.

I got up, found the chair in the living room where I'd flung my suitcoat, and fished my notebook out of the pocket. I dialed a number I'd scribbled into it. The telephone rang three times, then a slow masculine voice came on and told me to leave a message after the beep. I hung up ahead of the beep and got dressed.

Royal Oak dozed fitfully. Dark houses were a thing of the twentieth century. Those that didn't leave all their lights blazing like Gatsby's featured the glimmer of a late-night talk show through picture windows or sent the turquoise beacon of a mercury bulb through the mosquito-ridden reaches of the night. Here and there a garage door yawned open, spilling dropcord yellow where some mid-level executive labored to reset a timing chain or polished the undercarriage of some obsolete two-seater, primping for the Woodward Avenue Dream Cruise. You needed a fifty-foot ladder and a telescope just to keep tabs on Ursas Major and Minor.

The Babbage house was a blaze of light. Every lamp was burning, even the one on the porch. For a home occupied by two senior citizens who had outlived most of the friends they would invite to a party, that was an evil omen. I sprang the Smith & Wesson loose from the trick compartment and stuck it under my belt in back as I approached the front door.

Once again, Winthrop Babbage answered the bell. Super-added age had gouged cavities in the ham face. Shadows pooled beneath his eyes and engraved new lines from his nostrils to the corners of his mouth, which hung open a little as if the springs that kept it closed had lost tension. The top button of his white shirt had come undone and the skin of his neck hung like bags of shot. His eyes were dull. I saw no recognition there.

"Amos Walker, Mr. Babbage. We met the other day. Is it too late to talk to your wife?"

"My wife is in the hospital."

That explained the lights. It's more lonely in the dark. "Is it serious?"

"They're setting up a cot for me in her room. I only came home to pack a suitcase with clothes and my prescriptions. It's not a good time, Mr. Walker."

"Which hospital?"

His mouth worked a little before words came out. "She hasn't much time."

"I'm sorry."

"Thank you." He started to close the door.

"I wouldn't be here at this hour if I didn't have important questions. Maybe you can answer them."

The door stopped. He drew his chin into the folds of his neck. "I don't owe you answers, Mr. Walker. You've gotten far more than enough at this address. In fact, I blame you for Regina's collapse. Since she spoke to you, the police have been here, because of information you gave them. She was severely upset by both visits. This morning she couldn't get out of bed. I had to call an ambulance. I've been with her all day, and now it appears I'll be with her until the end." The door thumped shut.

The clock in the dash read 12:35, but the traffic was as heavy as at noon. The factory shifts were changing and speed limits were shattering all over town in the race to get home. My eyes smarted from lack of sleep. Oncoming headlights starred out across my corneas and I blinked hard to squeeze moisture into them. The gun was gouging a hole in my back. I unbelted it and laid it on the passenger's seat. I was beyond exhaustion. But my heart was kicking my ribs sixteen beats to the measure. It was a good thing I was headed to a hospital.

When it comes to serious care, emergency or long-term, and you live in Royal Oak, there is only one place to go. The local branch of Beaumont Hospital is one complicated cell in a system that has absorbed most of the best-trained doctors, nurses, and technicians in the health community of Southeastern Michigan. One or the other Babbage would fix on Beaumont as if no other facility existed.

If Winthrop hadn't exaggerated, Regina's thirty-four-year reign of hatred for Delwayne Garnet was drawing to a close. When Winthrop joined her—soon, if what I'd seen in his face wasn't just a reflection of another death nearby—no one would be left to care or even remember how Karl Anthony Mason had blown himself and his colleague to pieces, leaving his mother to fill the vacant space with rage for the one who had survived. What it had to do with the murder of a forgotten fighter nineteen years before that was only a few answers away.

Maybe. Detecting isn't an exact science. Nothing is, including science.

At night the sprawling medical complex burned enough electricity to illuminate Afghanistan. There were lights in all the windows and you could have played a night baseball game under the floods in the vast parking lot. I found a space within twenty miles of the entrance and legged it up the wheelchair ramp. The steps took too long; I was racing the Reaper.

The nurse on duty at the first station I came to was a pretty, round-faced brunette with a distracting scar slanting two inches across her chin. The degree came with combat training.

"Regina Babbage's room number, please." I spelled both names.

"Are you a relative?"

"No."

"I'm sorry. Visiting hours are over. You'll have to come back in the morning at eight A.M."

"That's when eight A.M. usually occurs. This can't wait." I showed her the county star.

She pressed her lips into a thin line, paged through a chart attached to a clipboard, and ran a short-nailed finger down the list of names. She paused long enough to make me wonder if I wasn't at the wrong hospital after all.

"She's in ICU. You'll have to identify yourself over the intercom."

I got the number of the intensive care unit, passed through a half-dozen doors equipped with bumper pads and cotton-covered hinges, scaled a long incline, and flattened my thumb against a button under a round speaker mounted next to a door. This time when a voice came on I broke the law instead of just nudging it. I said I was there to see patient Babbage on police business. I was asked to wait one minute.

One minute later a buzzer razzed and I pushed through the door. The lighting here was soft, as if it were some kind of salon instead of an arsenal of monitors, instrument panels, defibrilators, oxygen tanks, and one-finger latex gloves. The lone party at the station was a young man with a headset clamped over his buzz cut. He murmured an apology into the mouthpiece, looked at the bit of tin in my hand, and asked for my name.

"Captain Hichens."

He asked if that was spelled with an *h* or a *k*. I told him and he wrote it down in a log, checking the time against a stainless-steel wristwatch and entering that. "She's in Three. I can't let you have more than five minutes."

"That'll be plenty."

I hoped it would be. If she was unconscious or didn't have the answers I needed, it would be a long time in a cell with nothing to occupy me but past failures.

The room was just big enough for the railed bed, the usual blinking and beeping equipment, a couple of cabinets for clothes and other personal items, and a narrow rollaway bed, made up as tightly as a bunk in a marine barracks. Whatever chairs there may have been for visitors had been removed to accommodate Winthrop Babbage for the night. Regina lay under a thin blanket, taking in and draining fluids through clear flexible tubes hooked up to the standard containers. In the light of a fluorescent panel behind the bed she looked as small as a child. Her pale blonde hair, washed out by the light, was nearly indistinguishable from the white pillowcase. She had a tube in her nostrils. Without the little touch of lipstick and blush her face looked pasty and sunken.

Time is a fascinating invention. A couple of nights earlier, I wouldn't have believed any pair of aluminum rails could have held her.

"Mrs. Babbage?"

Her eyes were open. After ten seconds they prowled my way. They looked alert.

I told her who I was. A vertical line appeared between her brows. It wasn't puzzlement, but annoyance. The brain waves were still strong enough to tip over a bus.

"Can you talk?"

She nodded once, a shallow movement. Her lips separated with a sound like pages peeling apart. In a voice like emory paper she asked for water.

I didn't know if she should have it, but there was a plastic cup with a straw next to a pitcher on the bedside cabinet. I filled the cup, pressed a button to elevate her top half, and held the cup while she drew greedily on the straw. She let go with her lips and I put the cup back.

"What name did you use when you sang professionally?"

She breathed in and out three times, her breath quickening on the third. "Peggy Yale. Yale was my real name, before I married the first time. The booking agent changed the other. He thought people would rhyme it with 'vagina.'"

Her voice was still hoarse, the sentences drawn out, with spaces to breathe in between.

"What band did you sing with?"

"Rex King and his Royal Athletics. It was the house orchestra at the Athletic Club."

The room's air current changed. Someone had opened the door behind me. I bent farther over the bed. "I saw the cufflinks you gave Curtis Smallwood that night."

"This man isn't a sheriff's deputy. He's trespassing."

I recognized Winthrop Babbage's voice.

Regina managed a small smile. Her teeth were all hers. They wouldn't have let her keep them otherwise. "Pretty snazzy, hey? I had them made at Enggass's. They didn't go with his outfit, but I didn't know what he'd be wearing that night. He took off the ones he had on anyway and put on the new ones. He was a sweet boy."

A hand gripped my shoulder. "Sir, you have to leave."

It was the male nurse. I shook off his hand. "Who'd you see that night in the parking lot?"

"Parking lot?"

I was starting to lose her. Her eyes had gone opaque.

"You have security, don't you?" Winthrop's voice shook. "Call somebody!"

"The Lucky Tiger," I said. "The roadhouse. Who killed him?"

The fog burned off all at once. She nodded again.

"Fair trade," she said. *"Exodus."*

THIRTY-THREE

I was still getting information when the security guard made his appearance, but Regina was growing incoherent, drifting away on the morphine tide. Even her husband's shouting wouldn't bring her back to shore. By then the nurse was more interested in calming him down than throwing me out. He'd gotten too intense for intensive care.

I couldn't blame him. I'd have screamed at me too.

The guard was a hard-faced black with a cavernous voice and a tribal tattoo on one wrist. He identified the source of the excitement without direction and asked me to come with him. I came with him. His face looked like a mortar and pestle for pulverizing knuckles.

Outside the unit he took my upper arm in a delicate thumb-and-forefinger grip that would have crushed an iron pipe. My arm went dead below the elbow. We went down the hall together like old friends.

"I'll just ask you to sit in the office till the police come," he said. "You can't just bust in. This is a hospital, not some blind pig."

We wound around a series of corridors and stopped before

an elevator. He pushed the Down button. He was still holding my arm but I couldn't feel it.

The doors rolled open and a doctor or something in a lab coat strode out without looking, the way some people will. I decided he was a doctor. The guard relaxed his grip and shifted to make room. I twisted loose, body-checked the doctor into the guard, and took off sprinting. I hit a pair of double doors on the fly. The guard's shout thundered after me, pinched off when the doors flapped shut.

I didn't know the way out from there, but all halls lead somewhere. When after a mile and a half that theory came open to question, I asked for directions from a rubber-faced old gent pushing a vacuum the size of an armored truck along the carpet. He answered softly and I had to ask him to speak up; my own heart and gasping breath drowned out even the bawling of the vacuum. He told me where I'd find an exit. I pounded on.

I had a hand on a glass door opening to the parking lot when two more guards in uniform came bounding across the side-walk. They had sidearms and walky-talkies flapping on their belts. I backpedaled into a visitors' waiting area and stepped behind a kiosk filled with magazines in Plexiglas pockets. The door whooshed open. There was an atoll of silence, then feet thumped the carpet going in two directions. I waited another beat, then stepped out and used the door.

Outside I took a minute to get my bearings. I'd exited through a separate wing from the one where I'd entered and had to cup my hands around my eyes to isolate the north star from the glare of the floodlights. At length I turned the right corner, found the section where I'd parked, and drove away, obeying the 15 MPH signs in the driveway. As I turned into the street, I heard a distant siren winding up. It probably hadn't anything to do with me. I only noticed it because I'd broken three laws in close succession, a personal best.

My building looked medieval at that hour. The street was emptier than usual and the sandstone box with its griffin-headed waterspouts stuck out in the ambient city light like a castle keep. By day it was just an obsolete brown pile. But just then it was the only place for me.

I was slowing to a stop in front when a square of yellow light breached the wall on the third floor. It was on less than a second, then the glass went dark and resumed reflecting the building across the street. The window belonged to my office. Someone inside had decided to check the time.

Accelerating gently, I turned the corner and bumped up over the curb and into the little lot I used most days. A sawhorse barricaded the entrance at night. I retrieved my revolver, left the car in a patch of thick shadow, went back on foot, and took up space in the deep doorway of the defunct laundromat across the street from my building. I got out a cigarette, just to be doing something. I didn't light it.

The window remained dark. There were no lights in any of the others; the cleaning crew had finished with everything up to eye level and gone home. Everyone had gone home except me and the character who had to know what time it was in the middle of the night. I had a pretty good idea who it was and that he wasn't alone. That made us three.

After twenty minutes or so a police cruiser glided down the street heading east, slow as the mail and aiming one of its swivel beams toward the odd shop doorway on either side, casting for prowlers. I backed as far as I could into the shadow. The spotlight on the passenger's side swung my direction. I ducked and stopped breathing as the beam grazed the crown of my head, paused on the corner entrance of the pet-supply emporium next door, then angled down toward the pavement and went out. The cruiser picked up speed and in the next block turned on its flashers and siren. The whooping dopplered away. Silence drifted back down like volcanic ash and covered the street. Behind it, tires hummed on the hard-hearted surfaces of

I-94 and the John Lodge, somewhere on the far edge of the next solar system. The air on that stretch of West Grand hung as quiet as the gardens of Babylon; quieter, maybe. For all I knew, that was where all the happy pagans went to blow out the carbons on Friday night.

I sucked hard on my cigarette, drawing in as many unignited poisons as I could and kill the more delicate brain cells. I was getting to be too romantic for the work. It was time to hang up the brass knuckles and write odes to glazed pottery.

More time gnawed at the mountain. I wondered if whoever had broken into my office had broken back out while I was parking the car. I wondered if he'd been there at all. Maybe I had a loose bulb, or the spy microphone had messed up the wiring. Maybe it was my own wiring that was messed up. I hadn't slept since Nixon.

The weight of the gun was pulling my spinal column out of line. I adjusted the gun and changed positions, leaning against the other shoulder. Now all I had to worry about was the weight tugging at my eyelids. The sleep that had hung back snickering when I invited it into my bed had come crawling back with the same rotten timing as ever.

My cigarette made a little tapping noise when it struck the rubber pad at my feet and rolled out onto the sidewalk. It woke me like a gunshot. My eyelids snapped apart. The door to my building was opening.

Reflected city light struck Shelly's silver thatch of hair first, then the V of Nicky's pale shirt framed by the open front of the glistening leather Windbreaker he'd put on in place of the suede jacket I'd ruined. They glanced both ways on the street, then started across directly toward me. I reached behind my back and drew the Smith & Wesson.

They stepped up onto the curb on my side and turned left, away from me. They hadn't seen me after all.

Nicky was talking. "Maybe he blew town with the girl."

"I don't think so. She wasn't with him later." This was Shelly.

"That was clumsy. You should of let me drive."

"You're lucky I let you handle a gun."

"Christ, I never seen a town this size so fucking dead. You could shoot craps on the center line."

The voices were fading. I had to lean out of the doorway to hear them.

"Where to now?" said Nicky.

"Back to his dump. Man's got to go home sometime. He wouldn't live in a shithole like that if he could go anywhere else."

"How long we going to keep this up?"

"Till we find out where he stashed the girl. Then we do them both."

"Dibs on Walker."

They were still talking as they moved off, but they'd passed out of listening range. I ran across the street to my building. I didn't know how close they were parked or if they'd swing past for another look on their way back to my house.

I had to fumble out my key to let myself in. They'd managed to jimmy the lock without breaking it. The story was the same upstairs. I don't know why I didn't just leave everything open. I was the only one who needed a key to get in.

The waiting room and the office seemed undisturbed. The file cases were locked and they hadn't taken a knife to the upholstery. They'd probably thought there was nothing worth taking. That made me mad, because they were right. Nicky wouldn't have been able to resist going through the desk, but I couldn't confirm that without turning on a light and I wasn't going to do that. I made a mental note to replace the bottle in the deep drawer. A guy like Nicky would carry around a bottle of rat poison for contingencies like that.

I filled the basin in the little water closet, again without turning on any lights, and plunged my face into the icy water. When I took it out my nerves were prickling. I mopped it off, closed the blinds in the office, and smoked half a cigarette in the dark.

Not quite dark: A little light leaked in through the pinholes where the cords passed through the louvers. I watched it, spun silver in the braid of smoke twisting toward the bugged fixture in the ceiling, and wondered what the joker on the other end had made of whatever conversation had taken place there earlier. I knew the joker wasn't Jeremiah Morgenstern. He'd wandered in from another deck. He was just beginning to realize it. Pet wasn't the only reason he'd put Bugs and Daffy on my case.

The telephone rang, loud as church bells in the desert atmosphere. I tamped out my cigarette and let it ring. There was only one party who would be calling my office at that hour. Shelly and Nicky had had enough time to find out I still hadn't gone home, and had decided to backtrack.

I figured I had just enough time to make the call I'd come there to make before they returned to the perch. I waited thirty seconds after the last ring, then picked up the receiver and dialed a number I knew by heart.

"Hichens."

I settled back in my chair. "You must have a bed and a hotplate in that office. I thought I'd have to have them patch me through to your house."

"Where the hell are you? I've been calling your house and office for an hour."

"You wouldn't have had much to talk about with whoever picked up. I'm at the office."

"Go again. I just tried there."

"I didn't answer. I thought it was someone trying to sell me local long distance."

"At three A.M.?"

"I had my watch on upside-down. Anyway, we're talking now. What's on your mind?"

"Where were you two hours ago?"

"Visiting a sick friend."

"Would this friend be in intensive care at Royal Oak Beaumont?"

I poked at a live spark in the ashtray with the eraser end of a pencil. "Who called you? Winthrop?"

"Male nurse at Beaumont. The switchboard gave him to me. It seems I dropped by the hospital a little before one, badged my way into ICU, disturbed a patient and upset the patient's wife, assaulted a doctor and a security guard, and scampered away. It seems I'm six feet, one eighty-five, with brown eyes and graying brown hair."

"Right up until the eyes I thought you were talking about me," I said. "It says hazel right on my driver's license."

"Shut the fuck up. I'm sending a car. If you aren't there when it arrives, I'll swear out a takedown. The boys get in a snit over phony cops; it's a reputation issue. They might bounce you a couple times."

"You'd disapprove."

"Not too loud. "I've got in my thirty."

"If you want them to find me, you'd better send the car someplace else."

"Someplace else such as where?" Suddenly a chair leg scraped the floor on his end. "Just a minute. Is that thing still—"

I cut him off. "I let my subscription lapse to the Bar Association journal. What's the latest on the validity of a deathbed statement?"

THIRTY-FOUR

P lymouth was asleep. Moonlight lay in pools near the park, where the only things moving were a man smoking a short stub of cigarette and a dog looking for the right bush. Dog and man looked equally intent. The man gave me a little wave as I drove past. I might be a neighbor.

I parked on the street and walked through the dewy damp of a warm summer evening, brushing at the occasional mosquito. The crickets all had chainsaws.

The split-levels were dark except for a single lamp burning in an upstairs window, where a shadow drifted past the gauzy curtain. It wasn't any less than I expected, nor any more. He was a quiet man, deliberate in his movements, the kind of neighbor you hoped you'd get instead of a house full of healthy teenagers or a tuba player with a day job. He would be a treasured figure on the block. A lifetime of training will show through decades of retirement.

The big pickup stood in the driveway pointed out. I'd expected that too.

The front door was locked. I turned the doorknob gently to confirm that. Any rattle, no matter how slight, would separate itself from the normal sighs and crackles of a fifty-year-old house settling into its foundation. Even an amateur house-breaker knows that.

I unfolded the worn suede case containing an assortment of instruments that could get me six months in county just for carrying them. They'd belonged to my late partner, who could pick any lock invented since before Houdini. They'd liked him in his neighborhood, too.

I'd never gotten the knack. Turning the tumblers took me ten minutes under the best conditions, longer when I had to worry about making noise. When the bolt finally slid back, there were scratches on the brass plate Stevie Wonder couldn't miss. But I wasn't trying to fool anyone who would see them. I put the picks back in their loops, fixed the snaps on the case, and slid it into a pocket. Then I drew the revolver and let myself inside. I didn't make any more noise easing the door shut than a head makes going into a hat.

I waited inside the entrance while my pupils made the necessary adjustment. Low-watt light from an under-the-cupboard fixture in the kitchen filtered out into the living room, outlining potential hazards while leaving others knee-deep in poured shadow. With the aid of memory I identified the sofa and recliner and dark TV set, and to the left the door to the den where I'd familiarized myself with the Delwayne Garnet fugitive case and encountered the name Curtis Smallwood for the first time, a hundred years ago. The polished wooden stair risers leading to the second floor gleamed in the reflected light, rose into a bottleneck of shadow, and picked up light again near the top, where lamplight slid out of a door and onto the landing. My path was clear.

The refrigerator kicked in with a gasp and a shudder, like an old man forcing his prostate. It bumped me out of my state of suspended animation.

I slipped off my shoes, crept along the runner to the stairs, and climbed, leaning on the bannister with my free hand in order to keep weight off the steps, which squeaked anyway. I let a minute go by after each complaint. A house will make such noises, but not as regularly as footsteps. No one ever took longer climbing the Statue of Liberty than I did those twelve steps.

In the second-floor hallway a T-square of light showed around a door standing partially open. I padded down six feet of pale wall-to-wall carpet, tightened my grip on the revolver, and pushed the door open the rest of the way on silent hinges.

The room was a bedroom, papered in faded brittle gold, with a double bed on a massive oak frame and a matching bureau and night tables at its foot and head. Two of the bureau drawers hung open. A fat brushed-brass lamp on the near table shed light onto an old-fashioned leatherette suitcase with straps, flayed open on top of the bed. Stacks of shirts, underwear, and neatly rolled socks lay around it on the spread. I was alone with all this.

The only other door belonged to a closet, where a robe and an assortment of sweaters and jackets hung exposed with the door open. The rest was a tangle of empty hangers. Across from me was the window I'd seen light showing through from the street, with its diaphanous pale-gold curtain to match the wallpaper, darkened at the hems with age. No one had touched the decor in the years since the woman of the house had died. It was a widower's room, utilitarian and lonely. I saw my reflection in the glass behind the curtain. Then movement behind it.

I sidestepped fast, but not fast enough. Something solid missed the crown of my head and struck the right side of my collarbone. An orange flash of pain soared to the top of my skull. The revolver dropped from my hand and I dropped right on top of it.

When I woke up, I smelled gasoline.

THIRTY-FIVE

The blow hadn't knocked me out so much as paralyzed me temporarily. It was a natural protective function, a signal sent from the brain throughout the central nervous system ordering it to shut down to prevent permanent damage from shock. A few inches farther to the left and the condition itself would have been permanent. I was a lucky man. And I smelled gasoline.

After two minutes my toes and fingers began to tingle and I was able to rotate my head and release pressure from the throbbing place where my neck sloped up from my bruised collarbone. In the meantime I felt myself being dragged and lifted into a sitting position, my arms forced behind my back, and something as hard and cold as Arctic ice clamping itself around my wrists. Then the sharp familiar sting in my nostrils. I had a sudden atavistic flash of my father filling the tank of a prehistoric Briggs & Stratton motor from a red metal can with a flexible spout, an unlit cigarette dangling from the corner of his mouth.

My vision cleared. The figure with the can was thicker through the waist than my father and older than he lived to be, and the thing clamped in the corner of his mouth was a cold cigar. He had on a knitted green polo shirt stretched tightly over the swell of his belly, pleated gray slacks, and cordovan loafers on his big square feet. The can was plastic. I saw all this just as he swung it back and then forward. Amber liquid erupted from the spout, drenching me from hairline to ankles and burning my nose and throat. I choked, hacked, and threw up Regular Unleaded. A thread of spittle glittered between my chin and the carpet between my thighs. I braced my stockinged heels against the floor and tried to stand up, barking my wrists on the underside of the bed. They were handcuffed behind one of the stout oaken legs.

"Federal issue," Randall Burlingame said. "They don't make carbon steel any higher. Careful, there. You don't want to strike any sparks."

I looked up at him. My eyes were stinging from the gasoline. "I wouldn't light that cigar, either," I said. "You wouldn't want to lose the house now that it's paid for."

"Who says it's paid for? It started out as a thirty-year loan and I refinanced it into the next century. But it won't be my problem after tonight." He set down the can and took the cigar out of his mouth. "Thanks, by the way. This is from the box you brought me from Canada."

"Sorry they aren't Havanas."

"Don't apologize. They're overrated. I did a little stint down there when I was in the field. How come you came here early? You asked Hichens to meet you here tomorrow morning with a warrant." He stopped, grinned, and screwed the cigar back between his teeth. "I get it. You were smoking me out. How'd you find out I bugged your office?"

"Just because I never clean out the fixture doesn't mean I never look at it. I should've figured it out sooner. A former FBI big shot would maintain some contacts with Special Ops. You knew I'd be tied up in Toronto all day. Once your spooks were finished, you'd be in on every conversation that took place near my desk. That's how you found out Garnet would be at the Marriott that day."

He sniffed at the hand that had been holding the gasoline can. "I need to wash up. Can't have airport security smelling Amoco on my luggage." He went out into the hall. I heard water running a moment later. He raised his voice. "Sorry about this, Amos. After what you did for my daughter I should've known you wouldn't walk away from the case just because you lost your client."

I experimented. If the carpet was thick enough I might be able to press the handcuffs down far enough to slide the chain under the leg of the bed. I braced my back against the frame and pushed down.

I kept up my end of the conversation. "That's the part I couldn't figure out without talking to Regina Babbage. I knew why you killed Curtis Smallwood. You blamed him for your sister's death. Even a teenage kid can work up enough hate to turn killer. But it wouldn't be strong enough to want to kill Smallwood's son fifty years later." I strained, relaxed. The bed had stood in one spot too many years. The leg had sunk through the pile. Only a thin layer of fiber separated it from the floor. There was no room to slide the chain between them.

"Him being Smallwood's kid had nothing to do with it. I'm sure Regina told you that. *There's* a lady who can keep a good hate going. Thirty-four years, and it was just as fresh as the day her boy blew himself to kibble." The faucet turned off with a clunk. He came back in, wiping his hands with a towel. He was still chewing the cigar.

"Not me," he went on. "Seeing that arrogant would-be Sugar Ray Robinson bleeding brains on the pavement satisfied me. You could say I even felt guilty. That's why I went back to school, studied law, and took my degree down to D.C. Thought I'd spend the rest of my life enforcing the law I broke. Opal would've approved. She never thought department-store model was as high as a Burlingame could reach." He swallowed. "That's why she worked so hard to pay for my education."

"Killing Smallwood didn't make you a killer. You couldn't

pull the trigger on Regina, even though she was an eyewitness."

"Peggy, she called herself then. Peggy Yale." He tossed the towel aside and picked up a stack of shirts from the bed. "I thought he'd be alone. I should've guessed he'd already have another one lined up when he dumped Opal. I didn't even know about the actress then. I'd been away at school. For all I know, he had that butcher who killed my sister on call." He threw the stack into the suitcase.

My eyes were streaming from the gasoline fumes. I twisted my head to wipe my cheek on my shoulder. The lock-picks in my pocket tinkled when they shifted. I might have been able to get at them and jimmy open the cuffs—if I chewed an arm off first.

"You're right about Regina," I said. "A band singer in nineteen fifty couldn't come forward saying she was out with a Negro boxer and stay employed. But she had a good memory. The FBI liked publicity. By the time you took over the Detroit office, your picture would have been in the paper plenty of times. She'd remember you; and after Garnet ran to Canada, she'd have come to you to collect on all those years of silence."

"She wouldn't let it go. And I can't blame her. May she rot in hell. Did she die?"

"She was sleeping when I left." I concentrated on those picks. They took my mind off the throbbing where he'd hit me with whatever he'd hit me with. I'd made more noise coming up those stairs than I'd hoped.

"Does she know she's dying?"

The eyes in the square face were hooked up to a mind that had been trained legally. I worked on that.

"It wouldn't hold up in preliminary," I said. "A deathbed confession needs two witnesses. Her husband and the nurse were too busy trying to get me out of the room. Everything else is circumstantial. Why do you think I used your own bug to draw you out? You can quit packing."

"Not while you're alive. We're too much alike. I didn't lift those files just to protect myself from the Bureau. Or even to convince Regina I hadn't forgotten her. An open case is like an open wound. It won't drain forever."

"Don't you want to get to know your grandson?"

"Kids these days have enough baggage without having a jailbird for a grandfather. I'll miss his mother. That's the hard part. But I'd miss her just as much behind bars."

I gave up then. He finished loading the suitcase, latched it, and buckled the straps. He carried it out into the hall. While he was gone I wriggled around, trying to jostle the case of burglar tools out of my pocket. They rattled around but stayed put.

He came back in and picked up the gasoline can. "The ironic thing is, if I'd just sat still for a week or two, I'd be free to enjoy my retirement. Who knew the old lady was so sick?" He splashed gasoline on the bed and slung it up the wall. It splattered against the window and streaked down the glass. There were more fumes in the room now than oxygen. I put my head down and breathed.

"Exodus," I said.

"What?" He stopped and waggled the can. There wasn't much left in it to slosh around.

"'An eye for an eye,'" I said. "I don't know the rest, but I know what book it's from. It's the one most people remember. It's the one Regina remembered. She sang in a choir before she signed with Rex King and his Royal Athletics. She brought it up when I was questioning her. 'Fair trade,' she said. She let you have your murder, but you had to pay for it with hers. A life for a life."

"That's not in the passage. The Chief expected all his agents to go to church. You're right, it comes up a lot. I made a point of memorizing it. 'Eye for eye, tooth for tooth, hand for hand, foot for foot.' *Exodus,* twenty-one, twenty-four. There's no 'life for a life' in it. But a lot of people have been killed for a lot less than a misquote." He spread his feet and upended the can. The rest of the contents spilled out onto the carpet.

While he was doing that I strained at the manacles. They say Billy the Kid could slip out of any pair they put on him. But he had small hands and big wrists. I only managed to scrape some hide off bone and put a kink in my back. I stopped for breath.

"Torching the place won't cover up murder," I said.

"I'm buying time, not a clean bill of health. When the DNA tests come back and they know the crispy critter in my bedroom isn't me, I'll be in a different hemisphere."

"Southern or eastern? Most countries extradite. The rest confiscate."

"Let 'em extradite. I cashed out my life insurance and stock portfolio the day after you came here asking about Delwayne Garnet. It's all in a bank draft in my wallet. I'm not a whole lot healthier than Old Lady Winthrop; I've got angina and both kidneys never work at the same time. By the time they find me and finish the paperwork, I'll be a corpse with a big fat smile on my face."

"It didn't have to be this way. You should've taken your lumps for Smallwood. Back then they were still lynching Negroes down South for looking at white women. Figure in a fatal abortion and a mixed-up kid, and you could've walked."

"Coulda, woulda, shoulda." He removed the cigar, peeled a slimy shred off his lower lip, and slid the cigar back into its groove. "I won't apologize again. We all pull our own strings, and sometimes we hang ourselves. You didn't have to come here tonight. Smallwood didn't have to play with blonde fire. I could've stayed at school. Garnet might have taken his chances with a jury back in sixty-eight, and Regina could have been a stand-up citizen and ratted me out to the cops on New Year's Eve. Everybody makes a wrong turn he can't forget. When they finally get around to building that time machine, you'll have to wait ten years for a seat."

"Backward is the new forward."

"What?"

"Something a lawyer told me," I said. "You don't have to

wait. You said it yourself; you're a sick old man. Most judges consider that when they hand down a sentence."

"Maybe so, but I'll be just as dead by the time it gets that far. This way I'll spend my last months on a beach instead of in a cell. Smoking a cigar." He stepped out into the hall, turned around, and fished something out of a pocket. It was a box of matches.

He paused, looked around. "I had a life here. Made love, raised a child. It's just wood and plaster and masonry now. I guess it always was. I hope whatever they put up in its place winds up with more to offer than a roof over a balding old hypocrite." He placed a match against the striker.

"First tell me how you got the gun into the hotel past security."

He smiled. He dropped the match back into the box and strode over to the bed.

"This gun?" He slid a .38 Colt revolver from under a pillow. The cylinder, frame, and barrel had the brown patina of the authentic antique. "It cost me twelve bucks in a downtown pawnshop in 'forty-nine. I don't know what it's worth now. Probably a lot more before I hit you with it. As for getting it into the hotel, that part was easy. It was always there."

THIRTY-SIX

lways there how?" I asked. "That checkpoint's been there more than thirty years."

"The gun was there when it came. It's been parked behind a ventilator grid since LBJ. I parked it there six months before the Chief made me Special Agent in Charge in Detroit.

"I don't remember what I did with it after I shot Smallwood," he went on. "That's the truth. I'm blank on everything that happened that night after I saw Peggy Yale staring at me over the body. I didn't know that was her name then. I suppose I threw the piece in a trash bin. Somebody rescued it. I never saw it again until it turned up in an illegal weapons cache in sixty-six. I was head of the Black Panther squad here. We got a tip some local Panthers had set up a meet with an out-of-town cell to lay off some ordnance in a room at the old Airport Hilton. We raided the place, made arrests. Then came the photo op. Well, you saw it in the file: federal men posing behind a bed with guns spread out on it in display. We were setting it up when I recognized this piece. See, there's a triangular chunk broken off the outside grip. I spent plenty of time stroking it with my thumb in my pocket while I was waiting for Smallwood to show up at the Lucky Tiger."

He thrust the butt under my nose. It was an old chip, dark and rounded at the edges. No one had thought a windfall piece found in the trash worth dressing up with a replacement grip.

"You'd be surprised what kind of junk came up in raids like that," he said. "Washington put out that the Panthers were mounting armed insurrection with state-of-the-art automatic weapons. Most of the stuff went back to Dillinger, with rusty actions and busted firing pins. It was all for show. Anyway, I panicked a little. I thought if Ballistics matched this to the Smallwood case, Oakland would reopen the file and dig up Regina. We hadn't inventoried the merchandise yet. I put it in my pocket when no one was looking. After the press left I told the others to pack the stuff up and used a dime to unscrew the grid off a ventilator in the hall and pushed it as far back into the shaft as I could reach. I always thought I'd go back for it when I had time. Well, you know how that is."

"So in time you forgot. Finding out Garnet was going to meet me at the Marriott—the old Hilton—reminded you. How did you know it would still be there?"

"I sure didn't expect it to be. I figured somebody probably found it years ago and kept it or gave it a toss. Maybe the vent got sealed up during a renovation. For the record, I never forgot. Never. As time went on it just got harder and harder to think about going back. Then I started to wonder if the Wayne County cops had found it and kept it quiet, and deputies were staking out the spot, waiting to bust whoever came for it. But after thirty-six years that seemed unlikely, so I made a dry run after I found out Garnet was coming there and before he was expected.

"Well, there it was. The grid had a new coat of paint, but whoever they've been paying to do the heavy cleaning is either slapdash as hell or his arms are shorter than mine. I had to reach farther in than I remembered, but no set of fingers were ever more surprised to close around the butt of that dusty old Colt."

"*I'm* surprised it still fired."

"They didn't know about planned obsolescence when they made it. I'd brought a handkerchief soaked in solvent and a handkerchief soaked in lubricant. I found a vacant room and gave it a good going over. It was dry in that shaft. The rust was just surface grit, harmless. The cylinder turned smooth as silk. I put the gun back for when I needed it and left."

"What about the cartridges?"

"Couldn't trust them after all that time. When I came back for real I brought two fresh ones with me, in the barrel of a fountain pen in case I was searched. But they weren't big enough to trip the alarm. I threw the old ones back into the shaft and reloaded. Later I just carried the gun out in my pocket. Nobody stops you on the way *out* of a secure area."

"Pretty lucky."

"No need. I'd have found another way if not that one."

I believed him. You needed a head for more than just politics to climb as high as he had in Hoover's FBI. I tried again to force my left hand out of its cuff. It's the smaller hand. Blood trickled into my palm.

"It won't matter now if they connect what's left of it to Smallwood and Garnet. I'd just have to ditch it between here and the airport anyway." He tucked the Colt back under the pillow and turned toward the hallway, sliding open the box of matches.

The window flew apart. He threw a hand up to his head, hit the wall with a shoulder, and slid down, rucking his shirt up above his pale hairless belly. Vermilion tadpoles fanned the faded gold wallpaper where it had been blank before. The report echoed like cannon fire in some deep valley.

I didn't look at Burlingame to see if he was breathing. I dug my heels into the carpet, braced my palms against the floor, and heaved back and up with my shoulders against the footboard. The bed moved half an inch and the headboard bumped the wall. I scooted the same half-inch, felt the shallow ledge along the top of the footboard with my back, notched my shoulder blades under the ledge, braced myself again, and took a deep breath. Downstairs someone threw open the front door hard enough to bang the wall on the other side. I hadn't relocked it when I broke in. I heaved. The leg lifted slightly. I strained to hold up the weight of the bed and slip the chain underneath. My shoulders slipped instead. The leg slammed back down.

I breathed in and out twice, mustering strength. Feet thumped on the stairs. I got back into position and pushed up with everything I had. The leg lifted. My arms shook and I had tremors in my legs. I dug my heels in deep, bent my elbows, and pulled my arms forward, all in one movement. The chain slipped under. I let the bed fall back with a bang and scrambled to my feet. My thigh muscles were cramped. I stumbled and almost fell over Burlingame.

I didn't know where he'd put my gun. I vaulted over him and dived for the bed. I twisted around to get my hands on the Colt. With just one free hand I'd have made it with a second to spare.

A roar shook the room and a hunk of plaster fell off the wall above the nightstand. It left behind a concavity the size of a Frisbee.

Shelly stood in the doorway with his fifty magnum leveled across his left forearm, a shell of smoke crawling out of the muzzle. When he saw me sprawled on the bed with my hands pinned under me, he smirked and thumbed back the hammer. The click fell on my thickened eardrums like a stone.

"Hold your fire, for chrissake! This place smells like a filling station. You want to blow us all to pieces?"

The white-haired man's face went flat. He relaxed his stance and stepped aside from the doorway. He left the hammer cocked.

Jeremiah Morgenstern followed his bray into the room. He wore a navy blazer over an open-necked shirt and gray flannels, very sporty. Behind him, Nicky slithered in, saw where Shelly was standing, and took up a position on the other side of the door. He was holding his Beretta. His eyes brightened when he saw how I was trussed.

"We'll let the room air out a little," Morgenstern said. "No need to open a window. I wouldn't of bet you could hit the sky with that musket. Guess it's okay I ain't going into gambling. What do you say, Red?" He put all his weight on one shiny-toed Oxford and kicked Burlingame in the ribs. Something popped.

The man on the floor groaned. Lying there with one side of his head stained almost black, he'd looked as dead as he'd left Curtis Smallwood. One leg was twitching.

Morgenstern squatted on his haunches, took Burlingame's chin in one hand, and turned the ruined head toward him. The ex-FBI man had lost an ear and most of his scalp. His mouth hung open. Grotesquely, the cigar was still in place, dry-glued to his lower lip.

"I'm too trusting," the gangster said. "My only fault. When a fed tells me he's got the gaming commission in his pocket, I believe him. I even agree to meet him on his own turf. Just a sucker for a title. A Girl Scout could rig me for a frame." He took the ragged stump of ear between thumb and forefinger and jerked. I turned my head away. Burlingame howled.

I looked at Shelly. "Good tail job. I never saw the Jag."

He thought before answering. "It's up on a hoist. You made me snap an axle on that train crossing."

Morgenstern wiped blood off on Burlingame's shirt and stood. He looked at me for the first time. "Where's Pet?"

"I don't know. I dropped her off in Windsor."

He nodded. Then he drew in a lungful of air through his nose and let it out. "Smells a lot sweeter now. Nothing like the night air in a small town." Without turning, he held a hand out toward Nicky, palm up.

Nicky took a beat, then laid his pistol in the palm. Morgenstern fisted it and pointed it at me. I shrank back against the headboard. My hands touched cold metal. I fumbled for the Colt's grip.

Morgenstern bent suddenly and jammed the muzzle under Burlingame's chin. The Beretta cracked and the top of the FBI man's head flew off.

I twisted onto my left side. I had the Colt in both hands and I strained my left shoulder almost out of its socket, bringing the barrel clear of my hip. As I squeezed the trigger I realized it wouldn't fire; Burlingame had pumped both fresh loads into Delwayne Garnet. The rest were in a ventilator shaft.

It pulsed between my hands. He'd reloaded, like any good field agent trained to respect firearms. Morgenstern was still bent over the dead man, with Shelly standing beyond him, looking down at his boss's handiwork. Shelly's white shirt blossomed red. I fired again, opening another bud high on his chest. His back struck the wall and the long silver barrel came up as if the gun were guiding the hand. The headboard splintered, a foot from my head. I twisted in the other direction now, throwing myself toward the floor. I took the nightstand with me, and with it the lamp. Red flame squirted in the sudden blackness. Morgenstern's bullet whumped into the mattress, but I was in the clear, scrambling for thinking space under the bed.

There was a little silence. It might have meant my eardrums were gone.

"Mr. Morgenstern?"

Nicky's voice. It sounded shaky.

"I'm okay. Where's Walker?"

"Shelly's hurt."

"Fuck him." He raised his voice. He hadn't been whispering to begin with. "Where'd you take her, Walker? Not Canada. I got people in every province. She knows that. She knows a lot more than she lets on. Or has till now."

I lay on my back under the bed, trying to breathe without panting. The gasoline stench was strong there. If I fired from that position I could barbecue myself.

"I won't hurt her," Morgenstern went on. "You either, if you tell me where she is. I just want her back."

I said nothing. I could make out the shape of the box springs. That wasn't good. Morgenstern's and Nicky's eyes would be adjusting too.

"Say something, you son of a bitch! You hit?" The Beretta cracked again. I heard plaster falling.

I tried to wriggle over onto my stomach. My sleeve caught on the end of a coil and I had to reverse directions to clear it without making a ripping noise. I gashed my wrist. Morgenstern heard me gasp.

"Where'd I hit you?" he shrieked. "The belly, I hope."

I stopped struggling and held my breath. My heart wouldn't cooperate. It hammered against the bedframe.

"Don't just stand there. Find a light."

Nicky said, "Not me, boss. If he can suck in air he can still shoot."

"So can I, you yellow bastard." Another shot. The bullet didn't strike anywhere near me.

"Jesus, you almost hit me." Nicky was as shrill as Morgenstern now.

"Next time for sure. Do what I tell you."

A floorboard shifted. The yellow bastard was more afraid of Morgenstern than a slug from me.

"Sing out, Walker. Otherwise I'll torch the place and you with it."

Nicky said, "what about Shelly?"

"If you don't find that fucking light they'll be saying, 'What about Nicky?' "

A shoe gleamed on the floor. If my hands were free I could have reached out and touched it.

"Don't think too long, Walker. They won't know a PI from a pot roast."

I got my sleeve free and squirmed into position by easy installments. There wasn't room enough for a decent-size monster under Burlingame's bed, let alone one hundred eighty-five pounds of red-blooded American detective.

Nicky's toe touched the lamp. Clothing rustled as he bent to pick it up.

At last I lay on my chest with my head toward Morgenstern's end of the room. If he was still *on* that end of the room; he might have been moving too. I used my toes and knees to push myself forward.

Nicky fumbled for the switch. The bulb was smashed. I saw a ghostly face beneath the bedframe.

"He's under the bed!"

Something struck sparks off the steel frame and chugged into the floor two inches in front of my face. I braced for the blast.

There wasn't one, but I couldn't lie still while he tried again. Once again I strained the Colt past my hip. Nothing to aim at; I was blinded by Nicky's muzzle flash. I squeezed my eyes shut. They claim you don't hear the explosion when you're in it, but what do they know? I tightened pressure on the trigger. It was slippery with my blood.

"Police! Drop your weapons!"

Captain Hichens' voice. It sounded like birdsong.

THIRTY-SEVEN

I finished my stand-up and got off the stage, just like George Burns said.

Hichens let the camcorder run another thirty seconds, then twirled the power cord around his ankle and yanked the plug out of the wall. The red light winked off and the motor stopped whirring. The remote was on the table right in front of him, but he'd have had to lean forward from his chair to use it. The arid eyes in the pale face looked as tired as I felt. In his case the condition was chronic.

"I never heard of an investigation like it," he said. "Not a single informed decision from start to finish. You just stuck your nose into the wind and stumbled after it, like a—a—" He looked to me for help.

"A hungry coyote," I said. "Wile E. Except it takes me longer to bounce back after the cliff falls on my head." I rubbed my eyes and yawned. I was crying pure gypsum and my breath would knock down a wall. Outside the room where we sat in the City-County Building, feet had begun to whisper along the corridor. The bureaucrats were reporting for work. Apart from being knocked silly in Randall Burlingame's bedroom for a few minutes, I'd gone around the dial without sleep. "It wasn't an informed-decision kind of a case. Most of the witnesses were dead and the only piece of concrete evidence spent the last half-century in a wall with Poe's black cat. The rest was instinct."

"You were a hair less dumb than Burlingame, if it means anything. If he hadn't got cute and tried to frame Morgenstern for Garnet, he'd be smoking that cigar of his on some beach right now."

"He trained under J. Edgar. Doubling the double-cross came as natural as shedding skin cells."

"Feds and gangsters. Yippies and prizefighters and whore-house madams. What year is it?"

"Backward—" I yawned bitterly. I didn't have the energy to finish the sentence.

"We've got the gun, and if Homeland Security cooperates we ought to find Burlingame on videotape at least twice going through the hotel checkpoint. That ties up the Garnet case. I doubt Smallwood, even if the gun checks out; hard to prove chain of possession after fifty-three years. That's Oakland County's headache. I don't guess they'll chew much aspirin. Their suspect's on a slab."

Hichens hadn't gone to Plymouth alone. If he had, he might have arrived in time to prevent bloodshed; or to make his own contribution to the pool. He'd stopped to alert the city police and make a courtesy call to Oakland, whose case Smallwood still was. Three departments had converged on the quiet residential street, and Morgenstern and Nicky surrendered themselves without gunfire. Shelly left strapped to a board in an EMS unit.

A perky Pakistani with the Washtenaw County Coroner's office had opened his bag next to Burlingame's body and confirmed he was dead. That ended the suspense.

"Be in your office this morning," Hichens said. "I'm sending a couple of deputies for that bug. There are going to be some vacancies in the Hoover Building when the feds finish tracing it—after we're through with it."

"Can you make it this afternoon? I get sleepy every twenty-five hours."

He made a magnanimous gesture with one hand. I asked him who gets Morgenstern.

"Plymouth, to start. They've got your statement and you'll be hearing from the county prosecutor. New York and Washington too, probably; they've been trying to twist him up in a RICO rap through three administrations. Don't be surprised if the Department of Justice offers you a free extended vacation, complete with new I.D."

"It's always been a dream of mine to sell plumbing supplies in Wichita."

"It won't come to that. I ran his name through the NYPD rackets division after I found out he was involved. He's been an embarrassment to the no-necks on the East Coast for years. They call him the Yiddish Little Caesar, not always behind his back. They'll do handsprings when they find out he got taken down on an operation that won't kick back to them. They'll have his territory all divvied up by this time next week."

"Edgar Croswell."

"Who's that?"

"He was the country cop who broke up Little Apalachia." He stared. I moved a shoulder. "Friend of mine knows the Book of Sicilians chapter and verse," I said.

"I guess I can take it into retirement. That and Delwayne Garnet. If I had any ambition left, you'd be showering at County right now."

"A shower sounds good."

"I'm glad. I didn't want to say anything."

"We through?"

His telephone rang. He held up an index finger and answered. He listened, said thanks, and hung up.

"I've been trying to reach Morgenstern's girl at the Marriott," he said. "I can't get an answer. Any idea where she got to?"

I glanced up at the clock. The Caracas flight was off the ground, barring delays.

"Not a one."

He gave me the bleak look. It didn't have to mean anything. "That was the Royal Oak substation on the phone. I asked Oakland to put a man outside Regina Winthrop's room. She died forty minutes ago."

"That ties up Smallwood." I peeled myself off the chair and cracked some bones. I smelled pretty stale, at that. "Thanks, Captain. You sounded good there in the dark."

"You ought to hear me in the tub. You're lucky that old Colt didn't blow up in your hand."

"They made them good then. Not much else. Abortion's as safe as root canals and no one cocks an eyebrow when a black fighter dates a white entertainer. None of this would have been necessary today."

"Yeah. They sure knew how to dress, though."

The same sweet-faced old lady took the slip Hichens had signed and gave me my Smith & Wesson. A cop had scooped it off the floor where it had fallen out of the drawer of the nightstand when it tipped over. I remembered almost nothing of the drive from Plymouth, but I found where I'd parked, snapped the revolver into its compartment, and drove away with the windows down to clear out the stink of my own corruption. My wrists were still raw from the cuffs. None of the officers present had had a key that worked on them, but someone had found the one that belonged to them in Burlingame's pocket. When I turned my head at intersections, I felt the tight soreness where the gun barrel had bruised my collarbone. Lately it seemed like every job I took left me damaged in some way. Maybe it always had, and I'd just been young enough to shrug it off. Now I wondered if each new ding would be permanent like the rest.

I stopped at the office to call my report into Lawrence Meldrum, who seemed relieved the firm wouldn't figure front and center. I ignored whoever might be listening on the receiver the cops had found in Burlingame's den. Next I called Barry Stackpole. I gave him the whole story on one condition: that he agreed to share a byline with Edie Van Eyck. He had no problem with that.

When we were through talking I worked the plunger and called my service. There was one message, from a Mr. Hale: "The bird has flown." I made a snarky laugh, thanked the operator, and hung up.

The State of Michigan tried Jeremiah Morgenstern, Sheldon Bardo, and Nicholas Delarocca separately for charges connected with the death of Randall Burlingame. I testified in all the proceedings. Shelly attended his preliminary in a wheelchair with I.V. attached, but by the time of his sentencing he was able to stand with the help of his attorney. He drew life for accessory to murder and most of the factory options, including the attempted murder of one Amos Walker, a misdemeanor. Nicky got seven to fifteen for commission of a crime involving a firearm, pled down from accessory to murder when he rolled over on Morgenstern. At his own request he was moved from the state penitentiary at Jackson to an isolation cell in the maximum security facility at Marquette in the Upper Peninsula, after he slipped in the shower and broke his jaw and seven ribs.

The judge in Morgenstern's case gave the defendant two life sentences to be served consecutively, for murder and conspiracy, then handed the gavel to the U.S. District Court, which scheduled him for trial on twenty counts of violation of the Racketeer Influenced and Corrupt Organizations Act. That was high and outside for me. I went home.

I didn't get any midnight telephone calls telling me to watch my step. No one kissed me on the mouth without my consent, sent me a dead pigeon by registered mail, or called my obituary into the *Free Press*. I felt like sending myself a funeral bouquet just for the anticipation.

My Luger was waiting for me behind the registration desk at

the Renaissance Center the day after I made my statement to Captain Hichens. None of the cartridges had been fired.

I saw Hichens just once after I left him downtown, but not to talk to. We were both giving evidence the same day, and he nodded at me from the gallery as I was looking for a seat. He'd bought a new black suit for the occasion. A week after the criminal trial I read a three-inch piece in the *News* announcing his retirement after thirty years with the Wayne County Sheriff's Department.

Regina Winthrop was buried in a Catholic ceremony in Royal Oak. I didn't attend, but I went to a memorial service in Dearborn for Edie Van Eyck, who'd died in her sleep from complications of diabetes in August. Someone had framed the front-page story she'd written with Barry and propped it on a table cluttered with pictures of Edie drinking beer with friends.

On July 1, I got a bill from Llewellyn Hale at the Loyal Dominion Enquiry Agency in Toronto, only part of which I charged to Meldrum & Zinzser, Attorneys at Law. No personal notes were exchanged.

And last Christmas a card came to the office with a foreign postmark, showing Rudolph and the rest of the reindeer sprawled in lounge chairs overlooking the heartbreaking blue of the Caribbean. It was signed "Duffy."

ABOUT THE AUTHOR

L oren D. Estleman, author of the acclaimed Amos Walker private detective novels and the Detroit series, has won three Shamus Awards from the Private Eye Writers of America, four Golden Spur Awards from the Western Writers of America, and three Western Heritage Awards from the National Cowboy Hall of Fame. He has been nominated for the Edgar Allan Poe Award, the National Book Award, and the Pulitzer Prize. His other novels include the western historical classics *Billy Gashade, Journey of the Dead,* and *The Master Executioner.* Detroit hit man Peter Macklin made his return in *Something Borrowed, Something Black* (2002), having previously appeared in three novels: *Kill Zone, Roses Are Dead,* and *Any Man's Death. Retro* is the seventeenth Amos Walker novel, his second for Forge Books. Estleman lives in Michigan with his wife, mystery author Deborah Morgan.